To Becky!
If you liked The Boss...
you're REALLY gonna "dig"
this one!

DEADFELLAS

by

Jon D'Amore

Based on a story
by
Steve Barr & Jon D'Amore

Jon D'Amore

Advice & Legal Stuff

Deadfellas ISBN: 978-0-9853000-5-0

Jon D'Amore and his writings are represented by Howard Frumes of the
law firm Alexander, Lawrence, Frumes & Labowitz LLP.

Cover design and graphics by Kelly Martin, kamdesign – www.kam.design

Print layout and formatting by Steven W. Booth, Genius Book Services –
www.GeniusBookServices.com

Back cover photo by Boncratious – www.boncratious.com

Cover art copyrighted © 2017 by Jon D'Amore

Published by JMD
Printed in the USA
Deadfellas – First Edition (a)

Table of Contents

Acknowledgments

As I've said before, all I ever wanted was to bring pleasure, entertainment
and a smile to the world…and to have a comfortable, relaxing life for
myself. But nothing is ever as easy or as simple as that. Know what I mean?

Yeah, I think you do.

Had it not been for Ann and Carmine *'Rocky'* D'Amore…this book and
all the things I've ever created could not have been conceived, produced
or put forth before the masses. I love them and they will *always* be in my
heart and mind.

Thanks to: Melicent D'Amore for…*everything*; Steve Barr, for his friendship
and for hanging out with me the day we decided to write *Mobsters &
Monsters*; Al & Carole Battisti, for being there with their kind hearts,
humor, compassion, and for allowing me to have their home in paradise so
the seed for this story could be planted. They will *never* be forgotten; Lisa
Tracy, for bringing out the writer in me back in 1977, and for her never-
ending love, faith and ability to push me to turn something good into
something great; and once again…all the cleaning ladies over the years for
coming to my residences to put creases in my pants and shirts, keeping me
clothed…and my living spaces habitable.

Stuart Aion; Glorie Austern; Bert Baron; Steven Booth; Tony Caputo
(whether he knows it or not); Jennifer Duke Anstey; Gail *'GB'* Geoia;
George & Eileen Herberger; Ray Koonce; Karen LeBlanc; Diane
Lombardi-Fleming; Irene 'Rene' LoPresto; Tony Onorato; Julia Peterson;

Louise Rittberg; Debbie Sparks; Tom Sullivan; Ed Wright…all believers in the dream, and caring friends for life.

The remaining space on this page is for "industry people" who deserve some ink: The Writers Group of Studio City, for being there so I could meet Steve Barr, making my Wednesday evenings worthwhile, giving me the creative support to believe in myself and my writing, and for inspiring me to bring each and every high point of my creativity to a higher level. And *most* importantly and sincerely, Howard Frumes, my legal representative and a dedicated believer who stood at my side knowing it would finally happen. He's truly one of the good ones.

vi

Dedication

Carmine '*Rocky*' D'Amore

December 20, 1925
to
January 30, 1994

"I'll be behind you in whatever you choose to do.
Just make sure you never do anything that will bring the police into this
house."

John Lennon

October 9, 1940
to
December 8, 1980

"The dream is over..."

FOREWORD
by
Steve Barr

The screenplay for Deadfellas started out as a laugh.

I first met Jon D'Amore when he was living in Los Angeles and we were members of The Writers Group of Studio City. He had recently written his excellent memoir, "The Boss *Always* Sits In The Back," and wanted to adapt it into a screenplay, so he asked me to co-write it with him.

After a few days of working on it, two things became clear: Jon didn't need anyone's help in adapting his book, and we enjoyed working together. So we decided he would continue with the screenplay for The Boss alone, but we'd come up with a different idea to work on together.

What were Jon's favourite movies? Morality tales of high stakes and broken trust among Men of Respect. You know…Mob movies.

What were my favourite movies? Morality tales of the best and worst of humanity, confronting the monsters we can all become. You know… Zombie movies.

And so we came up with a Mob/Zombie story, a morality tale of connected men forced to fight monsters outside the house…while being betrayed by mobsters inside the house. It let us play with the tropes of both genres in a fun way, and we got to resurrect some of our favourite whacked characters from the Mob movies of the last 50 years.

Developing the story was easy. Writing the screenplay was fun. Selling the screenplay was neither of those things.

The zombie genre, we were told, is dead. The genre's DVD bonanza of the 90s is over. There hasn't been a successful zombie project in decades… as long as you don't count the Dawn of the Dead remake, and Zombieland, and World War Z, and the Resident Evil franchise, and Warm Bodies, and

Pride And Prejudice And Zombies, and Ash Vs Evil Dead, and iZombie, and the Santa Clarita Diet.

Oh, and The Walking Dead, which is one of the most successful shows in the world, was so successful that they made a spinoff called Fear The Walking Dead. I mean, c'mon, they resurrected the idea of spinoffs!

Hollywood is known for a lot of things, but internal consistency isn't one of them, especially since this apparently-dead genre just keeps getting up and walking around.

We really like Deadfellas, so Jon decided he'd stop waiting for a movie to happen, and instead he'd tell this tale in a different fashion…leading you to now have this book in your (presumably not-dead) hands.

It was fun to co-write the screenplay version, and I'm sure Jon had a lot of fun writing the book version. Now you should have a lot of fun reading it.

If not, we'll send a couple of guys (or zombies) to come and talk to ya's.

Steve Barr
New Zealand
2017

Preface
A few things you need to know

What made me decide to turn the 90 page screenplay Steve Barr and I wrote into a book?

To answer that, I need to give you a little backstory.

Initially it was thanks to the good luck I had with my memoir, **The Boss *Always* Sits In The Back**. But whenever I was asked about the subject of my next book…I could hear the disappointment in their voices when I'd say it wasn't going to be mob related.

I wanted to complete a fictional novel I had started a long, long, long time ago, but my desire to give something new and humorous to those who enjoyed The Boss had become paramount, though I didn't have true stories to tell like I did the last time.

But I *did* have the screenplay for **Deadfellas**. And it certainly *is* mob related.

Deadfellas is *not* a true story…though maybe it is or could be someday. Who knows?

This book is the full story based on a screenplay Steve and I began writing one Saturday afternoon while sitting on the expansive two-level deck overlooking the San Fernando Valley of a home I was living in off of Hollywood's Mulholland Drive.

Steve had co-written a screenplay called *Plant Life* which Disney bought for six figures. But to this day it's *still* sitting on a shelf somewhere in Burbank, California. Waiting.

At the time, another slew of low-budget (and we're talking two million dollars or less) slasher/horror/gore-fest films were coming out. It wasn't the genre we'd normally run out to see, but we were smart enough to know about their substantial earnings.

We each agreed that producers wanted cheap projects with a minimum number of locations, not a lot of speaking parts, writers they can fuck over, and women who show their breasts. Maybe even a little girl-on-girl action before they get stabbed, devoured or ripped apart.

Steve loved the screenplay I had written for The Boss *Always* Sits In The Back, and he had one I thought was great called *Love Among The Lycanthropes*. So we knew we had to do *something* together. We each thought the same thing…we'd come up with a story that combined the best of our talents, hold back every opportunity to bring the production costs up…and get those topless girls in when it made sense within the plot. Or…as often as possible.

We started writing what would become the beginning, middle and finale, while also keeping it open for a sequel (or sequels), of a screenplay called *Mobsters & Monsters*. Three months later we had a script that worked, followed by a few table readings cast with actors from numerous films and TV shows. With each reading, Steve and I honed, tweaked and edited the script before we were sure it was complete.

And then we changed the name to *Deadfellas*.

Okay, now I can answer the question posed at the beginning of this Preface.

Deadfellas was the perfect foundation for a book. It's an intelligent and hysterically *funny* concept…and I always wanted to tell the backstory that couldn't be told within the confines of a screenplay. Oh, and I wanted to give those who enjoyed my writing something along the lines of The Boss to thank them for their support and for making *my* life happier.

I guess I'll get to that fictional novel once things settle down from Deadfellas.

The names in this story have been made up, *or* their names have been taken from my personal phonebook…but they are *not* intended to be, in any way, conducive to the characters in this fictional story (or any film or sequel of any kind) they portray. There *is* a Gabbs, Nevada, but the people represented in this story and its premise has no bearing on the town whatsoever.

I use ***italics*** and ***ellipses*** (such as: …). Why? Because *that's the way we* (Italians) *speak!* They are there to alter the way you read.

Italics *emphasize* the specific word.

Ellipses are used as a timing rest…while staying on the same subject.

Deadfellas is a story primarily about Italians, who, as everyone knows, are *very* animated in the way they speak and emphasize their words. The italics and ellipses will make the reading of this story more enjoyable…and will bring the characters to life (which is very ironic, considering the plot).

If some of the names become a little confusing for you, I've included a ***Cast of Characters*** at the end of the story (and it's in alphabetical order… just in case you need to reference it once in a while).

Oh, and if those last six paragraphs sound familiar…check out The Boss *Always* Sits In The Back. Enjoy!

Following the Cast of Characters is something special you wouldn't normally find in a book like this. Chickie hopes you'll enjoy it.

CHAPTER 1

It was just another late summer Thursday afternoon for four Jersey guys picking up the monthly tribute from Alphonse '*Little Allie*' Salvucci, the 42 year old son of Alphonse '*Big Allie*' Salvucci Sr…head of the family that bears their name and controlled the mob rackets from Clifton to Belmar.

Driving his new red-and-silver 4 door 1956 Chrysler Imperial Custom with Dean Martin's "You Belong To Me" flowing from the AM radio and out the front windows was 23 year old Enzo Paldino.

Enzo was a tall, dark, well-dressed Italian who always had a cigarette in his hand or mouth and a smile on his face. Sure, it was the sick smile of a second-rate thief, but he was also a first class killer.

Well, at least *he* thought so.

In addition, no matter what he wore there was the ever-present and obnoxiously oversized, *very* shiny gold crucifix around his neck. And he made sure it was always visible thanks to his top three shirt buttons purposely being undone.

Also…Enzo talked too much and was an asshole. But the other three guys in the car needed him to make sure things never got out of hand during these pick-ups.

Things never had a reason to go wrong with Alphonse Junior *or* Senior. The Salvucci family had loyally been paying their tribute to the Ponti family for the last eleven years.

Vincenzo Ponti controlled all of New Jersey for Antonio '*The Big Hand*' Agostini, the don of one of the original Five Families out of New York City. Ponti's territory included the Jersey shore…from Sandy Hook down to Cape May, which included Asbury Park, Belmar, Point Pleasant, Ortley Beach, Seaside Heights, Long Beach Island, Atlantic City and Wildwood.

2

The tributes from Memorial Day to Labor Day by all the "local" families, like Salvucci's, were much larger and *always* in cash thanks to their "games-of-chance" and pizza stands on the boardwalks that lined every beach visited throughout the summer by *all* of New Jersey, plus another several hundred-thousand sun-and-sand seekers from Philadelphia, Baltimore, New York City, Long Island and upstate New York.

Vincenzo was known as '*Don Ponti*' to those smart enough to show him respect. To everyone else he was simply '*Mr. Ponti.*'

For running the Jersey operation, Vincenzo would take his family's piece from the tributes, then once a month drive into Manhattan to kick the rest up to Don Antonio Agostini...usually handing him close to one hundred thousand dollars in a leather satchel.

The *tribute* was a rule set by Charlie '*Lucky*' Luciano back in 1941 when the bosses started slicing up the boroughs of New York City, the whole state of New York, everything north along the coast to Massachusetts, south to Baltimore, and as far west as Ohio.

The Chicago, St. Louis and Kansas City bosses ran everything west of there...except for the casinos and hotels sprouting up in the desert, lake and mountain areas of Nevada.

By the early-to-mid-1950s, Nevada had become the new profit-playground for the big bosses. But New Jersey was a stone's throw from Manhattan...and other than "the city" itself, Jersey was the mob's second biggest cash factory.

Sitting in the Chrysler's passenger seat was 27 year old Mike Santorella.

Mike had been part of the Ponti family since he was 19 when he was brought in by his father Carmine, known as '*Big Carmine*,' a loyal family captain who hustled, robbed, bootlegged and killed with Vincenzo's father during Prohibition and the Great Depression.

Like the others in the car, Mike was dressed to impress. Even for an afternoon pick-up they dressed like they were on their way to Sunday mass. These guys *always* dressed to impress.

Conversely, Mike had another reason for being there. Don Ponti knew Mike would always take care of the other two guys in the car...the don's two sons; 31 year old Giuseppe, known to everyone as '*Joey*,' who sat behind Mike...and sitting behind Enzo was Joey's slightly younger brother Carmine, named after Mike's father.

Mike and the don's sons had grown up together and were the best of friends. Vincenzo knew his boys were in good hands.

As the Chrysler cruised west on Route 3, Dino's song ended and the news began. Enzo ground out his cigarette and lit another as he reached for the volume knob, turned the radio off and asked, "Why Clifton? We always went to Newark for this. Since when do we meet Little Allie at a fuckin' hot dog stand?"

Carmine answered, "He said he was gonna be in the area and it was easier for him. What the fuck's the difference? A bag of cash is a bag of cash. Don't matter to me *where* we pick it up...as long as we get it."

"Besides," Mike chimed in, "This way we don't need to go all the way to Newark. *Rutt's Hut* is right off the highway...and I gotta take my wife to the doctor's when we get back. This'll save us an hour or so."

"How many months along is she, Mike?" Joey respectfully asked.

"Three, and the doctor said everything's fine," he replied. "Besides, Diana's a friggin' clean freak. She thinks *everything's* got germs. So she enjoys stayin' home cleanin', ironin', cookin'...*all* that shit." Mike turned to face Carmine and said, "Seein' as *my* old man was *your* Godfather, me and Diana would like you to be Godfather to *our* kid."

Carmine beamed with pride. The mood in the car went from jovial to one of "traditional Italian respect" as Joey leaned toward his brother, grabbed his head and kissed both cheeks. Then Joey extended his right hand over the front seat to Mike, who clasped and kissed it.

The Godfather-to-be reached over the seat, kissed Mike on the cheek and said, "It would be my honor, paisan. And if *anything* ever happens to you, I promise to take care of that kid like a Ponti."

Those were the words Mike Santorella wanted to hear as he leaned back into the leather seat. He knew his child would be safe in a world filled with guys like them.

And like *any* typical asshole would do, Enzo took a long drag on his cigarette and chimed in, "I think I'll find me a fuckin' wife someday, knock her up and have a couple-a little guineas runnin' around the house, too."

Then he looked in the rearview mirror and continued, "Either of you two wanna christen *my* kids?"

The answer took a few seconds as each Ponti looked at the other and knew they had no option. So they *both* responded with a half-hearted, "Yeah. Sure."

Enzo could hear the hesitation and bullshit in their answer…so he kept his eyes on the road.

After they exited the highway and drove along River Road approaching the glorified hot dog stand, Enzo asked, "We gonna get a couple while we're here?"

Carmine quickly replied with a sarcastic laugh, "You fuckin' kiddin'? Hot dogs? *Us?* Head up to Bergenline Avenue for some pizza after we finish here." Then Carmine shook his head, looked at his brother and said under his breath, "Fuckin' hot dogs. What's this guy? Stoonad?"

Joey hunched his shoulders and shook his head.

Though there were a few cars in the parking lot, it wasn't hard to spot Little Allie's shiny black Cadillac in the distance.

As Enzo's car approached, Little Allie and his driver opened their doors, stepped out and waited for the Chrysler to come closer. Allie, eating a hot dog, was holding a brown paper bag with the monthly cash.

Enzo pulled up with the passenger side next to them as he always did, then took another long drag on his cigarette before flipping it out the driver's window. As he had done dozens of times in the past, Mike exited the Chrysler to take the bag and Allie greeted him in the usual manner.

"How you doin', Mike? The wife okay?" Allie asked as he handed Mike the bag. It was the standard weight. That was always a good sign.

"Doin' good, Allie. Doin' good. Thanks for askin'," Mike replied as he handed the bag to Joey through the open rear window.

But unbeknownst to the Ponti brothers, who were now opening the bag to look inside, Allie's driver put a pistol to Mike's head when he stepped away from the window.

Little Allie was pointing *his* pistol at a speechless and completely caught off guard Enzo as he was adjusting the gold crucifix on his chest. Allie knew Carmine and Joey wouldn't have weapons. That's what Mike and Enzo were for.

Carmine reached in the bag and pulled out a handful of folded newspapers.

"What the fuck is *this*, Alphonse?" Carmine asked as he and Joey raised their heads.

There was silence. They saw what was happening.

Little Allie was now pointing his pistol at *them*.

"If your driver makes a move for his gun, I'll blow you *both* away," Allie said loud enough for Enzo to hear, then continued. "I guess you boys didn't know my old man had a heart attack this morning. He's gone. And now...*I'm* in charge. *I'm* Big Allie now!"

Joey leaned forward and tried to calm things down.

"Alphonse, listen. We're *very* sorry to hear about your father. He and our dad were friends for a long time. If the don had known, he would have told us. We would have said something as soon as we got here. We...*none of us*...meant no disrespect."

It didn't matter what Joey or *anyone* said...*none* of it mattered.

"I don't give a fuck about *that*. All you gotta know is...*I'm* runnin' the Salvucci family now, and we ain't payin' nothin' to the Pontis, or The Big Hand, or to *anybody* who thinks they're gonna take our money. You got that?"

Joey nodded his head and leaned back in the seat. He had nothing else to say about the situation and knew he'd have to bring this bad news back to his father.

"And just so you know I mean what I'm sayin'," Allie continued as he leaned toward the open window and raised his gun, "Make sure *everybody* knows I ain't my father...and I ain't takin' orders from Vincenzo Ponti *or* his fuckin' kids."

Then he fired three bullets into the car.

Two hit Carmine in the head and chest, killing him instantly. The third caught Joey in the left arm, but he barely flinched. All he could see was his brother's motionless body.

Once Allie fired his gun, Mike grabbed the distracted driver's hand, forced his body against the passenger side door and grabbed the pistol. Seeing his back-up was now disarmed, Allie jumped into the driver's seat of the Caddie and slammed the door.

Enzo pulled a .32 from his shoulder holster, pointed it toward the open passenger window with the driver's body sticking though it and fired twice. Blood sprayed the interior of his car as he roared, "My motherfuckin' seats!" Then he fired another shot into the already dead body still being held up by Mike…causing *more* blood to gush onto the leather bench-seat.

Salvucci put the car in Drive, then careened wildly through the parking lot and into River Road's traffic as Mike fired the driver's gun, breaking the Caddie's rear window.

"Fuck him, Mike! Get in the car!" Joey loudly commanded. "We gotta get Carmine to the hospital! Enzo! *Drive!*"

By now they could hear police sirens in the distance. It was time to go.

Mike opened the passenger door and jumped in the seat…*very* unhappy about sitting on the fresh blood. Enzo's tires screeched as he jammed his foot on the accelerator to put as much distance between them and the dead body in the parking lot.

Joey was in shock…cradling his younger brother.

"I'm gonna kill that fuck! I'm gonna kill him, Mike! Look at Carmine! Look what he did!"

As Mike turned to look, Joey yelled to Enzo, "Drive this motherfucking car! Get to a hospital *now!*"

Mike put his hand on Enzo's arm, looked at him and solemnly shook his head. There was no reason to speed.

"Giuseppe," Mike sorrowfully whispered as he looked at the two brothers. "Carmine's gone. We can't go to a hospital. We'll only get in *more* trouble." He looked at Joey's arm and watched blood come out of it. "C'mon…we gotta get you to the doctor." Then he looked at Carmine's dead body…the man who was going to be his child's Godfather, and said, "Don't worry about Alphonse-fuckin'-Salvucci. He'll pay for this."

Enzo slowed the Chrysler just as two police cars sped in the opposite direction…heading to *Rutt's Hut*. Though probably not for hot dogs.

CHAPTER 2

"You know what has to be done, Mike. Show Alphonse Salvucci who's in charge, and make sure he knows it's not *him*. It will *never* be him...or *anyone* from that family. Do it."

Those were the words Don Ponti whispered to Mike Santorella as Carmine's casket was being lowered into the ground at the family's burial plot in Fairview Cemetery.

The number of attendees, cars, limousines, flowers and FBI agents were beyond impressive and not unusual for the son of a don. Vincenzo's wife and assorted women loudly wept and screamed. The endless line of mourners...mafiosi, politicians, policemen, businessmen and civilians... came to pay their respects as much to the don as to his murdered son. The mere fact they attended registered in the minds and hearts of the Ponti family.

As each person passed before Vincenzo and Giuseppe, whose left arm was now in a sling, to shake their hands or kiss them, Mike stood to their right...his mind racing...thinking of how and when he'd make the now-*Big Allie* Salvucci pay for the death of the don's son...and the loss of one of his lifelong friends.

About 30 miles south in Colonia's St. Gertrude's Cemetery, the body of Alphonse Salvucci Sr. was being put into the family crypt, but the only people in attendance were the forty-or-so family and crew members who came to pay their last respects to their patriarch and boss.

The newly self-appointed Big Allie scanned the small attendance...and it pissed him off. He knew *everyone* was at Carmine Ponti's funeral...and it was Allie's own fault Carmine was buried on the same day. That pissed him off even *more*.

The Salvuccis were expecting a rapid retaliation. They already had extra muscle on the street waiting…and Mike was well aware of it.

He knew he'd have to wait.

Meanwhile, the pick-ups from the other families continued without any problems, though under orders from his father, Joey never took the rides anymore. After Carmine's death, Enzo and Mike would *always* have two other guys with them on pick-ups, and everyone was on high-alert and heavily armed.

The consensus of the New Jersey families was that Alphonse Salvucci *always* wanted to control their family, but his father knew he was wild and too fast to kill instead of working out a deal. In the end, his old man was right.

It only took two weeks for Mike's first show of revenge.

Late Thursday night before Labor Day, each of the Salvucci-controlled game stands and pizzerias along the shore were set on fire so they wouldn't make a penny over the summer's most profitable weekend.

Though the papers said it appeared to be, "…*arson by a series of unknown perpetrators*," everyone, including the police, knew who was behind it and why it was done. But since no other businesses were damaged or people hurt…the authorities never pursued the investigations. Besides, they knew Don Ponti would show his appreciation around the Christmas holidays… like he *always* did.

None of that sat too well with Big Allie and his inner crew, which now included his 21 year old son Alphonse, who overnight acquired the alias 'Little Allie.' Word on the street was that he was as ill-tempered as his father.

It was around noon on February 14th, 1957, Valentine's Day, when Mike and Diana Santorella announced to the world…or at least to northern New Jersey…they were the parents of Carmine Santorella, named in honor of Mike's father, and his departed friend.

A month later Giuseppe Ponti held infant Carmine, who Vincenzo had started calling '*Chickie*,' over the baptismal in Union City's Holy Family Church.

The don loved little Chickie…and that made Mike *very* happy.

Time passed. Things quieted down.

In New York City, Antonio Agostini wasn't happy about Big Allie not paying his monthly tribute to Don Ponti from the Salvucci family's businesses…loansharking, extortion, hijacking trucks, paid hits, prostitution, car theft for international sales and parts, sports betting, *the numbers*, hotel room craps and poker games, kidnapping, *anything* where money can be made illegally…or legally such as the pizzerias.

Vincenzo assured Agostini things would eventually be back to normal. He was leaving it up to his man…Mike Santorella.

By this time, Vincenzo liked the way Mike worked. He was the brains behind the Salvucci-Labor Day fires, and the don admired that it was done with no one getting hurt. Over the last two years Mike had also become a trusted hitman for the family and, like his father a couple of decades earlier, was promoted to lieutenant. This started his path to being *made*.

Because none of the other families backed Salvucci when he wanted to break away from the Pontis, Big Allie consistently drilled into his son the need to, "…always bring in new talent. New men. A new guy *always* wants to prove himself. He wants to show you what he's got. How much balls he's got. Who he knows. Which enemy of yours he fucked over. How much he can earn. How much he can bring in. The guys that've been around a long time…yeah, they're good, they're loyal, but they get lazy. They don't wanna expand. And the one thing you always gotta remember, Alphonse… is never stop growin'. It's our goal…it's *your* goal to wipe out the Ponti family. We gotta be a thorn in their side until we wear 'em down to nothin'. *And most of* all…don't trust *nobody*."

Sure his last sentence was grammatically incorrect…but Little Allie knew what his father meant.

It was now mid-1958, almost 2 years after Carmine Ponti was killed. The pick-ups continued without a problem…but Salvucci still wasn't paying his share. Everyone saw his family as renegades…and this wasn't how things were supposed to be. But nobody wanted a war on the streets of New Jersey.

The businesses Big Allie had his fingers in were afraid to stop paying his "protection fees" or to go with another family still aligned with the Ponti family. Alphonse Salvucci was now running wild and doing everything he could to operate *the business* his way…and making sure *everyone* knew his family was in charge of their territory.

To prove his point, Big Allie torched or blew up six businesses who tried to switch.

Everyone else caught on real quick.

It was Sunday morning, August 10th, when Big and Little Allie, each smoking cigarettes and smartly dressed in slacks and sport jackets, stepped from the passenger doors of the same shiny, black Cadillac used that day at *Rutt's Hut*. They were in the front parking lot of *The Tick-Tock Diner* on Route 3 in Clifton, the same town where Carmine was killed. The Caddie's rear window had since been replaced with bullet-proof glass.

As the father and son entered the diner, their driver pulled away and backed the car into a spot between a dozen others…then waited for his bosses to have breakfast and get their protection payoff from the owner. Knowing they'd be at least 30 minutes, he lowered all four electric windows, turned off the engine and lit a cigarette. He picked up a copy of The Herald News, opened it wide and laughed at one of the headlines on the second page that read, "*Mob violence down since gov't hearings.*"

He didn't see Mike Santorella walk up to the Cadillac or hear the three bullets from a .22 silencer that tore through the newspaper into his head.

Mike reached in the window and pushed the driver's dead body over so no one would see it…then turned and waved to Joey Ponti sitting in the back of Enzo's red-and-silver Chrysler on the other side of the lot. Joey waved back as Mike walked toward the rear of the diner.

Inside, the Salvuccis, still smoking, strode past the teenage cashier as Little Allie told her, "Let your old man know we'll be in a booth. And tell him we're in a rush, so move his ass."

She nervously chewed her gum, nodded her head and took off to find him in the kitchen.

Once they slid into a booth, Big Allie ground his cigarette into the ashtray as a familiar waitress brought menus and coffee to the table.

"We know what we want," came from the father and son in unison as she poured the coffee. They pushed the menus back and ordered, then

Little Allie arrogantly told her, "Go tell that Greek boss of yours he's got a couple of friends waitin' and we ain't got all day."

She cordially replied, "You got it, hon. Lemme get your order in…and I'll find him. And let me know if you need more coffee," then she walked away.

Waitresses shuttled food from the kitchen to customers at the counter and booths…but the owner still hadn't come to their table. Little Allie was getting pissed. His father was more concerned about his son's short temper.

"What did I tell you, Alphonse? Relax. Where's he gonna go? He's in the kitchen. You see these people? What the fuck you think they're comin' here to do? He's feedin' 'em. Plus, he's makin' money…and you know what that means for *us*. So calm down…it'll fuck up your appetite. And put that fuckin' cigarette out."

Even after those uncharacteristic words of wisdom from his father, Little Allie's tough-guy attitude took over while he dragged on his cigarette and waved off the advice. As the youngster started to slide out of the booth, Mike Santorella, holding a pot of coffee, approached from behind Big Allie and sarcastically asked, "How you doin', guys? Want me to warm those up for you?"

It took the Salvuccis by surprise. Big Allie didn't see any guns pointing their way…just a pot of coffee, so he knew Mike only wanted to talk.

Little Allie didn't take it so calmly. "Holy shit!" he said as he threw his cigarette on the floor and bolted from the booth, leaving his father behind. He ran through the diner, past the cashier and out the front glass doors toward the Cadillac.

A look of sadness came over Mike's face as he ground out Little Allie's cigarette with his shoe. "Shit, Allie. It wasn't supposed to work out like that," he said, regrettably.

"Whatdya mean?" Salvucci asked…nervously.

Two quick and loud shots rang from the parking lot.

Customers jumped from their seats to see where the shots came from.

Big Allie quickly-but-unsuccessfully tried to stand while still in the booth. Then his hand went for the gun in his shoulder holster. Before he could get there, two men were on each side of Mike with silencers pointed at Salvucci.

"There's too many people around for you to kill me, Mike. What's goin' on?" Allie nervously asked.

Standing over Little Allie's near-lifeless body in the parking lot and with his back to the onlookers was Joey Ponti with a .45 in his right hand. He looked at the crying Salvucci and had no qualms about putting the final bullet into his head...but not before he said, "This one's from me, my brother Carmine and my father." Then he walked to the two-tone Chrysler, got in the back and was driven away without anyone seeing his face.

When Big Allie heard the third shot, he knew what had happened.

Everyone was at the front door and windows shocked at what they had just seen. That was when Mike said, "I expected to have this conversation with you *and* your kid. But I guess that's changed now." He sorrowfully shook his head, took a deep breath and continued. "*Still* think you can fuck Don Ponti and New York outta their money, Alphonse? Or do you want your family to bury *two* of ya's on the same day?"

Salvucci sat...weeping. Afraid. Beaten.

Unable to speak through the tears running down his face, he waved his hand, signaling he got the message and would do what needed to be done to pay the monthly tribute to the Ponti family.

"Good," Mike said as he put the coffee pot down. Then a side of him came out no one knew existed as he said, "I'm sorry about your kid. We didn't mean for it to go that way. Now go take care of him...and let's get back to business."

Before Mike and his two soldiers left, he put his hand on the distraught man's shoulder and softly said, "Seriously, Alphonse...I'm sorry."

Once again, police sirens could be heard in the distance. Mike motioned to his men. They put their weapons away and within a minute were out the back door and into another car speeding west on Route 3.

Even though Big Allie agreed to do business as before, Mike knew this was the beginning of a long personal vendetta between Alphonse Salvucci and the Ponti family. He also knew if someone did the same to *his* son Chickie...he'd never rest until the people responsible were eliminated.

On a sunny Columbus Day afternoon, Sunday, October 12th, 1958, Don Ponti brought his son Giuseppe and Mike Santorella to Manhattan's Little Italy to meet *his* boss, Antonio '*The Big Hand*' Agostini, for the first time. It was a special occasion. They were bringing the normal monthly tribute, plus Mike had Alphonse Salvucci show respect to the family by including *all* the money that would have been collected throughout that summer. There was over three hundred and fifty grand in the leather satchel.

Agostini was called '*The Big Hand*' because he didn't want his name mentioned in public. When anyone spoke about him, they simply raised their hand and nodded toward it.

Though it was an Italian holiday, the streets of Little Italy were relatively empty. The locals, and there were thousands of them, were uptown at 59th Street and 8th Avenue where the statue of the famous Italian explorer has presided over Columbus Circle since 1892. It wouldn't be until that evening when the celebration would drift downtown. Italians love to eat, and the best places were in Little Italy.

Dennis Dragona had been driving Vincenzo Ponti for twelve years. He knew every possible route to cruise his '58 black Cadillac Sedan DeVille in and out of Little Italy and return to Jersey with the least amount of traffic, problems or people tailing them. He also carried an arsenal of pistols on him, under his seat, above the sun visor and in the glove box.

During World War II, the U.S. Army trained Dennis to be a marksman and small weapons expert. Those were certainly a couple of the reasons Vincenzo chose him as his driver.

In addition to that, Dennis's favorite singer was Nat '*King*' Cole. As they cruised south on Broadway, Nat's "The Very Thought Of You" was on the radio…and Dennis sang along with cool charm and professional precision. Everyone, including the don, loved to listen to him.

He was as loyal a driver as any mob boss could hope for, and Vincenzo had plans for him to move up when the time was right.

Dennis knew where the meeting was being held and drove directly to the Mulberry Street restaurant's door. He stayed in the car and eyed the street and sidewalks in front of him and in the rear-view and side-view mirrors as he held a .45 on his lap…always expecting the unexpected.

Mike exited the front passenger door, turned and opened the don's door. Joey stepped from the rear driver-side door holding the leather satchel.

There were two large, well-dressed men standing on each side of the eatery's entrance. Vincenzo knew them as Agostini's bodyguards. They all acknowledged one another as one of them held the door open for Don Ponti, his son and Mike.

Once Dennis saw them go inside he pulled the car away to find a parking spot.

Rosemary Clooney's "Mambo Italiano" was playing through the speakers as the men entered the smoke-filled dining area. Don Ponti immediately spotted the man they came to see.

It wasn't hard.

Antonio Agostini was seated alone at a table for four against the back wall, away from everyone else...and flanked by two men who physically looked just like the two outside.

Once they reached the table, Vincenzo introduced Mike Santorella and Giuseppe to Don Agostini. After handshakes, hugs and kisses all around... they sat. That was when Giuseppe handed the satchel to his father, who handed it to his boss, then respectfully leaned close and whispered the total in his ear. The Big Hand leaned back, smiled, looked at his dining companions and happily said, "Buono. Molto buono."

After the four men devoured a variety of Italian food and wine, Agostini motioned to one of his men. The tall muscular bodyguard reached down, picked up a briefcase and handed it to Vincenzo.

Vincenzo looked at Agostini and asked, "What's this, paisan?"

"My gift to you for decades of loyalty to *my* family..." Agostini lowered his voice and continued, "...and to this thing we do."

Vincenzo popped the latches and opened the top as Mike and Joey, sitting on each side of him, leaned to look in.

It was filled with files, legal documents, a corporate seal, and on top... an envelope. Vincenzo was confused as he closed the case to look at his boss and said, "Non capisco."

"I'm giving you The Cactus Flower," was the response.

A *big* smile came across Vincenzo's face.

"What's 'The Cactus Flower'?" Mike and Joey asked quizzically.

Agostini looked at the younger men and told them about how Nevada had been broken up into territories by the five families once they found out gambling was legal there. Las Vegas, Lake Tahoe, Laughlin and Reno were chopped up among the mob families from New York to Kansas City. Unbeknownst to most people, the rest of the state was divided only among the New York City families.

"I got Nye County. That's where The Cactus Flower is. A little town called Gabbs. Nothing big. Just enough to stay below the radar and bring in a nice piece every month with very few headaches. And now…I want you to have it. The paperwork's in there…all signed. What that place brings in every month will make sure the Ponti family lives on forever." Then Agostini leaned forward, lowered his voice, looked at Vincenzo and said, "Just make sure five points goes into that satchel every month. Capisce?"

Don Ponti reached across the table, grasped his boss's hand and replied, "Capisco, Don Agostini. Grazie."

After the men enjoyed some espresso and a cannoli or two, Mike stood up, left the dining room, walked past the other patrons along the bar and out the front door where Dennis had been standing with the two bodyguards.

"We're finishin' up, Den."

That's all Mike had to say. The driver took off in the direction of the parked car. Mike reentered the restaurant knowing that when he returned with the don, the car would be waiting exactly where they had been dropped off.

Vincenzo and Joey were already standing and kissing Don Agostini before they departed. Mike joined in the traditional Italian hug-and-kiss ceremony. Joey picked up the briefcase filled with paperwork, again thanked the boss and followed his father and Mike.

A Nat 'King' Cole tune was playing as they walked toward the door. It gave Vincenzo an idea, so he quietly said to Giuseppe and Mike, "Once we get this casino in order, I'm gonna put Dennis in charge of it. He's good. He's ready…and we know we can trust him."

The two men agreed as Mike held the door open to see Dennis with the car waiting at the entrance. The rear door was open for Vincenzo as Dennis stood with his right hand in his jacket ready to pull out a pistol if needed. He watched the passersby on both sides of the street and the cars coming down the one-way block. Mike nodded to the father and son that it was safe to walk outside.

Vincenzo stepped out of the restaurant with his son behind him. They didn't know where it came from, but Don Agostini's bodyguard on Vincenzo's left forcibly fell back against the brick wall as blood sprayed from his head. Everyone looked at him in shock.

The next silent bullet hit Vincenzo in the right thigh, causing him to fall back into Joey's arms.

"Pop! Mike! Pop's hit!"

It was less than a second before Mike and the remaining bodyguard had their pistols out and looking for the shooter. Dennis had a gun in each hand.

The restaurant patrons near the front door watched as Joey pulled his father's wounded and heavily bleeding body inside. Those near the window scrambled to the back of the room.

One of the bodyguards still inside with Don Agostini said, "Stay here. Don't move," as he ran to see what was going on. He saw Joey on the floor holding his father in his arms, then yelled to the bartender, "Call an ambulance!"

Outside, another silent bullet ricocheted off the top of Dennis's Cadillac, causing him to look up in the direction it was fired from. There was a sniper with a rifle and silencer atop the three story walk-up across the street. The men raised their guns and began shooting in his direction. The shots echoed up and down Mulberry Street as civilians ran or ducked behind parked cars.

The sniper backed away from the edge of the roof as bullets flew toward him.

That's when things got worse.

As the three men were looking up, two figures with machine guns exited the walk-up and sprayed the front of the restaurant. Agostini's bodyguard took several rounds and fell dead onto the cement. Mike took a couple of bullets to his right arm and shoulder, causing him to fall and drop his pistol.

Dennis threw his empty guns to the ground, then reached into the Caddie and grabbed two more from above the sun visor. As a barrage of bullets whizzed past him, he pointed each pistol and fired...killing both shooters at the same time.

Agostini's other bodyguard stepped onto the sidewalk with his pistol out…unsure of what was happening, but ready for *anything*.

"Mike! You okay?" yelled Dennis as he looked at the dead machine gunners.

"Yeah…I think so! Where's the don?" he called back as his left hand painfully pressed against his right shoulder.

"Inside with Joey!" came from the bodyguard.

No one noticed the sniper reappearing at the edge of the roof. He put Dennis's head in his scope and squeezed the trigger.

The silent bullet caused the driver's skull to explode. The bodyguard spied the sniper and fired several quick rounds that hit him in the head and chest, causing him to fall three floors and land on the spiked fence in front of the building.

Suddenly…all was quiet. Only the smell of gun powder filled the air.

The silence didn't last long as women screaming at the horrific scene on both sides of the street mixed with the sound of police cars and ambulances heading toward Mulberry Street.

Inside, Vincenzo was angry that he allowed himself to be shot as he grimaced in pain.

Don Agostini and his other bodyguard came up behind them. Agostini quickly got down on his knees.

"Who, Vincenzo? Who did this?" he asked in tears as he saw what happened to his longtime friend.

Pain and certainty were on Vincenzo's face as he whispered…"Salvucci."

Police cars and ambulances pulled up as Mike crawled into the doorway to see his wounded boss in Joey's arms. It brought back memories of Carmine.

Mike knew who arranged the hit, too. He and Joey looked at one another, distressed by what had started as an afternoon celebration…that turned into an arranged massacre.

CHAPTER 3

It was Tuesday, May 1st, 1962, when Don Vincenzo Ponti, Mike Santorella and Enzo Paldino were being driven by Giuseppe in his father's new Fleetwood to Idlewild Airport in Queens, New York. This was the start of a two-day, three-flight trip and four-plus hour drive, eventually getting them to Gabbs, Nevada, to pay a visit to The Cactus Flower.

The don's son was staying in New Jersey to run things while his father was away. Vincenzo was now approaching sixty-three and a little slower since the attack four years earlier, so he had been priming his remaining heir to carry on *the family.*

Typically, it was Mike or one of the other trusted lieutenants sent to bring home the casino's profits every three months. But Don Ponti told Mike to arrange three hotel rooms for a few weeks…and a rental car. That was the reason for bringing Paldino along…to drive and handle the luggage. He just didn't know that yet.

"Make sure it's a Caddie or Lincoln," Mike recalled the boss saying. "Like there was ever an *option?*" he thought.

But the don now needed the room a wide back door and seat allowed him since the Columbus Day ambush, causing him to walk with a limp and use a cane.

It didn't take a lot of investigating to find out who was behind the Little Italy surprise attack.

Alphonse Salvucci made it known to *everyone* that he orchestrated the afternoon gunfight and wore it like a badge of honor. He even turned his tale of the failed assassination into successfully sending Don Ponti a message that, "…the Salvucci family wasn't gonna take any shit *or* orders from him…or *anyone.*"

Big Allie had been paying the monthly tribute to Vincenzo's pick-up men, but it was always short the amount that would have gone to the Ponti family.

Allie didn't mind pressing his luck with Vincenzo, but there was no way that he wanted Don Antonio Agostini pissed off at him, though the wiseguy *was* heard to say disparagingly, "…and *fuck* The Big Hand."

The missing money never mattered to Don Ponti. As long as The Big Hand's piece was there, Vincenzo made sure Salvucci knew he didn't give a shit about the shortage. Ponti was making more than enough from the rest of the Jersey families, plus his family's territories of Hudson and Bergen Counties…along with The Cactus Flower tucked away in Nevada.

Mike personally wanted to whack Big Allie…and on several occasions followed and observed the renegade in situations that would have made killing him easy. But Don Ponti wanted to wait before taking revenge for the death of Dennis Dragona, a beloved member of Vincenzo's *family*. Mike felt four years was long enough to wait. The don said it wasn't. That was as far as *that* conversation was going to go.

Since the killing of Little Allie in 1958, Big Allie took his sister's son, Luigi Colucci, known as '*Little Calooch*,' into the family's inner circle. Now 24, Luigi was running the extortion and loan pick-ups. He had already made a couple of successful hits for his uncle, and handed off the monthly drop-offs to whomever Ponti sent for them.

The next day, the shiny leather shoes of the three sharkskin-suited New Jersey mafiosi touched the tarmac of Hubbard Field, a few miles from downtown Reno.

Of the twenty-plus passengers getting off the 10:35AM United prop-job and walking toward the tiny terminal, the apparel, jewelry and attitude of Vincenzo, Mike and Enzo showed them to be exactly what *those kinds of guys from New Jersey* looked and acted like to the rest of the world.

Enzo lit a cigarette within seconds of getting off the plane, then picked the large, gold crucifix from his exposed chest and admired the sun's reflection off of it.

As they walked, he scanned the mountainous horizon and said, loud enough for everyone to hear, "What kinda idiot's gonna go through all this just to gamble? Not for nothin', but you can gamble in *any* big city. I can run a card game in a hotel room and make more than these joints out here."

Those near the arrogant Paldino stepped away shaking their heads, causing Mike to grab his arm hard enough so the tall fool grimaced in pain, then whispered angrily, "*Shut the fuck up, asshole!* Don't we stand out *enough?* Didn't I tell you I don't want you doin' anything that'll call attention to us bein' here? And *you* already fucked *that* up." He let go of Enzo's arm and ordered him to, "Get the rental car, then put the luggage in the trunk and meet us at the bar."

The driver took a drag on his cigarette as he quickened his stride into the terminal, while Mike and Vincenzo enjoyed the quiet and took their time. Besides, due to Vincenzo's limp, he couldn't walk as fast as he used to…and that didn't make him happy.

As they entered the terminal, Vincenzo said, "I'm hungry, Mike. You been here. They got any decent seafood out this way? Any calamari?"… though he pronounced it with the New Jersey Italian flair of "*galamod.*"

"I know a place south of here," Mike responded. "They make a lobster fra diavolo…not bad for two hundred miles from an ocean. We gotta go that way anyway. But once we leave there…there's *nothin'* until Gabbs. And the hotel we're stayin' at…well, I just hope you'll be comfortable. It's *nothin'* like the places back home."

As soon as they got to the sparse airport bar and sat at a table, a cute, smiling waitress came over.

"We'll have two chiantis, sweetheart," Mike ordered with a flirtatious wink.

Her smile disappeared. Mike thought it was the wink. Then she uttered, "Chianti?"

Vincenzo lifted his head and an eyebrow as he said…almost involuntarily, "Seriously?"

The girl's look turned to embarrassment, so Mike jumped in.

"Bring us two glasses of a good red wine, please. Dry, not sweet."

She jotted it on her pad and smiled at Mike, then headed toward the bar. It only took a couple of minutes before she returned with their wine. Once she was gone, the don looked around to make sure no one was within hearing distance…but spoke softly anyway.

"You know, Mike…I haven't been to Gabbs since me, you and Giuseppe came out after we took over the casino." Mike nodded in agreement as the don continued. "In those four years…Tahoe, Reno, *all* these little towns have been growin' and earnin'. And *Vegas?* You *know* how *that's* doin'."

Mike sat back and looked at his boss. He knew there was *something* going on in the don's head.

"What are you thinkin', paisan?" Mike respectfully asked.

Next to his son, Mike was one the *only* man the don would tell his plans to…and trust they'd go no further.

"It's time to take the money The Cactus Flower's been earnin' and invest it back into the place…and maybe a place for *our* people to stay when they're out here on business," Vincenzo said, ending with a sly wink and a raise of his glass.

"You mean a motel? A house?"

The don thought for a few seconds, then sat back, looked at Mike with a grin and said, "Yeah…somethin' like that."

Mike raised his glass, toasted with, "Salud," and now understood why this trip would be a few weeks…not days.

A couple of minutes later Enzo appeared holding the keys to a Chevy.

"What the fuck is *that?*" Mike asked.

"No Caddies or Lincolns," was the response. "The luggage is in the trunk and on the back seat."

"Yeah, well fuck that. I ordered one and the manager told me it would be here," Mike growled…and that was a bad sign. He grabbed the keys and said, "Wait here," then headed toward the Hertz Car Rental desk….getting more pissed off with each step.

About ten feet before he reached the counter, the mob lieutenant held up the Chevy keys and started talking to the pretty woman sporting a bee hive and yellow vest.

"You got a boss here, sweetheart?"

"Yes sir. Is there a problem?"

"I called about two weeks ago and ordered a specific kind of car and was told it would be here," he said as he reached the counter and dropped the keys on it. "And this ain't the car I ordered."

She looked at their tag and sternly retorted, "Oh, yes. I told your associate this was the biggest car we have on the lot. I'm sorry, but that's the best we can do."

Her words slid off Mike. He didn't hear them.

"Get your boss."

Her demeanor changed to defensive.

"You mean the manager, sir?"

Mike leaned across the counter and quietly said, "Don't correct me, sweetheart. Just get the guy who's gonna fix this stupid mistake you made." Then he backed up and barked, "*Now.*"

It was something one never wanted to hear Mike say twice.

She nervously backed away and went into the small office behind her. It only took twenty seconds before the six foot, early 30s manager stepped up to the counter. The woman stayed in the office, but watched through the window.

"Is there a problem, sir?"

Mike looked at the man's name embroidered on his shirt, smiled, then reached inside his sharkskin suit jacket, startling the manager. Instead of a gun coming out, it was a piece of folded paper. Mike visibly held back anger as he quietly read it to himself, then lifted his head and asked, "You're Frank Temple, right?"

The manager looked down at his shirt. There was no backing out of this one. Before he could answer, Mike continued.

"You remember me?" Again…he left no time for a response. "A couple of weeks ago I told you the kind of car I needed. I was assured *by you* there'd be one here. You even charged me five bucks a day *more* because you said it was a 'special order.' Remember that, Frank? Then you told me you liked Lincolns so much that you recently bought one. Remember *that?*"

This time Mike waited for a response, but the best the now-very-nervous manager could muster was a nod of the head and a low-level, "Uh-huh."

"So I have my *associate* come over to get the car I ordered…the car *you confirmed*, and guess what? Your girl in there made the mistake of takin' our money and givin' him the keys to a Chevy. Can you imagine that, Frank? A *Chevy.* And she didn't even give him a discount for it *not* being a *special-fuckin'-order*. It sure sounds like you're tryin' to fuck me, Frank. Is that true?

Is that how you were able to buy your *own* Lincoln? By fuckin' people? Did you really think you were gonna fuck *me and my friends*, Frank?"

The intimidated manager was speechless.

Mike walked around the counter, put his hand on Frank's shoulder and led him into the small office, but not before he held the door open for the woman to return to her post. As he closed the door behind him, Mike said, "Now here's what I expect you and Hertz to do to make me and my friends happy."

Meanwhile, Enzo smoked and rambled incessantly about nothing-in-particular as Don Ponti gulped a second glass of wine and looked in the direction Mike had walked, hoping his buffer-to-Enzo would return.

Eventually the driver got around to asking, "How far is it to where we gotta go?"

Vincenzo had no option but to respond.

"It's about a hundred-and-sixty miles from here to the casino. According to Mike, it'll be a good four hour drive. Maybe more. These roads sure as shit ain't like Route Three…and we're gonna eat first."

Enzo lifted his head to see Mike approaching behind the don…and counting cash.

Once he got to the table, the lieutenant held up the cash and placed two sets of keys in front of Enzo.

"What's that?" asked Enzo, pointing to the money.

"The cash you paid for the Chevy."

The driver looked at the two sets of keys and noticed one was for a Lincoln Continental. He held it up.

"And this?"

"The manager…my friend Frank, he felt bad about not honorin' Hertz's promise, so he's lettin' us use *his* car while we're here. *He* can use the fuckin' Chevy."

After two seconds all three men burst out laughing…and just as quickly got quiet, though still smirking.

"The other set is for the Chevy. Find the Lincoln in the lot. I don't think there's too many of 'em out there. Put the luggage in it, then get the Chevy keys back to the Hertz counter. We'll meet you outside."

Enzo heard his orders, ground out his cigarette and took off.

It was nearly 11:30AM by the time they were on the road. Enzo was driving, Mike was in the passenger seat and their don stretched out his right leg on the backseat.

Unlike the Chevy, all the luggage easily fit into the trunk.

"Twilight Time" by The Platters played on the radio when the white Lincoln Continental pulled into *Nick's Seafood Restaurant* a few blocks off Route 50 in South Lake Tahoe.

As Mike helped Vincenzo out of the back via the Continental's unique rear suicide door, Enzo exited from the driver's seat and took a few steps back to look at the car. After a long drag off his cigarette, he remarked, "White, huh? I drove a lot of cars. *Stole* a lot of 'em…but never a *white one.*"

Mike laughed, "It's a different fuckin' world out here, *that's* for sure."

As they made their way into the dining area, Vincenzo noticed more than three-quarters of the tables were filled, which wasn't bad for 12:30PM on a Wednesday in a place not on a main street.

A pretty American Indian woman in her late 20s, dressed in tight jeans, a flannel shirt and sporting a tasteful array of silver and turquoise jewelry, approached them with a smile. She picked up three menus, said, "Right this way, gentlemen," and led them past a few empty tables…directly to one for four against the back wall.

Mike, ever being the ladies' man, asked, "What would make you think we'd like *this* particular table, sweetheart?"…then finished it with a wink.

"It was something my husband taught me when I see folks from back east."

Normally, Mike would have questioned the words, "my husband," but he went in a different direction this time.

"You never heard us speak until we got to the table. What makes you think we're from 'back east'?"

As the three men waited for her response, she smiled, took one step back and spread her arms to show *her* appearance, and then *another* step back so the men could see the casual western attire of everyone in the place. The guys then looked at each other…and started laughing.

As Vincenzo slid onto a chair, he asked, "So…where's your husband from?"

"New Jersey. Some little town I can never remember the name of…but he said it's an Indian word. He'd still be living there with his mother if I didn't get him out here about six years ago to open this place."

Vincenzo pointed to Mike and said to the hostess, "My friend here says this place has a good lobster fra diavolo. Is that true?"

With a smile she answered, "You'll have to decide for yourself. People 'round here think it's the best thing my husband makes. Can I start you boys with some drinks?"

Mike winced, hoping there wouldn't be a repeat performance of the airport bar as Vincenzo slowly asked, "Do you have any--"

She cut him off and said, "Let me guess…chianti."

Mike and Enzo looked at her and let out a "Holy shit!"

Vincenzo asked, "How'd you *know* that?"

Without missing a beat, she answered, "You mean *besides* the Jersey-or-Brooklyn accent, the sharkskin suits, the pinky rings, you pulled up in a Lincoln…okay, it's a *white* Lincoln, but it's still a Lincoln…and that *cross on his chest?* C'mon, guys…I might have been born on a reservation, but that's not where I grew up."

The don smiled and said, "Bring us two good bottles…and three lobsters, please."

She winked at him, turned and walked away.

He watched until she was no longer visible, then said to Mike, "Okay, let's see how these lobsters are."

A few minutes after the perfectly prepared crustaceans were delivered to the table and the guys started enjoying them, the hostess returned with her husband, a thin, bald man more than twenty years older than her, still clad in his chef's apron, and said, "Gentlemen, I hope you're enjoying everything. My name is Annette, and this is the man who cooked your lobsters, my husband Nick."

As the men raised their heads, Nick was already open-mouthed and staring at the boss.

"Holy Christ, Mr. Ponti," Nick nervously and quietly said as he pushed his wife aside. "I had no idea those were for *you*. I would've come out to show my respect earlier. I'm *very* sorry."

Vincenzo was unsure how to react, seeing as he didn't know who this guy was. So he looked at Mike and shrugged his shoulders.

Nick looked across the table to see Mike and said, a bit too loud, "Holy shit! *Mike Santorella!* I don't believe it. I don't fuckin' believe it!"

Enzo Paldino was hurt Nick didn't know *him*. "After all," he thought. "I *am* a killer."

Mike looked at the chef closely, then recalled in a flash, "Nick? Nick Oliveri? Jesus Christ! It's been years. You had that joint in Secaucus, right?"

"*That's it!*" Annette jumped in. "Secaucus! *That's* the Indian word where he lived. How come I can't remember that?"

Nick turned to his wife and said, "Honey, give us a few minutes, will ya?"

She smiled at the men, kissed her husband on the cheek, then turned to deal with two customers who had just walked in.

Nick sat in the fourth seat, held Vincenzo's hand and quietly said, "Don Ponti, I'm honored to have you in my restaurant."

The don placed his hand on Nick's shoulder. That was a good sign...a blessing-of-sorts coming from someone of the don's level.

Nick told them about meeting Annette, the 21 year old, one-hundred percent Shoshone Indian, while driving back from San Francisco seven years earlier. One thing led to another and they fell in love, but he felt the Italian sections of northern New Jersey in the mid-1950s, along with their belief of marrying within the culture, wouldn't be too pleasant for a young American Indian who grew up in the wide open spaces of Nevada. So after a short discussion, Nick and Annette got married at the Immaculate Conception Church right in the heart of Secaucus.

It really pissed off Reverend Fitzpatrick O'Reilly that Annette couldn't produce her Baptism, Communion or Confirmation documents. He seemed to have doubts about her *really* being a Roman Catholic...which she wasn't. But Nick wanted to get married in the town's Catholic Church to please his mother Mina.

Mina wasn't too happy about it. But then, she also knew her son was in his early 40s and didn't want him to spend the rest of his life alone...though she certainly didn't expect him to find, "*some-a puttana Hiawatha*," as Mina would call her. The idea that her son would be closing the restaurant and moving 2,700 miles away to some little town in Nevada was crazy to her.

But after Nick resolved the church *situation* by slipping the honorable reverend an envelope with $250 in fifties, and assured His Holiness two free dinners with the tip included, the marriage took place without a problem.

A couple of weeks later, Nick and Annette packed up the little Secaucus eatery, drove west and opened *Nick's Seafood Restaurant.*

The capper to the story was that the day before the guys from Jersey walked in, the 50 year old chef and business owner was told he was going to be a father in several months.

After "Congratulations" from the others, all in Italian, the chef went back to work and the guys enjoyed their lobster. Of course, now that Nick knew they were there, he sent out a platter of lasagna, an antipasto for four and a third bottle of wine.

Then came the cannolis and espresso…and time for the guys to get to Gabbs before sunset. Out of respect, Nick wouldn't give them a bill. So Mike left a crisp one hundred dollar bill on the table as a tip before they left.

Vincenzo was sitting comfortably in the backseat as Enzo, already with a cigarette in his mouth, pulled the Continental out of the parking lot. That was when Mike turned to the boss and said, "You know *who* this guy was back home, right?"

With interest, Vincenzo looked at Mike and asked, "No. Who?"

"Well, I don't know…maybe with the wife and *this* place he's gotten better. But he pretty much fucked up everything he ever touched. He's the guy everybody back in Jersey called '*Nick The Dick.*'"

CHAPTER 4

With Don Gibson's "Oh Lonesome Me" coming from the speakers, the Continental cruised into Gabbs, population 783, at the legal 35mph along the mostly unpaved Brucite Street, until Enzo parked it in front of the three-story Gabbs Hotel at 6:22PM, and as the sun slipped behind the distant mountains.

There were motels several blocks away on Route 23, but this was where Mike booked the rooms. According to the billboards along the way, the Gabbs Hotel was supposed to be "the tallest and best place in town."

As they each stepped from the car, Mike tried to soften any potential problems or comments by telling Vincenzo and Enzo, "I stayed at a few of these joints, but always for one night and then I'd head back to Jersey. Same as the other guys. But I figured *this* would be the most comfortable if we're gonna be here for a while. They got air-conditioning, a restaurant, a bar, phones, TVs, and it's not far from The Cactus Flower."

"Don't worry," the boss assured Mike, then leaned on him for support as they slowly walked to the curb. "That just might be one of the problems we're gonna solve while we're here. Let's check in, wash up, have dinner and a couple of drinks, then start fresh tomorrow." He looked at Enzo and Mike, and asked, "Good?"

They each nodded.

Mike helped Vincenzo walk up the three steps to the hotel entrance, leaving Enzo with the luggage. That didn't make him happy. He was, after all…a killer. But they were treating him like the second-rate hood he really was.

Mike checked in while Vincenzo strolled through the lobby, enjoying the old photos of Gabbs that lined the walls. By the time they got the room keys, Enzo had found a cart, loaded it with the suitcases and they headed up to the third floor.

Don Ponti had the corner suite, which meant it had a large bedroom, a bathroom and a living room with a sofa, three chairs, a coffee table and a 12-inch TV with rabbit ears. Mike had the large bedroom next door, and Paldino had the room next to Mike. His was smaller. Again, it pissed him off, but he kept it to himself.

They turned on the air-conditioners in each of their rooms and began the process of cleaning up before having drinks and dinner.

Mike had just put the straight razor to his sideburns when there was a knock on the connecting door to Vincenzo's room. With Old Spice shaving soap on his face and neck, the razor in his right hand and wearing only dress slacks, he walked to the door and opened it. Vincenzo, now in a comfortable robe and slippers, strode in.

"I don't mean to bother you, Mike. It's just…I don't wanna tell you this around the *stroonze*. He's got big ears and a bigger *mouth*," the don said while pointing to the room Enzo occupied.

Mike laughed and answered, "I know whatcha mean," then pointed to a chair in the corner and said, "Please, Don Ponti…sit. Talk while I finish."

The lieutenant returned to the bathroom, leaving the door open. He stood at the mirror and sink to continue where he left off as his don sat, made himself comfortable and said what was on his mind.

"Tomorrow, I want you to find this guy…William Dunay. The locals call him '*Willie*.' He's the mayor, and if we plan to make the changes I wanna make to the casino, we're gonna need him to see things our way." Though he didn't have to say it, the don got a laugh out of finishing it with, "Know what I mean?"

Mike's laugh reverberated from the tiled bathroom.

"Let him know we're plannin' on puttin' down some roots. You know, buy a place or maybe build somethin'. See if he can recommend a real estate agent we can trust." Again, he chuckled and said, "You know…the *usual* bullshit story."

"Got it," said Mike while shaving the last strip of soap and whiskers from his neck.

"Then I wanna meet with the real estate agent. Oh, and we'll see if the mayor knows any reputable contractors."

"To build a house?" asked Mike as he rinsed his face.

There was silence. Mike stood straight up and waited for Vincenzo to continue.

"Somethin' like that. In a little town like this, the mayor usually has most of their family on the payroll…just like Jersey," Mike eventually heard his boss say.

Mike entered the bedroom patting That Man after-shave on his neck and face as the don stood up.

On the way to the connecting door, Vincenzo said, "If we play this right, we just may put half the mayor's family to work over the next six months. And six months after *that*, we'll be bringin' a *whole lot* of legal cash into town from people comin' to gamble and stay here. He's gonna *love* havin' us around. Maybe we'll even get him to pave some of these friggin' streets."

"He probably has a relative who does *that* too," Mike replied.

The men laughed as Vincenzo stepped into his suite to get ready for dinner.

It was 9:20AM the next day when Mike did everything he could to hold back his excitement as he stepped away from the hotel's front desk to return to the breakfast table in the dining room.

He didn't even notice the warm mid-spring sun bathing the lobby's terra cotta tiles and adobe walls, or the breeze that was comfortably passing through. Normally, he'd stop and appreciate all of that.

But not today.

Not now.

Though it was hard, with each step he made his way without expressing *any* of the luck he was feeling.

The waitress had just arrived with their order, so he had to sit…and wait.

Once the food was on the table and the coffee cups had been refilled, she left. Mike leaned in a little. The others followed suit, though Enzo, with his gold crucifix dangling over his plate, started eating.

As he spoke, Mike's excitement became apparent to the don.

The lieutenant pointed over his shoulder and said, "See the guy behind the front desk?"

The don turned his head slightly, looked into the lobby and saw a tall man in his late-40s.

"G'head," whispered Vincenzo.

Mike got *more* excited and continued, "So I go there to find someone who'd know where I could find the mayor."

None of this mattered to Enzo as he interjected, "Yeah, so?" with a piece of omelet and toast in his mouth and a cup of coffee in his hand.

The don's left eyebrow rose as he looked at the driver and said, in a tone one would never want to hear a second time, "Shut the fuck up, Enzo. If you don't know what we're talkin' about, then shut your fuckin' mouth."

Enzo knew he had just overstepped the line and retreated like a wounded dog…not like the killer he felt he was.

Mike was *also* pissed at Enzo for taking the focus off of what he wanted to say, but Vincenzo and Mike knew Enzo was the only one at the table packing a gun. So it made sense not to piss this psycho off any further.

Vincenzo looked at the driver and said, "Enzo, mangia," then turned and raised his head, letting Mike know to continue. Enzo went back to eating.

"Anyway, I ask the guy at the desk, 'Where can I find Willie Dunay?' So he looks me right in the face and says, 'What can I do for you?' So like a stoonad…I ask him again, 'Where can I find Willie Dunay, the mayor?'" Mike laughed to himself and shook his head.

"Yeah, so?" asked the don.

Enzo raised his head and looked at the boss as if asking, "Why is it different when *you* ask him that?" but he was smart enough to keep his mouth shut this time.

"He says, 'That's *me. I'm* Willie. What can I do for you?'" Mike focused directly on Vincenzo and said, "I couldn't fuckin' believe it. You wanna find this guy? He *owns* this joint, and his wife and daughter run it. His son runs the Road Department for the town. Can you believe this shit? His family's been in Gabbs since eighteen-fifty-eight, and *owned this hotel* since eighteen-fuckin'-eighty. Before *him?* His father was the mayor. And before *him?* His *grandmother* was the mayor, *and* she ran the town's brothel about seventy years ago."

Enzo quietly asked, "Is that…good?"

Vincenzo smiled and slowly said, "Buono, Mike. Molto, molto buono."

About an hour later, Enzo Paldino, wearing a guinea-tee shirt, dress slacks, leather shoes and smoking a cigarette, sat on one of the wooden benches on each side of the steps to The Gabbs Hotel hoping to get a tan on his already naturally dark body. He was transfixed by the way his crucifix would shine in the Nevada sun. It never shined like that in New Jersey.

Inside, Vincenzo and Mike were entering Willie Dunay's hotel office.

The walls were covered with framed documents, along with family and political photos. One embossed parchment showed someone in the Dunay family was the mayor of Gabbs on November 31st, 1864, as the Civil War raged and Nevada became the 36th state. There was Willie's 1937 diploma from Pennsylvania State University for a Bachelor Degree in Engineering and next to it was a 1960 diploma for a Bachelor Degree in Business from Rawls College of Business in Lubbock, Texas, bearing the name of Sheila Dunay.

What the guys from Jersey didn't know was that besides the federal government and the Shoshone reservations, Willie's family were the largest landowners in all of Nye County's 18,000 square miles.

As the mayor stepped behind his desk and eased into a high-back leather chair, he asked, "So, my friends...what can our little town do for you?"

Mike sat in one of two comfortable leather chairs facing the desk.

Vincenzo walked around the room admiring what was in the frames as he answered the mayor with only the slightest of a north Jersey accent... which he maintained throughout the meeting, "Mr. Mayor, my name is Vincenzo Ponti. You may recognize that as being the owner of The Cactus Flower for the last few years."

Willie leaned back in his chair and from a hand-carved stand on the desk he picked up a dark red, half-filled Meerschaum pipe with an elk etched into it that easily looked to be more than a century old. He lit it and took a deep puff.

When he exhaled, he had a sly grin on his face as he said, "I know who you are, Mr. Ponti. I also knew the previous owner, your friend Mr.

Agostini. He and my father, who passed a few years ago, were 'goombahs,' as you folks say. I hope you and I can maintain that *same* relationship. I also know your associate Mr. Santorella from our records of the last few times he's stayed here. It's a pleasure to have the both of you come all the way from New Jersey to stay with us. I notice you're registered to be here for a bit." Dunay took another long pull on the pipe and slowly exhaled, letting the smoke surround him before he spoke. "So let me ask you again, what can Gabbs do for you?"

Mike said nothing as he leaned back into the leather and watched. He wanted to see how this would play out. Dunay's face was hard for the Jersey guys to read, and they knew they were dealing with a different kind of animal in Nevada.

It was the *idiotic* wiseguys who'd go out west to be *tough guys*, and before they knew it they'd wind up about 65 miles out in the middle of the high desert. East coast mob guys weren't meant to be stranded with no clothes, food or water and be up against rattlesnakes, scorpions, cactus... and the sun.

The guys heard these old-time Nevada lawmen and politicians weren't friendly to the mob-connected casino owners *or* Italians who hadn't already been in the area for seven or eight decades. The *last thing* these good ol' boys wanted to hear about was a bribe or payoff of *any* sort...*especially* from these "*Greasy Eye-talians.*"

The families with casinos in these little towns were best to keep quiet, keep legitimate books, pay the correct taxes and make sure nothing illegal was happening to screw the locals *or* the people passing through.

But keeping legitimate books, paying taxes and not doing something illegal to make even *more* money just wasn't a normal way of life for these guys in *the business.* Hence, the occasionally missing mobster. It seemed every culture, including those living in what was still the Wild West, sent a message in their own way.

Vincenzo wanted to avoid *any* of these possibilities, so after a few seconds of silence he answered, "Mike stayed *here* and he stayed at a few *other* places. Their records show that, too. When I told him to set us up in what he thought would be the most comfortable hotel, he could have picked a location closer to the casino or even a cheaper one. But Mike knows what I would have wanted…and he picked *this* one. He didn't have a clue it was *the mayor's* place."

Willie took another draw from his pipe and nodded to Mike as he exhaled.

Vincenzo came closer to the desk, rested his hands on the back of the empty chair, looked at the mayor and continued, "The reason we plan to be here for a few weeks is because I want to make some improvements to The Cactus Flower…and to bring more people and money into Gabbs." He paused for a few seconds to read Willie's face. It didn't look like it was saying, "*Oh no you won't!*" to the don…so he added, "If that's alright with *you.*"

Again, the pipe was inhaled and exhaled before Willie asked, "What exactly you lookin' to do, Mr. Ponti?"

Vincenzo stepped away from the chair and again strolled the office looking at photographs and documents as he spoke.

"I'm a man who appreciates family. Family…and the *longevity* of that family." He stopped walking, turned, looked at Willie and said, "It looks like you are too, my friend. Is that true?"

This time there was no pipe smoking, just a straight answer.

"Yes sir, it is."

The don turned to look at the wall and continued, "I thought so."

Mike looked at Willie. He was smiling…but to Mike, that didn't mean a thing. Vincenzo proceeded with what he came to talk about.

"I like what I see here, Mayor Dunay…and I think you're a man I can talk to. So I'll make this fast and simple."

Mike *and* Dunay looked at Don Ponti…each not knowing what to expect.

"Like I said, I plan on fixing up my casino. It's old and it needs to be updated. Not like the ones on The Vegas Strip, but something pleasing to the eye that would attract people."

The mayor nodded his head and said, "Sounds reasonable," then relit his pipe, drew long on it, sat back and exhaled before he said, "And I suppose you'd like to work out some arrangement with my hotel to accommodate and feed these folks who'll be coming to gamble in your renovated casino."

Mike knew Vincenzo had just found their 'in' to working with the mayor. Business…but it had to be a *legit* business, or at least it had to appear that way.

Then the don took it one step further when he responded, "Not exactly, Mayor Dunay."

Willie's eyebrows rose as he waited to hear what this mob boss wanted to do. Mike sat quietly, *also* waiting to hear what his don was going to say…though showing no facial expression at all.

"Along with the casino, I want to build a hotel with thirty rooms on two floors, plus a café, a restaurant and a three-hundred seat theater to show movies…maybe have some performers come to town. And…"

The room went quiet. Even the don's lieutenant was visibly stunned… now hearing this for the first time. He quickly caught himself reacting and went back to a face of unreadable stone.

Vincenzo walked to the empty leather chair, lowered himself into it, looked at the mayor and said, "I want to hire *you* to oversee the contractors and the new construction, and I want your daughter Sheila to run the hotel and café. I'll cover all the costs and she'll pay me fifty percent of what they earn after all expenses. She keeps the rest. The casino, restaurant and theater are mine."

Before the mayor could respond, Vincenzo continued…but now, even Mike's eyebrows were raised from what he was hearing.

"I'd also like you to set me up with the best real estate agent you know. I'm thinking of building a place outside of town for me and my family when we come to visit."

Again, before the mayor could respond, Vincenzo kept talking.

"If you can make all that happen, when it's done…I'd like to donate twenty-thousand dollars to the town and have it go toward improving the roads around here. How's that?"

Vincenzo sat back into the leather and adjusted his bad leg. It was time for the mayor to respond. Mike felt they were either going back to Reno Airport in that white Continental right after the meeting, or they were going to be stripped and hogtied by thirty-or-so locals, put in the back of a truck and dropped off in the desert, *or*…the Ponti family was going to have a new partner in Nevada. But as good as Mike was at reading people, he couldn't predict which way this was going.

Once again, the mayor lit the pipe and took a deep draw as he eyed his visitors. When he exhaled and the smoke dissipated around him, he spoke.

"That's a mighty generous offer you put out there, Mr. Ponti. Of course, I'll have to think on it for a bit, talk to my daughter, and I'd need to make sure everything was done legally and aboveboard."

Vincenzo didn't blink as he returned, "I wouldn't want it any other way, Mr. Mayor." Then he leaned toward the desk and continued…but uncharacteristically *didn't* lower his voice, "I don't know what you may think of us from the east coast. Yeah, we look and talk different from the people out here…but then, so did *your* people when they first got here to set up shop on land owned by the Shoshones for thousands of years. My ancestors may've come from a different part of Europe than yours. But make no mistake, we still want the same things…a comfortable life for ourselves, and to know our families will be taken care of long after you and I are gone. Am I right?"

The man from New Jersey *knew* Willie couldn't answer it any other way.

"You're correct, my friend. And I'm impressed you know something of the local tribe and their history," he respectfully answered with a smile.

The don sat back and continued, "I'm glad you see it that way, Mayor Dunay. But as you know, Mr. Santorella and I are registered to be here for a while, and I'd like these projects to be underway before I leave. So if your decision is going to take longer than the next minute or so, let me know so I can have my driver pack our luggage and load the car."

The mayor didn't react. Again, he lit the pipe, inhaled and held it just a little longer. As the smoke drifted upward, his right hand replaced the pipe to its stand, then reached across the desk to clasp Don Ponti's hand.

Willie smiled as he said, "I'm familiar with how your organization works, Mr. Ponti…and no one can ever say they've been lied to when a man of your position offers something and shakes on it. I know your word is your bond."

"Grazie," the don respectfully acknowledged, then winked as he asked, "Capisce?"

To his surprise, the mayor returned with, "Si, capisco," then put his left index finger and thumb close together and said, "Solo un poco."

As they released their handshake, Willie continued, "Just to make sure there aren't any problems with anyone asking questions down the road that can affect *either* of us, I'll have my lawyer draw up something simple. Why don't you and Mr. Santorella come by tonight for dinner, meet my wife, son and daughter and look over the paperwork. I'm sure Sheila will be happy to meet her new partner."

That was it. By the two men shaking hands over the desk, the don had secured a *business* relationship and a friendship with the only person in Gabbs that mattered.

With a smile, the mayor said, "And since we're now friends and partners, Mr. Ponti and Mr. Santorella, from now on…please call me Willie."

Vincenzo replied, "Thanks, Willie. That's good to know. And from now on you can call him Mike…and you can call *me* Mr. Ponti."

The way he said it was not to be questioned. The mayor simply nodded his head. Mike smiled while saying to himself, "This guy should be grateful he doesn't have to get down on one knee and kiss the ring."

Don Ponti rose from the chair to signal the meeting was over, then said, "I'll check with the front desk in about an hour for the real estate agent's information and your home address. Is six o'clock for dinner good?"

Willie rounded the desk to walk them to the door and answered, "Perfect. I'll take care of the agent right away."

As Mike and Vincenzo walked out they all shook hands and said gracious goodbyes. It was very different from anything back east. No hugging, kissing or cheek pinching. Yes…it *was* a different world out there for these guys.

Before Willie closed the door to retreat inside, he made sure his visitors were far enough away, then looked at the 20 year old Shoshone girl in jeans and a flannel shirt working the front desk and said, "Laura-honey, get cousin Antoinette on the phone, would you please."

She looked up and smiled, "You got it, cousin Willie."

Once the mayor was at his desk it was only a minute before his phone rang.

"Mornin', cousin," Willie said with a big smile. "How are you and the family today?"

"The kids and Ray are fine…and I don't know if you know this, but I have my grandfather with us now," replied the perky voice.

"No, I didn't know. I always liked White Elk. How old is he now? Seventy-six or so?"

"Eighty-three! His health is fine, but since my mom died he hasn't been happy on the reservation without her. I figure he'll be here a while. A couple of months or so. But it'll be good for him to be around the kids to give them a sense of our heritage and this land."

Suddenly Willie's voice changed from cordial to business as he said, "Listen, the reason I called is because I think I found someone who'd be interested in that big piece we've been looking to sell."

"Happy Trails Road? Seriously?" Antoinette asked as if not believing him.

"Mr. Ponti, the owner of the Cactus Flower, wants to buy some property, build a house and put some money into our little town. I think we'll *all* be a little better off because of it."

"But that land is over forty miles from the center of town, Willie. Why would he want to live all the way out there?"

The mayor thought about it for a few seconds before he answered, "In this particular case it works both ways. I think these folks want to be a fair distance from any population, and the local population may think it's best to have them a fair distance away. The point is, I'd like you to show it to Mr. Ponti tomorrow morning."

"Well, the kids will be at school and Ray has work, but I'll have my grandfather with me. Is that okay?"

Again, Willie thought for a few seconds before he answered, this time with a chuckle, "Sure, why not? He'll add a little local flavor for these folks."

Concern then became evident in Antoinette's voice.

"As beautiful and scenic as that property is, it sure would be nice to sell it, but…" Her voice quivered as she took a deep breath and began to ask, "But, Willie…what about the--"

He abruptly cut her off with, "That's never going to be an issue with this buyer. These people like to deal with their *own* kind. Not yours." Willie hoped that calmed her down, then continued. "Laura will give him directions to the property. I'll set it up for eleven in the morning. Is that good?"

He could still hear the concern in her voice as she slowly replied, "Yeah…that's good."

"Look at it this way, Antoinette," he said, still trying to appease her. "If you make this sale, the commission will be your biggest in years. Plus, once this guy starts building his house, he plans to do a *lot more* in town…and since your husband has the only lumber yard and construction company in eighty-three miles, who do you think is gonna benefit the most?"

She knew what he said was an absolute fact.

"You're right, cousin Willie. Let him know I'll be there at eleven."

"Great." Having gotten past that hurdle, he turned on the friendly charm, wrapping up the call with, "Don't forget to tell White Elk I said 'Hey,' and I'll be comin' to see him real soon."

Before she could respond, he returned the handset to its base…then the mayor sat back and smiled.

While Enzo Paldino ate dinner in the hotel, Vincenzo and Mike showed up at the mayor's home at exactly six o'clock wearing sharkskin suits, silk ties, pressed shirts and handkerchiefs…bearing flowers for his wife Vivian and their daughter, and for Willie, the best bottle of wine that could be found in Gabbs…though when they bought it the don said to Mike, "*This is what these cowboys call wine? I wouldn't have this shit near my house.*"

Also in attendance was Dunay's son, 26 year old Willie Jr., the head of the town's Road Department and the spitting image of his dad. Not knowing what to bring for him, Vincenzo said, "There's a hundred dollars in chips waiting for you at The Cactus Flower…on me."

That made him a *lot* happier than getting a bottle of wine.

As promised, Willie handed over four copies of a three-page document detailing the specifics discussed earlier that afternoon, thus making it legal and easy to understand in case anyone ever asked questions….and they were already signed by Sheila.

Vincenzo looked a copy over as he sat at the dining room table with the mayor, Willie Jr. and Sheila while Mike, ever the gentleman, got the obligatory tour of the house from Mrs. Dunay.

"It reads exactly as we discussed, Willie. It looks fine." Vincenzo folded the pages in thirds, slid them into his jacket pocket, then continued, "I'll sign these and get them back to you as soon as all the permits are approved for the house and casino projects. Once I know everything is moving forward, we have a deal."

The don turned his head and looked at Sheila. At 24, she was a younger version of her mother, standing at 5'9 with shoulder-length brunette hair and brown eyes. Though she wouldn't be considered beautiful, her education and business acumen showed through more in her than anyone else in her family. And *that* impressed Vincenzo.

She returned his look as he spoke.

"I hope you know the great things you and your father are about to do for Gabbs, Sheila," he said almost paternally. "If we do this right, in less than a year people will be coming here for shows, food and a great time."

"Looking at it that way, Mr. Ponti, I'm happy to be a part of it. But…" then she hesitated and with seriousness in her voice, looked even deeper at him. "I'm just concerned you may have *other* plans. Plans that may make our town the *wrong* kind of place to visit…and causing us to regret what you're telling us here tonight. It's no secret who you are and the people you're involved with in New York and New Jersey. They have a history of--"

"*Sheila!*" Willie nervously jumped in. "That's no way to speak to Mr. Ponti."

Vincenzo held up a hand to calm her father down and looked at Sheila with a little more respect as he answered, "I know what and *who* you're talking about…and I know *why* you're saying it. I'm personally assuring you, Miss Dunay…we aren't here to do that. The fact is…gambling's legal in certain counties of Nevada, and as you know, Nye is one of them. People like me and those in my employ have the knowledge and experience in running that kind of operation efficiently and profitably. All I want is to run an honest business in an area that hasn't been overrun like some *other* towns in this state. By fixing up the casino with a hotel, plus a couple of places to eat and a theater to see a show…there'll be nothing like it for a hundred miles in any direction. With what I'm planning, and with the help and partnership of you and your family…people will be talking about Gabbs for years. *Years.*"

He placed his hand on hers and continued, "I promise you, Sheila, The Cactus Flower will be one-hundred percent legitimate. You have *my* word, and the word of my family."

In reality, Sheila had no idea what that speech from a person like Vincenzo would mean to someone back in New Jersey, but at the moment… those words worked, and as Willie and his son watched, Vincenzo and Sheila shook hands.

A moment later, Vivian Dunay and Mike returned from viewing the house and property as Willie Jr. popped open the wine and filled glasses to toast having the men from Jersey at their home, then Sheila and her mom went into the kitchen to work on dinner.

Vincenzo and Mike had a hard time swallowing the vino…so each had only one glass throughout the evening.

Earlier that day the mayor had called home and told his wife to make, "…spaghetti or something. They like that stuff." But Vivian was smarter and prepared her specialty…elk, baked potatoes, and asparagus with a dried cherry demi-glaze. The Jersey guys had never eaten elk meat, and they devoured it.

The remainder of the night was perfect. The same couldn't be said for things back in New Jersey.

Luigi *'Little Calooch'* Colucci was getting cockier over time. On the monthly tribute pick-up while Vincenzo was in Nevada, the young, brazen hood was nearly an hour late and verbally disrespectful about the Ponti family as he reluctantly handed over the bag of cash, then flipped his cigarette into the car onto one of Joey's guys.

"That little prick put a hole in my silk-fuckin'-*shirt*. It was *only* 'cause I know the don would be pissed off if I put a fuckin' hole in Calooch's head that I *didn't* do it," Joey was told when his men returned with the money.

During a brief call from Vincenzo to see how things were going in his absence, Joey told him what happened. Though it pissed the boss off, it pissed Mike off even more, and he vowed to resolve "…all the *problems* with those wise-ass, low-life guinea pricks," once he got back to Jersey.

Nothing more was said about it during the trip, but Mike was already planning on paying Big Allie and Little Calooch a visit.

From time-to-time, Mike would call to see how Diana and their now-five-year-old Chickie were getting along without him. It was the first time Mike was away for more than a few days.

All was well in their Englewood Cliffs home, though Diana said she'd prefer a single-level place to the sprawling two-floor one they were currently in.

"First, I gave Carmine a bath and got him ready. Then I started cleaning as soon as I got back from dropping him off at kindergarten. I've got the washing machine with whites going in the basement and hung the colored clothes in the backyard. Then after vacuuming the first floor, I had to lug that goddamn Hoover upstairs. I sure hope they figure out how to make those things lighter someday. Then I ironed clothes, sheets and pillowcases for two hours. After that, I cleaned the kitchen so it would be ready for when I make dinner…and then I had to pick up Carmine. Right now he's outside playing in the backyard…getting dirty, so I'll have to give him *another* bath in an hour or so."

Mike just chuckled, more to himself than over the phone to his germophobic wife, as he finally got in, "How often do you need to give him a bath? Or vacuum the whole friggin' house? Or sterilize the kitchen?"

He knew *exactly* what he was going to get as a reply, but loved hearing it anyway. Diana was an old-school Hudson County Italian girl from Jersey City, and had no problem dishing it out just as fast as it came at her…and with more authority.

"Yeah, so? Your house is immaculate when you bring your friends here, ain't it? Your clothes are spotless and creased, and your son is probably the cleanest and heathiest kid on the block. So don't gimme any of your shit."

To call Diana a germaphobe was an understatement. And that was just *one* of the reasons Mike loved her.

Another reason their marriage worked was because from the day they met, Diana knew he was part of something bigger than most people could understand, but she fell in love with *the man*, not what he did. He treated her with more respect than the average guy at that time, and he gave her the life and family she cherished.

Respect was one of the primary traits Mike was already instilling into his son.

Respect was paramount…and protecting the women in your life was even higher than that.

Conversely, Diana was teaching young Carmine about germs, bacteria, cleanliness and a neat appearance.

Diana also knew never to ask about Mike's business or his *other* family. He always told her what she needed to know...and no more. Often, the less one knew, the better off they were.

Diana lived by those rules.

CHAPTER 5

The guys finished breakfast at The Gabbs Hotel and returned to their rooms to clean up and dress for the day. It was exactly 9:30AM on Friday, May 4th, when Don Ponti slid into the backseat of the Lincoln and laid a briefcase next to him. Mike took the passenger seat and Enzo got behind the wheel, then asked, "Where we goin'?"

Mike reached into his sport jacket, took out the directions Laura provided the day before, and answered, "According to this, it's gonna take about an hour-twenty, more-or-less. All local roads, nothin' fancy. If we do it right, it says it's gonna be forty-six-and three-tenth miles."

"And we're going there for…?" Enzo inquisitively asked.

"None of your fuckin' business. Drive and you'll find out when we get there," came from the backseat.

Mike pointed to the right and said, "Go north on Brucite Street to Route Twenty-three South. Take that for…" He looked back at the paper. "Thirty-one-and-six-tenth miles…then make a left. What's with these friggin' 'tenths'? They must really get lost out this way and need these down-to-the-fuckin'-inch details." He looked at Enzo and continued, "I'll tell you more when we get there. Just make sure you watch the mileage gauge…and get gas. I don't want us gettin' stuck somewhere out there."

After filling up at the Sinclair station, Paldino pulled the Continental onto Brucite and started their journey, no one being exactly sure where they were going or what they were going to see when they got there.

It took about an hour on the mountainous two lane highway that was more dirt and sand than blacktop before the car made a left onto Old Shoshone Road…where it turned into a one lane dirt road.

Louis Prima's "That Old Black Magic" was the last song they heard before the radio signal disappeared. Out of nowhere and very uncharacteristically, the boss said, "I never thought that girl he sings with got enough credit."

They patiently cruised along the empty road while remarking on everything from the scenery, to the need for paved roads, to having to take a leak. Then Enzo slowed the car as they passed a large wooden sign that read, "Entering Historic Shoshone Tribal Territory."

"Whatdya know about *that*. This is fuckin' Injun land," came from the none-too-smart Enzo.

In unison Mike and Vincenzo said, "It was *all* their land, you dumb fuck."

The mob lieutenant and his boss turned to one another and simultaneously broke out laughing because they had said it together. Paldino wasn't as happy about it.

"*All* this land, the whole fuckin' country was theirs before Columbus and the Pilgrims and the Spaniards decided *they* wanted all of it. Didn't you go to fuckin' school, *stoonad?*" came from Mike...but once again, he and Vincenzo remembered their now-pissed off driver was the only one carrying a gun, and they were too far from civilization if he decided to do something crazy.

So again, they shut their mouths as the car continued for 12.2 miles before turning right onto Happy Trails Road for the last two-and-a-half miles.

At that point there was nothing as far as they could see. No homes. No cars. No people. Just tall pine trees, the unpaved road they were driving on and the occasional screech from the regional birds of prey.

The now dirty-and-dusty white car approached the long unpaved driveway with a wooden post bearing the address, 16, and a "For Sale" sign from the Shoshone Realty Company. Enzo looked at the mileage gauge and announced, "This must be the place. Forty-six-and-three-tenth miles...on the nose."

Mike looked at his watch and said, "And eight after eleven. Not bad for not havin' a friggin' clue where we were goin'."

"No chance you wanna tell me what's up this driveway?" Enzo asked.

"Not a clue," said the boss. "So let's see. Drive."

Enzo turned the car into the majestically forest-lined driveway and drove just over a mile to a five acre clearing. There was a blue 1959 Dodge pick-up truck with the Shoshone Realty logo on the doors parked along the tree-line. Standing next to it was 33 year old Antoinette Goode, the peppy Native American realtor Vincenzo had come to meet.

Kneeling in the center of the clearing with his back to the new arrivals, holding small gardening shears and pruning some shrubbery was Antoinette's aged grandfather, White Elk. Just short of six feet tall, he wore denim pants and a tattered denim jacket with no shirt, and seemed to purposely avoid acknowledging the guys.

Antoinette anxiously smoothed her blue jacket as the completely-out-of-place sedan drove into the clearing and pulled close to her. Mike and Enzo, dressed in the height of early-1960s New Jersey fashion, right down to their perfectly polished Italian loafers, stepped from the car.

Mike opened the backdoor and assisted his boss. Once the don was on the ground and took a few steps with the help of his cane, White Elk stood and made eye contact with him…and Vincenzo returned the look.

It wasn't hard for the Italian from New Jersey to see the struggle of White Elk's people carved into his face.

The sound of Antoinette's voice brought the don's attention back to the reason they had made the long drive as she said, "Gentlemen! You found it," and approached to shake his hand.

"You must be Antoinette. I'm Vincenzo Ponti and these are my associates, Mr. Santorella and Mr. Paldino. Mayor Dunay said you're the person to talk to about finding a piece of property outside of town to build a house, so you come highly recommended." Then he chuckled, "I guess you can't get more outside of town than this, huh?"

Antoinette politely nodded. Mike and Enzo didn't make a sound.

"So…what are you going to show me?" Vincenzo asked, getting to the point.

She proudly waved her arms and answered, "You're standing on it. Two-hundred-and-twenty-five acres of untouched land. A mile long driveway, and best of all…seclusion. *Total* seclusion."

Surprisingly, Vincenzo looked around and said, "Not bad. Show me more. Show me why I want to build a house here for my family."

Of course, she had no idea which *family* he was actually talking about. But since he was the buyer, she focused her attention on him as she said, "Why don't we take a walk around the acreage so you can get an idea of what can be done here, as long as it's not a problem with your cane."

Vincenzo agreed and signaled his men to follow as he and the real estate agent leisurely strolled to the center of the clearing.

Mike and Enzo, about fifteen feet behind their boss, looked closely at White Elk as they approached him. Mike nodded his head to show the normal respect given to an older person. White Elk didn't respond. Enzo, of course, couldn't keep his mouth shut as he walked past the old man, raising his hand and saying in a TV-Indian voice, "How!"

White Elk remained stone-faced...his disdain for the men was undeniable.

As they continued walking and were out of earshot, Mike quietly snarled to Enzo, "How many times we gotta tell you to shut your fuckin' mouth and stop makin' the rest of us look bad?"

Again, Enzo was pissed off at being talked to like that...but he knew not to reply.

Not far from the center of the clearing where the driveway ended, Antoinette again opened her arms wide, spun around and said, "*This* would be the perfect spot to build your home...and as big as you'd like, though the county code says you can't exceed two floors. I hope that's okay?"

Vincenzo nodded his head, so she continued.

"Your nearest neighbor is more than twelve miles away. So if you're looking for peace and quiet, Mr. Ponti...you found it."

Vincenzo stood for a few seconds looking at the trees, the large clearing and the blue sky, then asked, "So...what's the owner want for this little piece of paradise?" Then he lowered his head and looked at her.

White Elk stopped what he was doing to turn and listen to the conversation as best he could.

"Sixty-five thousand dollars, or a little over two-hundred-and-eighty-eight dollars an acre."

"Who's the seller?" Vincenzo asked.

"On paper the owner is The Shoshone Land Trust."

"Which means?" the don pressed.

48

"The Trust is overseen by Mayor Dunay, since his family and the local tribe own various parts of the county…and this is one of them."

From about ten feet away Mike asked, "Is this sacred land or somethin'?"

White Elk leaned a little closer, wanting to hear Antoinette as she hesitated and had to cover a little nervousness as she answered, "*Something* like that. It's just folklore from a long time ago."

Vincenzo turned to Mike to seek his opinion. Enzo felt snubbed the boss didn't look at him, *too*.

Mike said, "The fact Dunay's involved makes it seem a little too convenient and too close to home, if you know what I mean."

Antoinette held back the sudden feeling that she had just lost the sale.

"On the other hand," Mike continued, "It comes down to if you like it here. Is this the place you want to build a house? And can everything you need to be comfortable be brought right to this spot to make it the house you want? If you can get those questions answered and if you're *happy* with the answers…what you do after that is up to you, paisan."

Vincenzo asked Antoinette, "Can everything needed to build a house to my specifications be brought all the way out here and then be constructed?"

"I can guarantee it…and I'd like to recommend the company to do it. All *you* need to do is supply the blueprints."

"What about electricity? Phones? Water?"

"I'm sure Mayor Dunay can arrange to have power and phone lines run right to the house. And as far as water, I'm glad you asked about that. Please, follow me."

White Elk watched as his granddaughter led them into the forest as she said, "Unlike New Jersey where your water services come right to your door, out here you'll need to dig a well and install a septic system."

As they continued to walk, slowly because of the don's limp, for about another 60 yards, Antoinette told Vincenzo the rudimentary things he needed to know about the land's water system, the simplicity of installing what was needed…and that her husband's company would be able to handle it while building the home to Vincenzo's specifications.

"This whole area has substantial aquifers to feed our wells, plus the property has its own freshwater pond fed by an underground spring." She smiled as she continued, "Though I guess you'd call it a small lake."

As she said that, they came upon the shoreline. It was a three acre, eighty-five foot deep lake. Antoinette proudly said, "Isn't it beautiful? You can build a small dock for a boat…and even stock it with fish."

They stood at the edge of the water trying not to get their loafers muddy as the don turned to *both* of his men, which made Enzo a little happier, and sarcastically said, "Yeah…fish," followed by the three of them laughing.

Antoinette didn't get it.

When they reappeared from the forest into the clearing, Vincenzo saw White Elk still working and sweating in the nearly-noonday sun. The old man stood, looked in the don's direction, then scanned the area as if saying goodbye to more of his tribe's land.

The four continued toward White Elk when Vincenzo asked Antoinette, "If this is such a good piece of property, why hasn't someone *else* come up here to buy it?"

"We *have* had a few offers over the last couple of years. But the Trust turned them down because they came from big companies working with the government. They said they wanted to build research labs and facilities. With all the atomic bomb tests going on, we had no idea what they were going to do to the land, the water, the air, the animals, how much of the forest they were going to cut down…it wasn't what the tribes wanted. I'm sure you can understand that."

And he did, but then asked, "And there's been no one else like me who'd want a place off the beaten path and would enjoy it out here?"

"I can honestly say, 'No.' It's only because Mayor Dunay feels you're going to be an asset to his town in the coming years, and I guess he wanted you to have the best."

As they walked past White Elk, Antoinette continued, "Besides, it's not like New Jersey, Mr. Ponti. It's pretty far from civilization…stores and things." Then she gave a nervous laugh and said, "And the locals around here can be, well…superstitious."

"About what?" Mike asked.

She was sorry she brought it up as she stuttered to respond, "Old tales. Folklore. Stories from years and years ago."

Once again, Enzo forgot to keep his mouth shut and said, loud enough for all to hear, "Dumb fucks."

Vincenzo and Mike didn't laugh, and before one of them could apologize for their companion, White Elk looked at Enzo and defiantly said, "Not so dumb, maybe."

Enzo frowned at the old man. He wasn't used to being contradicted by anyone other than his bosses, so he stood face-to-face with White Elk and asked, "You got something you wanna say to me, Chief?"

Antoinette jumped in.

"Grandfather, please!"

She turned to Vincenzo and said, "I'm sorry. I brought him to help tidy up so everything would look nice."

The old man angrily matched Enzo's gaze for a few seconds, then glanced at his granddaughter...and forced himself to look down.

"That's enough, Enzo," the don commanded.

The driver backed off as the realtor tried to lead the guys toward their car.

"Why don't we step over here and talk a little business?"

White Elk kept quiet and wiped the sweat from his brow with his right forearm as Enzo mumbled, "Nice goin', Tonto," and slapped him on the shoulder, causing the gardening shears in his hand to make a small cut into his aged face.

The old man winced in pain, causing the realtor, Mike and Vincenzo to quickly turn around.

"Grandfather! Are you okay?" Antoinette nervously asked.

Mike yelled to Enzo, "What the fuck did you do?"

Staring with hate at the three men, White Elk used the blade to scrape some of the blood gently rolling down his cheek.

Antoinette panicked as he held the blade over the dirt and a bead of blood ran toward the tip.

"No!" screamed Antoinette as she rushed forward, pushing Mike aside, just as a drop seemed to fall in slow motion from the blade toward the thirsty soil.

As if she were a wide receiver becoming airborne for a pass, the realtor dove to catch the droplet a mere two inches before it hit the ground.

Without saying a word and breathing heavily, she knelt in front of White Elk, her slacks and blue jacket now covered in dirt.

Mike rushed over to help her up as Vincenzo angrily asked, "What the fuck's goin' on?"

Antoinette took Mike's hand, got up on her feet and thanked him, then stared at her grandfather as she answered the question, "Nothing. Nothing, Mr. Ponti. I'm…I'm sorry about that."

White Elk looked disgusted at *all* of them and angrily walked into the forest.

Antoinette regained her composure, then put on her best smile as Mike handed her his silk handkerchief to wipe the blood from her palm.

"Keep it," the lieutenant respectfully said.

She looked sorrowfully at Vincenzo. Her *sales persona* seemed to disappear as she apologetically said, "Please don't let his behavior ruin what you think of this beautiful property and the home you can build here, Mr. Ponti."

The mob boss looked around one more time, not thinking of the event that just happened before him…then winked to his underboss.

Mike walked to the car, took out the briefcase resting on the backseat, placed it on the hood of the Lincoln and backed away.

"So you said they want sixty-five grand at two-eighty-eight an acre, right?"

She nodded her head.

"Tell you what, seeing as I *still* have to build a house, a septic system, sink a well, buy furniture and get everything delivered here, and most likely pay through the nose to get all this done in three or four months, besides the fact that it looks like I'll be using your husband's company to do about ninety percent of everything I'm gonna need done, how about you tell the owners I'll take it for two-forty an acre." He turned to Mike and asked, "What's that come to, Einstein?" Then he turned to Antoinette, winked and said, "Watch this."

"Two-hundred-and-twenty-five times two-forty?" Mike thought and calculated for only a few seconds before saying, "That's fifty-four grand on the nose." Antoinette was impressed.

Vincenzo looked at Antoinette and asked, "Think the Trust and Willie will accept *fifty-four?*"

"Well, based on getting a mortgage through the bank, then finding out about the permits, I could probably get an answer by this coming Tuesday or Wednesday at the latest."

It was as if Don Ponti didn't hear a word she said as he led her to the hood of the Lincoln, then unlocked and opened the briefcase loaded with one hundred dollar bills wrapped in stacks of five thousand dollars each.

He counted eleven stacks and said, "We won't need a mortgage, and I've already made arrangements with the mayor for all the permits I'll need."

As he put the eleventh stack down, he looked at her and said, "Bring the papers to the hotel and we'll have breakfast while we sign 'em. Tell your husband I'll have the blueprints there, too…and be ready to start work by the middle of the week. Capisce?"

She stood there unsure what to say, so the don continued.

"Look at the extra grand as a bonus to make sure it all happens." Then he reached into his front pants pocket, pulled out a wad of cash wrapped with a rubber band, slid two one hundred dollar bills off the top and said, "Take your grandfather to a doctor and get his face looked at. Whatever's left over, take your husband and kids, if you have any, and go out to dinner."

She was now holding the two hundred dollars and *still* unsure what to say.

"So…we got a deal?" he asked loud enough to snap her out of what seemed like a trance…or a real estate agent's dream come true.

Numb by what had just happened…she smiled and replied, "Yes. *Yes*, Mr. Ponti…I think it's safe to say you just bought 16 Happy Trails Road." She smiled *bigger* and said, "Congratulations."

Enzo and Mike came over, hugged, kissed and congratulated the don. Antoinette had never seen something like that before, but kept her reaction to herself by looking at the eleven stacks of cash on the hood of the dirty white Lincoln.

Vincenzo turned to Antoinette and said, "Okay, we have a lot of work to do and it's one hell of a drive back to town." He shook her hand and asked, "You got something to put that cash in, honey?"

Again, she was too stunned to know what to say, but shook herself back to reality and asked, "Don't you want to sign something *now*, or get a receipt?"

The men behind him held back their laughter as the don looked at her and chuckled, "Why? You gonna steal from *me?*" He winked at her and continued, "Now go look in your truck to see if you have something to put that cash in."

And she did.

CHAPTER 6

Again remembering Enzo Paldino was the only one carrying a gun, during the drive back to the hotel Vincenzo didn't bother giving his driver any grief for acting like his usual no-class-wiseguy-self. The don knew he'd have more opportunities...*and* be in the company of *others* with guns who'd be happy to take Enzo for a ride. One way, of course.

Instead, the boss had other things to think about. Things even Mike had no idea of.

"Wanna tell me how you're gonna get these *blueprints* here by tomorrow?" Mike asked.

"Brought 'em with me from Jersey," came the response from the backseat, and that was all anyone in the car needed to know. Then the boss said, "It should be around two-thirty when we get back to town. We'll clean up, eat at the hotel, and then I wanna go to The Cactus Flower."

After that, it was quiet. As the car cruised along Route 23, the three men again scanned the scenery, remarked on the dusty, dirt roads...and the wide open spaces for one to take a leak.

Once they were parked in front of the hotel, Mike helped Vincenzo from the rear seat. The boss handed him a piece of paper from the briefcase and quietly said, "George's phone numbers."

Mike knew he meant George Pipher, an old *family* friend from New Jersey. Prior to the don moving George to Gabbs and making him Casino Manager of The Cactus Flower, he oversaw the Ponti family's roving card games, along with backroom and basement "casinos" all over Hudson and Bergen Counties. George held that position because he ran everything legitimately and was *always* straight with the family's money...especially since five points of The Cactus Flower had to be kicked up to Don Antonio Agostini.

"He knows we're in town and that I wanna see him," Vincenzo softly said. "Call him from your room and tell him to be in his office with the heads of each department at four o'clock. No questions. No options. Just be there."

"Si, padrino," was the simple response.

With Enzo holding the hotel door open as his crucifix reflected in the sunlight, the men walked slowly to the entrance. Enzo didn't mind waiting. He was grateful for getting a *pass* about not keeping his mouth shut and his hands to himself back at the clearing.

George Pipher, wearing an unpressed off-the-rack suit and easily showing his 53 years, most of them spent in bars and rooms filled with cigarette smoke, met the don and Mike at the casino's entrance. Enzo was told to wait in the car.

The old friends hugged and kissed as George whispered to his boss, "Don Ponti, I was at a loss for words when you told me you'd be here personally instead of one of your guys." George was speaking from his heart. Though his heritage was German, he and the don had formed an instant bond based on mutual trust and honor. It always worked for them. "Whatever I can do during your visit…just say it."

Vincenzo stood at the entrance looking over the casino. It was exactly as it was when he was there in 1958, only with a few more layers of nicotine on the ceiling and walls. Most of the hanging fans weren't moving, which meant they were broken. It was the same with the lighting. Some of the slot machines had rust on their metal faces. The aging bar was just that, a twenty-foot stretch of weathered wood with 10 stools, of which 8 were empty, and only three tables to sit and eat, which were also empty. Though there were two tables of craps and poker, and one roulette table filled with local gamblers…even the gaming tables were worn out.

Leaning on his cane, the don walked along the edge of the room and asked, "You have your people together?"

George realized his employer was in no mood for pleasantries and wanted to get down to business.

"In my office, Don Ponti."

George became uncharacteristically nervous seeing Mike, a man he'd known and broke bread with for *years*, but now feared was there to do more than just assist the don.

When they reached the office, there were three men in their 40s, casually attired and wearing cowboy boots, sitting on a couch.

The men from New Jersey were introduced as "Mr. Ponti and Mr. Santorella." Then George introduced his employees by name and their titles of Credit & Operations Manager, Food & Beverage Manager, and Employee Manager. Each was a local, none of them Italian, and having never met their employer before but knowing who he was, they looked concerned about their future.

Mike helped Don Ponti into George's leather chair behind the desk, then stood next to his boss. There was a hard-shell Samsonite briefcase atop the desk that Vincenzo put on the floor next to him. George stood by the closed door. Once he was ready, Vincenzo, with an unreadable expression, spoke slowly and clearly, using *none* of his Jersey accent.

"Thank you for assembling on short notice. I promise not to keep you long."

The men on the couch didn't know what to say...or if they *should* say anything.

"I came from New Jersey to make some changes at The Cactus Flower. *Big* changes."

This time, one could hear the proverbial pin drop from the silence in the room.

Emotionless, Vincenzo continued, "Since I've owned the casino and Mr. Pipher has been running it, I've never complained or been concerned about the way things were going." He shifted in the seat and sternly announced, "Until recently."

George took a shot and jumped in.

"I'm sorry for interrupting, Mr. Ponti. But we've been doing everything the same as usual. The books show that."

The boss raised his hand and said, "Let me say what I came to say, then if you *or* your people have something...let me hear it."

And once again, Mike had no idea what was going to come out of the don's mouth...but whatever it was, he couldn't show a reaction to it.

"It's apparent that if we're doing well based on the current conditions, then by improving and promoting those conditions, we should do considerably better. So I'm going to close down the casino for a couple of months, gut it and remodel it with new equipment, lighting, air-conditioning, tables, seats...everything. I'm also building a thirty room hotel onto the casino. The new place will be open twenty-four hours instead of noon to midnight. It will also have a restaurant, a theater and a round-the-clock café. When you come back to work, you'll be proud to walk in the front door." Then he pointed to the men on the couch and continued, "I want you to buy some suits, ties and *real* shoes. If you show up dressed like that in my place again, you'll be fired on the spot." Then he looked at George and said, "You got that?"

George didn't need to respond. He knew he was just given an order, not being asked a question.

Vincenzo leaned back, looked at the four men and asked, "Any questions?"

They were speechless, so George felt he should be the one to break the silence.

"This all sounds great, Mr. Ponti. But...do you think you can get the construction passed by the local politicians and the town's planning board?"

Vincenzo looked at him, and with no emotion, answered, "Yes."

"Will the employees still have their jobs when the remodeling is done?" came from the Credit & Operations Manager.

"Good question...and here's the answer. Yes. Anyone working for us at the time of the closing will be able to collect Unemployment Insurance, plus..." He stopped, looked at the Employee Manager and asked, "What's the average weekly salary for our people?"

The manager stumbled from nervousness for a few seconds before answering, "Anywhere from seventy-eight to about a hundred dollars a week, depending on their position. Unemployment will give them around forty-four to eighty dollars."

"Good. Tell them they'll collect Unemployment, plus you'll *subsidize everyone* with an additional fifty in cash every week. *But*...when this place reopens, I want *the best*. And that includes each of *you*." Vincenzo looked at the Employee Manager again and asked, "How many people are on the books?"

"Counting us in this room and in all of the departments…thirty-three," was the response.

"We'll triple that within the next year. And if it's not run right…*that* is when people will lose their jobs. But as long as it's run professionally and honestly, everything will fall into place. I want to make The Cactus Flower a reason for people to come to Gabbs. I figure we'll close in four months. The work should take five to eight weeks before the casino can re-open. The rest will be constructed after you're back to work. Does anyone have a problem with that?"

Again, no one said a word. They were just grateful to still have their jobs and to not have been taken for the proverbial "one way ride."

Vincenzo rose from the chair with Mike's help, then said, "Mr. Pipher will update you as things progress. In the meantime, thank you for the good job you've been doing since you've been with us. Now go buy some *real* clothes. I'll be in town for a few weeks and plan to stop by. I expect to see professionals working for me. Capisce?"

The three managers may not have known what "capisce" meant, but were wise enough to smile and nod their heads.

That was it. The meeting was over.

The don looked at Mike and then down at the briefcase. Mike picked it up and carried it. It was Ponti's profits that would normally be delivered every three months by Mike or one of the other lieutenants. It easily contained seventy-five thousand dollars in hundreds and fifties…but only George, Mike and Vincenzo knew that.

The managers approached their boss, shook his hand and thanked him as Mike led him out of the office.

Once Vincenzo was far enough away, George shut the door and looked at the others. Thinking they were called together to be fired, each couldn't believe what they had just witnessed.

Saturday morning breakfast at The Gabbs Hotel was a festive event with nine in attendance. Vincenzo sat at one end of the table with Mike and Enzo on each side of him. Of course, Mike took Enzo aside beforehand to remind him to keep quiet regardless of where the conversation might lead, and to, "…cover up that friggin' crucifix."

The mayor sat at the other end with Willie Jr. and Vivian on each side of him. Sheila sat next to her mother, and Antoinette and Ray Goode, visibly of Anglo decent, sat across from them.

In a conversation before breakfast, the Dunays and Goodes agreed not to mention their family affiliation.

On the *other* side, Vincenzo, Mike and Enzo made a similar pact before coming down to the dining room. But *they* were speaking of a completely *different* type of family.

Out of the blue and as the waitress was placing the plates of food on the table, Vincenzo picked up his coffee cup, took a sip, then looked at the real estate agent and asked, "Antoinette..." She smiled and looked at him as he continued. "How's your grandfather?"

She stiffened slightly and he could see it was a touchy subject. What he didn't know was that White Elk and Antoinette argued all the way home after showing the guys the property. But it wasn't the aged grandfather admonishing Antoinette. It was she who was angry with *him* for what he dared to do.

She sucked up her nervousness, graciously smiled and answered her client.

"He's fine, Mr. Ponti. That's very nice of you to ask. He's home with the kids so Ray and I could be here."

"Please give him my regards," the don said, then raised his cup as a toast to her grandfather.

"Thank you. I will," she replied, and hoped the conversation moved on to something else.

Throughout the meal, Vincenzo didn't discuss business. He patiently watched and listened to his guests, though he was impressed most by his new partner, Sheila.

It was *after* breakfast when things moved fast.

Enzo was told to find something else to do as Mike, Mayor Dunay, his daughter Sheila and Ray Goode were invited up to Vincenzo's suite to begin working.

Willie Jr. went to his office at the Road Department, while Antoinette and Vivian took a walk around town.

Once in the don's living room, the coffee table was cleared off and detailed architectural blueprints for a *very* large two-story cabin with a full-size basement were spread out. Vincenzo turned to Ray and said, "I want this built in the center of the clearing."

The exterior had a wide and expansive two-sided wraparound porch. The ground floor consisted of a large entrance foyer, a full kitchen with an eat-in dining area, a formal dining room to accommodate a table for sixteen, a bathroom, a massive living room with space for two full-size sofas and more than enough room to spare, plus a large stone fireplace. There was also a utility room for a washing machine, another bathroom, a rear door to the outside and a door to the stairs leading to the basement.

A wide stairway from the living room rose to a sizable landing on the second floor with a long hallway that ran from the master bedroom suite at the rear of the home, to two large guest bedrooms facing the east side and front of the house, each with its own bathroom.

Attached to the west side of the house where the driveway ended was a three car garage.

As Mike, Willie and Sheila watched, Vincenzo looked at the builder and said, "The mayor and your wife tell me you're the best in this area, *and* you can do what I want right down to these specifications. Is that true, Ray?"

The builder looked over the plans, then answered, "These are *extremely* detailed. A lot of time was put into them and it appears you want this building to be around for a long time. A lot of things here show heavier-than-normal beams and joists. I'll have to order some out of Denver." Then he looked through the pages a few times before saying, "But, yes...I can do it."

"And you'll start by the middle of this week?" Vincenzo asked.

Ray held the plans up and said, "We'll have to wait for you to get these approved by the building inspector and the planning boa--"

The mayor interrupted, "Consider them approved and ready to go. They'll be stamped when you bring them to Town Hall tomorrow."

Ray smiled, looked at Vincenzo and said, "I'll get the equipment and lumber there, then start digging out the basement and begin building the foundation this coming Wednesday. All that should take five to seven days."

"Good." Then, being somewhat vague, the don threw in, "I'll make arrangements to have something delivered from San Francisco around that time. Something for you to install in the basement before you cover it up, okay?"

Unsure of what he was agreeing to, Ray's answer was a simple, "Sure."

"I'll *also* order all the doors and windows. Just make sure you build the jambs exactly the way it's detailed in those blueprints. Got it?"

"No problem at all," the builder answered as he looked closer to see that the wood around the windows and exterior doors were heavier and stronger than normal.

"Just remember, I want it built within three months after you start. You do that, and there's a two grand bonus in it." Vincenzo looked at Willie and winked. The mayor nodded his head in approval.

Ray said nothing. He just smiled.

That's when Vincenzo pulled out a much thicker set of blueprints and sprawled *them* across the coffee table. They were for the casino, hotel, café, restaurant and theater.

"What's *this?*" Ray asked, while trying not to act too stunned.

Vincenzo, Willie and Sheila told the builder about the new Cactus Flower, what it was going to mean to the future economy of Gabbs, and that Ray was going to construct it as soon as he finished, "Mr. Ponti's home."

The builder was told to take the blueprints home to, "…start figuring out how much everything is going to cost, how much you'll need up-front, *and* get them stamped for approval."

Afterward, they went downstairs to the bar and at exactly noon on Saturday, May 5th, they each had a shot of the mayor's private stash of Mexican tequila, with a bite of lemon and lick of salt. It was a first for Vincenzo and Mike, who promised to bring a few bottles of anisette on their next visit.

It was a little after 2PM on Tuesday, May 15th, as the flatbed tractor crept up the driveway of 16 Happy Trails Road and pulled as close to the basement construction site as possible. Lying on the bed with its roots wrapped in burlap was a twenty-three foot California White Oak Tree, and something else about nine feet tall in four big segments covered and secured in heavy tarps.

The three guys from Jersey were there, along with Ray and a dozen of his workers.

As promised, the enormous basement had been dug out and lined with cement blocks as its foundation. There were no support poles or interior walls yet. They'd go in after the installment of what the tractor had traveled from San Francisco to bring.

As the workers removed the tarp and Vincenzo signed the truck driver's delivery receipt, Ray approached his employer and politely asked, "Mr. Ponti, is that what I think it is?"

Vincenzo handed the driver the signed paperwork, then replied, "What? The tree?"

"No. The *other* thing."

"That depends. What do *you* think it is?"

Ray took Vincenzo by the arm, led him away from the others and whispered, "Is that a fallout shelter?"

With a straight face, Vincenzo answered, "Yeah...it's a fallout shelter. Problem?"

"No, Mr. Ponti. Not at *all*. With all this A-bomb testing goin' on in Nevada, I was *wondering* when I was going to get to put one in somewhere."

Vincenzo was amused by Ray's excitement, but he was on a timeline, so he returned the contractor to his crew and watched as the "fallout shelter" was removed in sections, then lowered and assembled in a designated corner of the basement. Then he had the workers remove the burlap from the tree's roots, dig a deep and wide hole fifteen feet from the front of the house between where the steps to the porch and the first door of the three car garage would eventually be, and planted the tall, strong oak.

That made Vincenzo happy. With nothing but pine trees around, he wanted an oak that would survive the terrain and climate...and he found the kind that would.

A few days later, Vincenzo and Mike handed the mayor and his daughter three of the four copies of their agreement as promised, each signed by Vincenzo.

Over the next few days, the guys drove to 16 Happy Trails Road to watch the progress on the house, and to make sure the tree was constantly watered. Vincenzo was also there for the delivery of the windows and exterior doors, and was adamant when he told Ray to follow every instruction regarding their installation. What the builder didn't know was that they were constructed of the strongest bulletproof, fireproof, small explosive-proof and axe-proof material of its day.

The guys also visited the casino a few times to stroll the acreage making sure there would be ample parking…and to see if the managers were coming to work dressed for business.

And they were.

It was a happy scene on the steps outside The Gabbs Hotel on Saturday, May 19th. The same nine met for breakfast before the guys from Jersey made their way to Reno Airport for the return trip to their Bergen County homes.

In the less-than-three-weeks since Vincenzo came to Gabbs, he purchased land, started construction on a *very* special home, established a partnership with the mayor and his family, and was happy about what his casino, which he now felt was ready for a name change, was going to do to this little town.

Enzo loaded the trunk with their luggage while Mike and Vincenzo said "Ciao" to everyone.

The Lincoln pulled away as Willie and Antoinette stayed on the steps waving goodbye. That's when the mayor asked his cousin, "You say White Elk was actually letting a drop of his blood hit the ground?"

Still waving, she said, "Yep."

"And it was a cut from that guy slapping him on the back?"

"Yep."

"White Elk knows full well what that would have meant." They stopped waving, then Willie turned to her and continued, "We can't let him do something like that again. You've got to keep him off that property. *Please*. I don't want what happened in Worley to happen here. It may have been eighty miles away and almost forty years ago, but we can't have that happen here…*ever*."

As they turned to walk into the hotel, Antoinette said, "Yep."

After they filled the Lincoln's tank at the Sinclair station and were on the road, Enzo turned on the radio hoping to find a signal with something other than cowboy music…and it didn't take long.

The disc-jockey announced a new song by Nat 'King' Cole called "Ramblin' Rose."

A minute or so into it, Don Ponti shouted excitedly from the backseat, "*That's it!* That's fuckin' it! The new name of the casino! *The Ramblin' Rose*…in honor of Dennis. I was gonna put him in charge of the joint the day Don Agostini gave it to me…" Then his voiced saddened as he said, "…the day Dennis died."

And now, The Cactus Flower was dead, too. From that moment on it was The Ramblin' Rose.

It was 3:12PM when the Lincoln pulled into the same spot as the last time they were in South Lake Tahoe to eat at Nick's.

The three guys entered another three-quarter filled dining room, though this time they were dressed a little more casual than the sharkskin suits they usually wore, giving Paldino's crucifix more of an opportunity to stick out.

Annette spotted them through the large windows, so once they entered and saw her, she yelled out, "What the hell did you boys do to that shiny white car you brought here last time? *Look* at that thing!"

Most of the patrons by the window looked at the Lincoln and laughed to various degrees, as did the guys. But it caused Mike turn to the driver and say, "I saw a car wash about three blocks back. Get it washed and make it look nice for when we drop it off. Then fill the tank."

Once again, Enzo felt snubbed.

Before he could say anything, Mike placated him with, "We'll order for you and it'll be here when you get back."

There was nothing Enzo could do or say except to turn around and do as he was told…even if he *was* a killer.

As Annette approached, Mike and Vincenzo saw the bump in her belly and gently hugged her.

While walking to the same table as their last visit, Mike asked, "Nick around?" She nodded her head, then he continued, "Can you two join us for a minute before we order?"

"Sure, let me get him."

On her way to the kitchen she spoke to one of the waitresses, who promptly put a basket of warm garlic bread, a bottle of chianti and wine glasses in front of them.

When the couple returned and sat after the normal formalities of the Italian hug-and-kiss, Vincenzo got right down to it, but quietly.

"I have a little casino in a town called Gabbs. Ever hear of it?"

Nick shook his head, but Annette said, "Sure. About a hundred-and-fifty miles southeast, more or less. Not much out that way. *Big* Shoshone land. It's *beautiful* up in those hills." As she spoke, she seemed to become filled with ancestral and tribal pride.

Vincenzo said, "In the next several months I'm expanding the place to have rooms. So if you two ever wanna go there, you know, to get away, consider it my gift. But don't expect the kind of the food you make here. They can cook up one hell-of-an-elk steak, but they don't know shit about clams, lobster or calamari," again using the New Jersey dialect of "*galamod,*" now including the traditional hand gesture of a pinched thumb and first two fingers pulsing back-and-forth toward the listener.

"Grazie, Don Ponti," Nick said quietly as Annette warmly smiled and kissed his cheek.

Vincenzo decided to order, so Nick went back to the kitchen as the boss told Annette, "Bring me and Mike some clams and linguini in--"

She cut him off and said, "Red sauce."

He smiled, nodded his head and continued, "And make a lobster for the other guy. Keep it warm 'til he gets here." After she left the table, Vincenzo said to Mike, "*That* should make him feel special for a change."

Mike just chuckled.

It *did* make Paldino feel special when he walked in and was served his lobster fra diavolo within two minutes of sitting down.

Frank Temple couldn't believe it when Mike bypassed the car rental counter and stepped into the little office. He started shaking when Mike put his hand in his pocket, but it was just to hand back the keys, then said, "Next time you're gonna do the right thing, right?"

The manager tried to answer, but could only stammer. So he aggressively nodded his head with a *very* respectful smile.

Mike winked, turned and walked toward the gate for their flight.

During the flight home, whenever Vincenzo and Mike were alone or not within earshot of Enzo, the don would talk about his plans for The Ramblin' Rose and his new home in the woods at 16 Happy Trails Road.

The United flight landed at Idlewild Airport at 6PM on Monday, May 21st, and Joey was there to meet them. On the drive from Queens, New York to New Jersey, Don Ponti didn't speak about the house *or* the planned expansion of the casino. Mike knew it was because Enzo was in the car, and the less he knew, the better.

Besides, Mike had other things to think about. It was time to kill Alphonse Salvucci and Luigi Colucci, plus he wanted to send a message to any *other* family or crew thinking of going against the Ponti family.

They dropped Enzo off at his Ridgefield Park home, but as soon as he put his luggage inside, he jumped in his Chrysler and drove to downtown Union City for a couple of drinks at *The Ichi-Ban*.

Acting like his normal self, he had no luck with the women there. So he worked his way up to the infamous *Transfer Station*, a four block neon-signed strip in Union City filled with mob-and-politician run nightclubs along the borders of Jersey City and North Bergen.

The Rag Doll was where he knew he'd find a few guys from Ponti's crew, seeing as it was rumored the don was a "silent partner." With a cigarette between his lips, the crucifix dangling from his shirt, along with the standard array of gold and diamond jewelry one would find on these guys, plus flashing a roll of cash, it wasn't long before he found what he wanted…a mildly drunk, pointy bra'd local, laced with the scent of Chanel, scotch and nicotine.

An hour later she was in his place getting drunkenly fucked, though she'd get pissed off every time he asked her name. "*Christine!*" she yelled by the third time and in between drags on her cigarette.

As Joey drove, the don told him about the house and casino twenty-six hundred miles away.

The Caddie pulled into the driveway of Mike's Englewood Cliffs home shortly before 8PM. He leaned over and kissed Don Ponti on the cheek upon getting out, then walked to the driver's window and did the same to Joey. But when Diana and little Carmine emerged onto the porch to greet them, the Pontis got out of the car to kiss and play with the child who ran to his *Uncle Vincenzo* and his Godfather, *Uncle Joey.*

"Madone!" the don said, "Chickie's gettin' *big!*"

Mike looked at Diana, knowing it irritated her. But she also knew who was saying it, so it was better to smile and let it go.

The don and Joey eventually left so the Santorellas could be together. Besides, after three weeks of Nevada food, Mike needed Diana's Jersey-Italian cuisine. As soon as he got out of the shower and went down to the dining room it was on the table. A platter each of antipasto, lasagna and a *real* bottle of chianti.

It was Friday, August 10th, 1962, when Mike drove the black Lincoln he rented from his *friend* Frank Temple at Hertz in Reno. During the call he made to reserve the car, the mob lieutenant was assured there would *always* be a Lincoln or Cadillac available for him and "Mr. Ponti" on future trips.

Sitting in the back were Joey and his father. They departed New Jersey two days earlier without their usual invisibility. Through their contacts at the local newspapers, small articles, but no photos, said nothing more than, "Union contract negotiators, Michael Santorella, Vincenzo Ponti and his son Giuseppe Ponti were seen at Idlewild Airport boarding a United flight to Chicago to attend the national Teamster convention." It never mentioned anything about the next day's flights to Denver and then Reno.

The point was, Mike wanted to make sure it was known the three of them were out of town that day…the fourth anniversary of the unfortunate killing of Little Allie in the *Tick-Tock's* parking lot.

After a few weeks of some low-profile observations and discreet inquiries through channels only these guys would know about, Mike had found a pattern in Big Allie's travels.

Every Tuesday and Friday morning, Alphonse and his nephew Luigi Colucci would be driven in a blue Cadillac from Allie's Freehold home along a six mile farmland road to eventually get to the Garden State Parkway, and always at the same time.

As the Caddie cruised with no one around but the car's occupants, the timed explosives placed under the car the day before while being serviced at a Cadillac dealership owned by a Ponti 'associate'…went off. When the police cars and fire trucks arrived, there was nothing left of the car, just the remains of *two* men. Allie and his driver. Mike wanted the count to be three.

Little Calooch was running late and Allie was on a set schedule, so they made plans to meet later that afternoon. It was the nephew's lucky day. But it pissed off Mike and the Pontis to no end.

Word on the street when Luigi was told of the explosion and death of his uncle was that he raised an eyebrow and coldly responded, "Whatever." He showed no respect, emotion or compassion in the slightest for a family member. He was perfect for the position he had chosen in life.

Before Alphonse Salvucci was placed into the family crypt alongside his father and son, Luigi let the Salvucci family crews know he was now in charge, though he'd keep the family's name. But there were men who were with Allie since the family's inception who were more deserving and capable, and everyone knew it. Little Calooch didn't give a fuck about what anyone thought, so he had the three oldest captains whacked within the following two weeks.

Joey Ponti stayed at The Gabbs Hotel for ten days, then went home to the everyday business of running their family. But while he was in Gabbs, he watched as his father and Mike oversaw the near-completion of what would become known as *The Cabin*.

It would still take about three weeks before all the work was done, but the don wanted to be there to make sure it met his expectations.

Ray Goode and his team of builders had done an outstanding job, right down to installing the special jambs for the doors and windows. The septic system was in, and the mayor made sure poles were installed all the way to Happy Trails Road so that electricity and phone lines could be run directly to the structure.

It was a week later, Friday, August 17th, when the guys arrived at the cabin and real estate agent Antoinette Goode gave them the first walk-through of the unfinished and unfurnished rooms.

As the men approached the front porch where she was waiting, they admired the tall, majestic California White Oak. Then Joey paused, turned to Mike and asked, "You heard about Paldino, right?"

A feeling of dread came over Mike, expecting to hear bad news.

"No. What?"

"He knocked up some puttana he picked up in the Transfer Station a few months ago. They're havin' the kid and getting married in a few days down in Atlantic City."

It caught Mike even *more* off guard. The don just shook his head.

"Holy shit!" Mike said, almost in shock. "Enzo Pal-fuckin'-dino's gonna be a *father?* Now *that* scares me."

He suddenly turned serious, then looked at Joey and asked, "You gonna be the Godfather?"

The three of them broke out laughing until they were atop the stone and cement steps to the large wraparound porch. Once there, they turned to enjoy the view of the mountains in the distance, the density of their own private forest and the solitude of where they were.

Mike introduced Antoinette to Joey, then she turned to the don and said, "I think you'll find it to be everything you wanted, Mr. Ponti."

Mike stepped in front of her and opened the solid front door, allowing her to walk into the large foyer that led to a long wide living room on one side, and the spacious kitchen on the other.

"Isn't this a nice area to greet your guests? And look at that living room. It's *perfect* for entertaining."

There was no reaction from anyone, so Joey broke the silence.

"I don't think my dad will be having a lot of guests come by. It's really more of a family getaway and a base of operations for his business in town."

The don nodded, smiled and patted Joey on the back.

The real estate agent caught on fast enough and made a mental note not to mention *"guests"* again, so she led them into the kitchen and said, "Besides the latest appliances, you'll find this has all the room you'll need to prepare a meal for the sixteen that will comfortably fit in your dining room." She stopped to think about the number of people, then turned to Joey.

He anticipated what she was going to say, so he quickly said, "We have a *very* large family. You know us Italians. Guests? Not so many. Family? That's something else. More than I care to count. Please, show us more."

The absence of rugs, carpets, artwork and furniture caused every word and step from their Italian leather shoes and Antoinette's boots to echo through the empty retreat.

They proceeded to the dining room and living room before making their way to the second floor where they stood on the expansive landing overlooking the doublewide staircase, making it easier for Don Ponti to walk up with his cane.

"Each of the bedrooms has your special doors," Antoinette said as she handed Vincenzo the labeled keys to the front and back doors, each of the three bedrooms, the three garage doors, and the ones he actually cared about as she held them up. "These are for the fallout shelter."

Those were the keys that made the mob boss smile the most. Then the four made their way to the lake to inspect the new wooden pier and 14-foot rowboat.

It was 5PM and the workers were packing up their equipment for the weekend when Antoinette said, "It was a pleasure seeing you again, Mr. Ponti. You made every part of this purchase and the building of your home easy for *everyone*. I know Mayor Dunay is expecting the construction of your casino project to go just as smoothly, and he wanted me to tell you that if there's anything you need, just let him know."

The don respectfully smiled at her, and though he said, "I'm grateful to *you*, your husband Ray *and* to the mayor for all your work and his kind offer,"…he truly expected no less.

But this wasn't New Jersey and he had to play the local game.

The sun was still in the sky as the guys waved to the trucks loaded with the work crew as they drove down the long driveway, not to return until Monday. Once they were alone, like little children they went into the cabin and made a bee-line for the kitchen, and then down to the basement.

Joey hit the light switch to the full-length cavern. There was a cement floor with heavy concrete block walls, *very* thick support beams holding up the building…and a solid steel room in one corner that took up a full quarter of the basement. Other than the stairs, there were no windows and doors to enter or exit from.

Vincenzo held up *the keys*, slid one into the lock and slowly pulled the heavy door open. Mike walked in and flipped on the wall switch, illuminating the all-steel interior with built-in cabinets and shelves.

Vincenzo grinned, "Bella. Molta bella."

Joey couldn't believe what he was seeing.

"You're right about *that*, pop."

Mike turned to his boss and with a straight face said, "A *fallout shelter*."

Once again, the smartly-dressed men stood laughing. The echo from the massive, bare basement, plus the steel room they were in, was deafening… and *that* made them laugh even louder.

A little later, Vincenzo looked at his watch and said, "C'mon, let's go up on the porch. The van should be here pretty soon. I told him six o'clock, but with *these friggin' roads*, who knows?"

"What van?" came simultaneously from the other two. They never got an answer. Just a grin and a wink.

It was a few minutes after six when the blue 1962 Chevrolet C10 Panel Van made its way to the cabin and parked next to the oak tree. Out stepped Tony Battaglino, smiling and nodding his head to the don. The don smiled and waved back. Both of those were good signs.

Mike and Joey, very surprised, turned to Vincenzo.

"What's *Tony* doin' here?" Mike asked, happy to see an old friend.

"What's in the van, pop?" asked Joey.

This time he answered, "You'll find out in a few minutes." Then he looked at Tony and loudly asked, "You bring the gloves?"

The driver yelled back, "In the back."

The don looked at his son and lieutenant and said, "Go help him bring what's in there down to the basement."

Without question, the two men in suits and leather shoes walked to the back of the van, put on work-gloves and helped bring in two dozen wooden crates filled with new pistols, rifles, shotguns, machine guns, a couple of boxes of hand grenades and cases upon cases of ammunition for every caliber weapon that would be residing in the steel room.

Tony Battaglino was one of Vincenzo's men who preferred to stay on the sidelines, but was always there when asked to provide his services. And those services always entailed a vehicle.

Everybody liked Tony.

Mike would often have him, his wife and their 1 year old son Bobby, over to the Santorella house. Although Bobby was a bit too young to play with 5 year old Chickie, the boys would grow to be the best and closest of friends.

A week earlier, Tony flew from New York to Chicago and then to St. Louis, where he was picked up by an associate from a local family the Ponti's often did business with. The Jersey driver was given the van stocked full of the weaponry Vincenzo had ordered and paid for beforehand. There were two sets of the vehicle's paperwork and registration. One showed Tony as the owner. The other was made out to a fictitious Illinois company. He was also provided with a phony driver's license. It was all *very* efficient.

Tony took his time cruising the eighteen hundred miles through Missouri, Kansas, Colorado and Nevada while transporting enough weapons and explosives for the Mexicans to win back the Alamo, plus... he was an Italian. Those things made for a bad Midwest-combination in 1962.

For his services, he was given $2,000, another $200 for gas and hotels on the drive back to New Jersey, and the Chevy C10.

He was told to be at 16 Happy Trails Road by 6PM so they'd be able to unload while there was still some daylight. Tony always did what he was told.

It took about an hour before the heavy boxes, crates and cartons were in, and from that point forward the armory would be known as *The Ponti Collection*.

After they stored each item in racks and cabinets, then stacked the crates of ammo and grenades along one of the walls, Joey turned off the lights as the men walked out. Vincenzo locked the steel room, then put the keys in his pocket

The lieutenant drove the Lincoln with Tony in the passenger seat and the Pontis in the back. They left the van in one of the garages, but not before taking Tony's luggage with them.

Upon arriving at The Gabbs Hotel, the new guy was given a suite, everyone showered, got dressed and went downstairs for dinner. Though he had driven the Chevy for days wearing work clothes, he came down clean shaven and wearing the sharpest of suits and jewelry.

As they sat to eat, Vincenzo looked around to see the attire of the locals, then eyed his well-dressed assemblage and said, "This *really* proves you can take us guys outta Jersey, but you'll *never* take Jersey outta us guys," then followed it with his wink.

Once the laughter died down, they had the waitress bring three bottles of chianti taken from one of the twelve cases Vincenzo shipped out a month earlier and stored in the hotel's basement. He wasn't going to drink the local stuff, "…ever again!" The guys also made sure Tony had the elk.

When they took the driver dressed in work-clothes to the clearing on Sunday to pick up his truck and head home, he didn't know the casually dressed don's son would be joining him. This meant more to Tony Battaglino than most people would understand. Having the boss trust you to deliver his Number One man, his *son*, back to New Jersey, even if it *was* in a Chevy Panel Van, was an honor and a show of respect.

Vincenzo and Mike stayed a few days after the cabin's construction was completed to make sure everything was perfect.

It was.

Ray was paid in full, plus given the promised bonus, then put to work on The Ramblin' Rose Project, as it soon became known to the locals.

And once again, as close to being on time, given the size of the vehicles and unfamiliarity with the roads, two A. Pensa & Sons Moving Company trucks out of Union City made their way up the driveway, parked close to the front door and the four workers began bringing in all the furniture needed to fill every room.

"Why did you have furniture delivered all the way from New Jersey, Mr. Ponti?" the mayor asked while standing on the porch looking at the .oak tree the day the four Dunay family members came to see the finished cabin.

Mike held the front door open as Vincenzo answered, "You think you can find furniture and artwork like *this* out here?" Everyone walked from the foyer into the living room decorated in Modern Italian, with plastic covers on practically everything. "Not a friggin' chance," continued the homeowner.

Vivian and Sheila visibly held back their reactions and comments, having never seen anything like it before.

The Italians proudly gave the Dunay family a tour of the first and second floors, then took a walk to the lake to stand on the pier and enjoy the view.

"Do you or anyone in your family fish, Mr. Ponti?" Sheila asked, as she looked at the rowboat. Then she looked at him and continued, "These waters run with Bull Trout at various times of the year. Great eatin'."

He simply said, "No. We don't fish." Then he limped toward her, put his hand on her shoulder, smiled and said, "Besides, if I want fish, I'll go to The Ramblin' Rose."

Only Vincenzo knew what that meant.

Of course, this was the first Mike was hearing about a fish deal, though he had a feeling about who the contact would be.

The group made their way through the forest toward the clearing and into their respective vehicles. There was no need to bring anyone into the basement, though by that time Vincenzo and Mike were sure everyone in Gabbs had heard about "the fallout shelter" anyway. But nothing was said about it that day.

During the remainder of their stay at The Gabbs Hotel, Don Ponti had a few packages from Chicago and San Francisco delivered to his room. They were replacement locks and keys for each of the doors in the cabin, garage and the steel room in the basement.

It was late in the afternoon on Monday, September 3rd, when Mike finished installing the last of the locks, much to the don's satisfaction.

"Did those cowboys think I was gonna let them make copies of my keys and rob the fuckin' place while I'm back home?" Vincenzo said as Mike dusted himself off and washed his hands in the kitchen sink. That was when the boss handed the other set of new keys to Mike. It took him by surprise.

"You're the only person other than me and my son with access to this place."

That was all he had to say. Mike bowed his head in respect.

The next day, Don Ponti and Mike walked into *Nick's Seafood Restaurant* to have an early dinner with the owner and his wife at their usual table.

"In the end," Vincenzo wrapped up the meeting, "You're gonna double or triple the size of the orders, so the prices should drop significantly based on what we both need. Then, twice a week somebody from The Rose will pick up our order and pay you. Good? At least I know I'll be gettin' some decent *galamod* when I'm there."

Nick and Annette were almost speechless after hearing the don's offer. It almost sounded too good to be true. But he kept going.

"So? Whatdya say? I want you to be my fish supplier. I don't wanna deal with these locals out here. They don't know how to do business with a guy like me. You *do*. Capisce?"

Nick finally came out of his daze and answered, "Si, capisco, Don Ponti."

Annette looked at them and politely interjected, "I know that one. That's Italian for 'Understand.' Right?"

"Yeah, honey. That's right," Vincenzo laughed, then continued. "You two wanna talk about it and let me know before we take off tomorrow? You can call the hotel in the morning."

Annette immediately spoke up.

"There's no need to think about it, Mr. Ponti." She looked at Nick, then rubbed her nearly third-trimester belly, returned her gaze to the mob boss and said, "We'd be *honored* to be your supplier. This is a *wonderful* opportunity you're giving me and Nick. You're the *only* person from New Jersey to show me *any* consideration because I'm not, you know...*one of them*." She leaned over, kissed Vincenzo's cheek and asked, "Do you have a middle name, Mr. Ponti?"

"Yes. It's Donatello."

"That's a *wonderful* name," she responded.

"Grazie, bella."

"I'd like to name our baby Donna if it's a girl, or Donatello if it's a boy...if that's okay with you."

Mike and Nick's head sprung up and eyed the now beaming don as he answered, "It would be an honor. That's very nice of you. Grazie."

This time, he reached over to her and kissed her cheek, followed by everyone toasting the new partnership and the naming of Nick The Dick and Annette Oliveri's expected child.

During the flights back to Jersey, Vincenzo told Mike his reasons and plans for building the cabin in the fashion he did, and why he wanted it to be so far from civilization. He then put Mike in charge of finding "a friend to work with" to perform certain services that would be required from time-to-time.

What Mike didn't know was that when the plane landed at Idlewild and Joey picked them up, they would take Mike to the don's Tenafly home and, along with a few other men of Italian heritage, status and power, including Antonio Agostini, they would put him through the traditional ceremony of being *made*, and named a family captain.

There was no greater honor among these people, though he could never tell anyone. Not even Diana.

CHAPTER 7

Mike, Vincenzo and Joey made a few trips to Gabbs during the renovation and new construction of The Ramblin' Rose to make sure everything was ready for the New Year's Eve Grand Opening.

To stay in Ponti's good graces, Ray Goode had his crew work around the clock to make sure it would be ready.

And it was.

The newly paved section of Route 23 passed in front of the casino and hotel, which were specifically designed to blend in with the aesthetics of the region. Unlike the flash and brightness of Las Vegas, the neon lights of The Ramblin' Rose were a subdued purple and red.

There was a crowd at each of the 19 gaming tables. Every new slot machine was being fed coins. The café, aptly named '*Sheila's*,' had a constant line of sandwich and burger seekers waiting for tables. The reservation book of '*Carmine's*,' the fine dining restaurant named in memory of the don's murdered son, had been filled three weeks beforehand. Every hotel room was booked, with one of the two suites comped to Nick and Annette Oliveri...and their new son, Donatello. Annette didn't mind everyone calling him Donny.

Through Vincenzo's Hollywood connections, Nat '*King*' Cole was the first act to perform to an intimate, yet Standing Room Only audience of three hundred in the Dennis Dragona Theater. But the don's *biggest* smile came at midnight when Nat brought in 1963 by performing "Ramblin' Rose," and the audience sang along. Without question, Nat was grateful to the Ponti family when he and his wife Maria were given the second suite for their four-day stay, especially because of the non-stop racism he and other artists were enduring.

Willie Dunay and his family were *also* very happy. Especially Sheila. Everything Vincenzo Ponti had promised was right in front of her, and she and her family were benefiting from it as much as the town because The Gabbs Hotel was full due to the overflow of travelers coming for the big night.

The town hadn't seen anything like it since the mid-to-late 1850s when silver was discovered in the surrounding Shoshone hills. The news increased the population by fourteen, along with two new prostitutes to work the local brothel. That's when Willie's ancestors set up their residency.

It wasn't called Gabbs back then. It was just one of a few hundred tiny settlements dotting America's frontier. They'd pop up wherever there was a mountain pass that serviced the great western expansion, cattle herds, wagon trains and eventually railroads. Being near clean, flowing water was *also* a big advantage.

By 1872, whatever silver existed in the hills was dug up, melted and taken away, causing the count of residents, which included three prostitutes, to drop by thirty-seven.

The number of Shoshone *also* decreased over those years. Though no records were kept, it was determined no less than 4,000 were slaughtered as they tried to protect their sacred hills from the invading population armed with repeating rifles, six-shooters, dynamite, Gatling guns *and* the U.S. Calvary, who were under government orders to protect all *white* citizens against the "...Godless, savage, crazed and ruthless redskins."

The mayor's ancestors were among those who stayed.

In the early 20th Century, a mining camp had set up in the area and was known as Brucite, for the magnesium oxide brucite found only in that region.

Gabbs didn't become a town until late 1941, and took the name from the valley it was located in, which was named after paleontologist William Gabbs who unearthed prehistoric fossils there years earlier.

By 1944, the mining camp closed and Gabbs became the quiet little community of 802 residents it was when Don Vincenzo Ponti came to town in May, 1962.

When Willie offered the don a piece of The Gabbs Hotel's unexpected New Year's Eve windfall, which *only* could have happened thanks to the sold out evening at The Ramblin' Rose, Vincenzo politely pushed the envelope aside and whispered in Willie's ear, "That's just *one* of the benefits of doing business with me, my friend." The boss backed up, slyly smiled and said, "Don't worry. When we do something I think I should get a piece of..." he winked, and just before he turned to walk away, finished with, "...I'll let you know," leaving the mayor a little shaken.

George Pipher and his managers wore tuxedos, and every employee was neatly attired in Ramblin' Rose shirts, pants and name tags.

At the end of the night, Mike walked with the Ponti men and quietly whispered, "It's a shame Benny Siegel's first night didn't go this well."

"Benny had the foresight, he just forgot to respect money *and* the people who gave it to him," Vincenzo replied, then looked seriously at them and spoke. "That was the lesson Benny learned the hard way. The guys who gave him the money felt he was fuckin' 'em, and if you let somebody fuck you once and get away with it, you just gave 'em permission to fuck you ·over and over. You gotta make sure they either never screw you the first time, or you never give 'em the chance to do it twice. The Commission thought Benny took his second chance. That was where he went wrong. He *was* a very smart guy. But he *never* should-a thought he was smarter than the people who financed him. Capisce?"

The don had just given them words he never wanted them to forget.

Vincenzo and his wife spent the next few days, along with their son Giuseppe and *his* wife, and Mike, Diana and the nearly six year old Chickie, at the cabin enjoying the solitude, the space and the beautiful night skies. Of course, before returning to New Jersey on Saturday, January 5th, they all enjoyed dinner at *Nick's Seafood Restaurant* in South Lake Tahoe.

It wasn't until Tuesday, February 5th, that Mike, now 34 and a *made man*, made his first trip to the cabin without the don, though he *was* with Andy Cappomaggi, the chosen associate he was ordered to find, along with a Rutherford, New Jersey wiseguy named Gary Gentile, a low-level soldier for Ponti family lieutenant Paulie Schielzo.

Gary had one job and one job only...to run the coin-operated toiletry machine business in Bergen County. All he had to do was make sure they were filled with cologne, perfume, combs, condoms and sanitary napkins. After expenses, he was taking in over $500 a week for himself, plus giving an average of $3,000 to his boss, who kicked $1,700 up to Don Ponti every week.

But after doing the job for seven months, Gary told Schielzo a dozen machines had been stolen from nine diner and gasoline station bathrooms along Routes 17 and 4.

It only took Schielzo a day to wait for Gary to leave his house and for Enzo Paldino to pick the backdoor lock so Paulie could go inside to find all twelve machines sitting in Gary's basement. He left the house just as found it, and it was never known the two men were there.

Therefore, Gary Gentile was made an offer he'd never *want* to refuse.

Mike told Gary about the toiletry contract Don Ponti wanted him to have at the hotel and casino in Nevada. The boss needed Gary to check the place out to see how many machines they'd require, and that the don, "...wants only the most expensive and the best." He was also told to, "...keep your mouth shut about where you're going and why you're going there. The don don't want any of his *other* guys knowin' it was *you* who got the contract," then he finished it with a friendly wink.

Gary was honored by the request, so he joined Mike and Andy on the two day trip to Gabbs. Of course, Mike made up some bullshit story about why the airline ticket was made out to Enzo Paldino, but Gary was so excited it didn't matter to him.

Gary Gentile also had a major flaw. He told the stupidest jokes, and only *he* thought they were funny.

Once they landed in Reno, Mike avoided the Hertz desk and had Andy rent an unassuming Plymouth. It wasn't long before they were heading south with Mike driving and The Rooftop Singers' "Walk Right In" pulsing from the AM radio. Upon arriving in Gabbs, Andy went into the local market to pick up everything they'd need for a few days at the cabin. Bread, milk, coffee, cold cuts and most importantly...toilet paper. Mike stayed with Gary in the parked car around the corner, but was forced to sit through a couple of terrible jokes which were nothing more than ones the jokester heard on The Ed Sullivan Show over the years.

Gary was visibly disappointed as they drove past The Ramblin' Rose.

"Fuck it, Gary. Let's get to the cabin to unpack and clean up. We'll come back later and have dinner. You like lobster fra diavolo?" Mike calmly asked.

"Oh, okay. And yeah, sure. I *love* fra diavolo."

Gary was told to lay off the jokes for the remainder of the ride, so the conversation was mainly about the scenery, the roads and the wide open spaces where one could stop to pee, until they arrived at 16 Happy Trails Road.

The two guys who had never seen *the cabin* before were visibly impressed as the car entered the five acre clearing.

Once they parked, Andy took his and Mike's suitcases while Gary took his luggage and the two grocery bags. Mike took out his keys, opened the front door and they entered the cabin.

Mike put the groceries on the kitchen counter as Andy and Gary went upstairs with the luggage, then he went to the basement.

Several minutes later, Andy and Gary made their way to the kitchen where Mike was putting away the contents of the bags.

"Christ, Mike! I would-a thought you'd have that done by now," Gary said, not thinking to whom he was talking.

Mike smiled and answered, "I had-ta check the basement for leaks, then take one myself," ending it with a wink as he put the last of the supplies away and excitedly said, "C'mon, you *gotta* see the lake."

"Okay, but you *gotta* hear this joke I remembered upstairs."

Mike, appeasing him, said, "Sure. What the fuck. G'head," as they laughed and headed toward the front door.

Gary was wrapping up the short joke as Andy held the door open for them to walk out.

"...so then the lumberjack goes, 'No, today's *your day* in the barrel!'"

No one laughed. Gary walked off the porch and took a few steps before realizing he was alone. He turned to see Mike and Andy on the porch... each pointing a shiny, new Colt .45 pistol at him. The thief froze.

"You know, Gary," Mike calmly looked at him and said, "You shouldn't-a put those machines in your basement and steal from the Ponti family. So, ya know what this means, right?"

Gary was about to speak, but Mike didn't give him the chance, and said, "It means, you're a funny guy and all, and none of this is personal, but it looks like today's *your* day in the barrel." Then he fired a round, but didn't see it hit Gary square in the chest and throw him onto the ground. Mike had immediately looked up, amazed at the way the surrounding forest kept the sound of the loud .45 from echoing off the distant hills.

Meanwhile, Gary Gentile lay dead and his corpse was bleeding onto the ground.

"What the fuck, Mike!" Andy said, bringing Mike back to the moment. "Whatcha fly me out here for if you were gonna do him yourself? You said we were gonna wing him a few times first."

Comically, Mike acted like a schoolboy being scolded as he lowered the gun, hung his head to his chin, swayed side-to-side and said, "I'm sorry. It won't happen again."

"Good," Andy said authoritatively while taking Mike's .45 away as if he were being punished.

After they had a laugh, Andy got serious and asked, "Okay, what are we gonna do with this fuckin' guy?"

Mike proudly said, "Watch."

They put the pistols on the porch, then Mike took out his keys as they walked to the third garage bay. Once he unlocked it, Andy raised the heavy steel door revealing a new John Deere backhoe.

"The keys are in it. You and me are the only guys the don trusts who know how to drive one, so let's get to work. We'll take care of this guy, clean up and go eat."

Andy drove the earth-mover out of the garage to the front of the cabin and expertly brought the wide front shovel to within an inch of Gary's body. Mike, avoiding the blood on Gary's clothes and the ground, flipped the body face down into the shovel, then raised his hand, signaling Andy to wait. He went into Gary's pockets to remove his wallet and cash, then lifted the money and yelled over the engine, "Casino money for later!"

Mike walked around the distant tree line before choosing a spot. Andy wasn't far behind with Gary's body slumped in the front shovel, until he raised it, tilted it and dumped Gary out. He maneuvered the earth-mover so the rear digging shovel was above where Mike chose and dug a hole about four feet wide by four feet deep. Then he swung the vehicle around and used the extended arm and rear shovel to push Gary in. It only took a couple of minutes to replace the dirt and pound it down.

Before the backhoe was put away, they hosed down the shovels and the ground where Gary died.

When they finally got in the cabin it was nearing 6PM. The sun would be gone by the time they were ready for dinner, but Mike had a couple of things to take care of first.

While Andy showered, Mike built a small fire in the living room with wood from the countless cords stacked outside the garage's back wall. While the fire was beginning to catch, he sat on a plastic covered chair, picked up the phone and called the local switchboard to connect him with his Englewood Cliffs home to say goodnight to his wife and son. Then he called Joey's house in Tenafly, two blocks from his father's place.

"Hey, goombah!" Joey said when he heard Mike's voice.

"Everything's fine. Me and Andy are goin' out to eat, and the new car works great."

That meant the hit went according to plan. Only two of them were going to dinner, not three, and Gary was buried. It made perfect sense to Joey, who would relay those details to Don Ponti.

But *no one* knew what would be in store now that Vincenzo's idea worked with the coin machine thief. No one except Vincenzo.

As with *all* heads of families, deals are made that even their closest people aren't aware of until they're part of them…or a victim of them.

Over the past few years, whenever Don Ponti would meet with bosses from Long Island, New York to Long Beach, California, he'd hear one constant complaint, but never heard an acceptable response.

In one version or another they'd say, "I wish there was someplace far from my territory where I could send some prick, have 'em whacked and never hear from 'em again. *That* would be a fuckin' service I'd pay for."

Vincenzo heard them…and he responded.

That was the reason for purchasing the massive piece of property in the middle of nowhere, then building the cabin and updating the casino as quickly as he did. Vincenzo Ponti began a service for the dons across the country to have "problem people" eliminated, but not by *any* of that particular don's crew, thus eliminating any implications. In addition, no one would ever know where the cabin was, and, it was said, no one *wanted* to know.

For this, the Ponti family, with the proper share being kicked up to Don Agostini, would collect a sizable fee. It didn't take long before Andy Cappomaggi was living at the cabin full-time, with Mike, Joey or Enzo making the trips to meet with the soon-to-be victim.

A couple of weeks after Mike returned to New Jersey, Mrs. Christine Paldino gave birth to Ricardo, son of Enzo. Or, as Mike sarcastically said upon hearing the news, "Another friggin' Paldino. Just what the world needs."

Though they may not have thought much of him, the Ponti crew gave Enzo and his new family the respect they deserved. He may have been an asshole, but Enzo was *their* asshole. They knew it would be better to have him on *their* side than on someone else's. And because of that, the guys watched little Ricardo, who would become known as *Richie*, grow up.

By the late 1960s everything was running smoothly for the Ponti family. The Ramblin' Rose and all its parts were operating without a problem. The cabin's murder-and-bury business was receiving two or three *permanent guests* a month, and the California White Oak was growing in height and girth with strong, thick limbs and branches extending in all directions. The New Jersey families were staying in line, and as Luigi Colucci gained a few years of wisdom while running the Salvucci family, he continued to pay the monthly tribute, but still kept Ponti's share out, knowing that's how his uncle would have wanted it. Plus, it meant more money in Luigi's pocket.

Of course, none of the smaller Jersey families trusted Luigi. They knew he was a cannon waiting to explode…and it was overdue.

The only problem that *did* exist for the Pontis was Vincenzo's rapidly failing health. Born in 1899, he barely lived through a handful of mustard gas attacks in Italy's Army during World War I, and the age-old lung damage and emphysema caught up with him.

Vincenzo Donatello Ponti died of a stroke in the fall of 1968 at 69 years old. Don Antonio Agostini gave the eulogy at the massive funeral as the entire Fairview police force controlled the parking and flow of traffic in and around the cemetery. It made the New Jersey and New York City six o'clock news, along with all the newspapers. The attendance was so large that the FBI couldn't get close enough to take photos of the faces they came to see. The man being buried was well loved by the community, his relatives and his *family*.

The only family not represented at the wake or funeral were the Salvuccis. Joey Ponti, Mike Santorella and *all* the don's men made note of it. So did the other New Jersey, New York and Philadelphia family heads who attended. This was Little Calooch's first show of disrespect that he didn't inherit from his Uncle Alphonse.

Mike had heard from a source inside the Salvucci clan that when Luigi was told of Don Vincenzo's passing, he coldly responded, "Whatever."

And for that, two of Little Calooch's men, Wayne 'CC' Welstone and Martin *Little Marty* McCarthy, each good earners *and* with murder records, were told by Mike, after a few social drinks in *The Rag Doll*, about, "…this casino in Nevada, out in the middle of fuckin'-nowhere where all the women craps dealers are former Vegas showgirls, and they're topless."

From the looks on their faces, Mike knew he hooked his fish. With a smile, he ordered another round as they listened to local band, The Blue Boys, play "Mustang Sally," and watched the white booted, miniskirt-and-bikini-top wearing go-go girls dancing in cages on each side of the stage.

Then, CC and Little Marty were handed a Ramblin' Rose brochure and told to mention Mike's name. "It's a great getaway for four, five days without the wives. You don't even need to tell 'em *where* you're goin'. I fuckin' loved it," Mike ended with a wink, then said, "But it's best we keep this between us. I don't think Little Calooch or Joey Ponti would be too happy knowin' we were talkin'. Know what I mean?"

Once Al and Marty agreed with him, it meant they had no idea the Ponti family owned the place. All they cared about was being in a legal casino where the crap dealers showed their tits.

Less than two weeks later, George Pipher let Mike know his name was used and the *"special New Jersey friends"* rate was given. George said the callers asked if the female craps dealers were topless, and they were told the affirmative. That's when the caller from New Jersey made reservations for two rooms the following week…just three weeks before Christmas.

Mike and Enzo made plans to leave sooner. They had no problem whacking these guys. Primarily because they worked for Little Calooch and he needed to be shown what happens to his money-makers when he doesn't show the proper respect for the death of a don. Another reason killing them wouldn't be difficult was because Welstone and McCarthy weren't Italian. The older guys, like Mike and Enzo, felt they belonged to a *closed club* for paisans only. It didn't matter that CC and Little Marty were Irish. It's that they weren't Italian, plain and simple.

During the drive from Reno to Gabbs, Mike asked Enzo, "You have any idea where these two got their names?"

Enzo lit a cigarette, then reached for the radio knob, lowered the volume on Marvin Gaye's "I Heard It Through The Grapevine," and said, "From what I heard, they call him *CC* 'cause he's a fat fuck who used to be a cop. They found out he was on the take and got fired. So the CC means Corrupt Cop. They say he's really nothin' but a fuck-up who inherited his spot from his old man who was with Allie's father when they started together in the thirties. I heard CC pissed in his pants once when Allie was fuckin' around and pointed a gun at him."

"The other guy?"

"*Little Marty?* Fuckin' guy thinks he's a know-it-all. He's nothin' but a wise-ass who's big on intimidatin' people. You've seen him. A big fuck about six feet. Muscular. More brawn than brains *or* balls, but it seems to work for him. They say he makes a nice pile of cash every month for Calooch. The name? According to my wife and some of the *other* girls down the Transfer Station, they call him *Little* Marty because he may be a tall guy, but that's where it ends…so I've heard."

Mike and Enzo had a laugh, and then enjoyed the rest of the ride to Gabbs.

As CC and Little Marty pulled their rented Chevy Bel Air into The Ramblin' Rose's parking lot at 4:07PM on Thursday, December 5th, Mike Santorella and Andy Cappomaggi, both friendly faces to the visitors, were walking to a Pontiac Catalina parked a couple of spaces away. They appeared shocked to see Wayne and Marty and said they had just checked in and on their way to a house where, "…a few of the dealers live. They invited us to come by for some *fun.*" Mike gave a wink and continued, "Why don't you guys come with us. I'll drive."

Wayne and Marty thought about it for a few seconds, so Mike persisted, "What the fuck? Check in when we come back. It's not like they're gonna give away your rooms. Plus, the *hot* ones work the tables later at night anyway." Short of shooting them in the parking lot, he had to do whatever possible to keep them from walking into the lobby to see the fully-clothed craps dealers.

Andy tossed in, "There's a heated pool in the house and they all go in bare ass."

That even caused Mike to raise his eyebrows.

The guys didn't need any more prompting. CC and Little Marty were Jersey guys who had never traveled west of Lake Hopatcong, so they were ready for a good time. Little Marty spoke for both of them.

"Sure. What the fuck. Let's go."

Though Mike could get to the cabin blindfolded by now, he took out a piece of paper with directions on it so Marty and Wayne would think it was his first time going there.

Around forty minutes into the drive, the new guys started getting antsy. Mike showed them the directions and assured them they were more than halfway there, so it appeased them a bit. Since the sun was still shining, they spent the rest of the ride looking at the scenery, talking about the quality of the roads, and how much open space there was for someone to get out and pee. Which they all did.

Mike noticed that whatever anyone spoke about, Little Marty would contradict them and act as if he knew the right answer, or at least more than the others might have known. More than a few times during the hour-and-ten-minute ride Mike and Andy proved him wrong, and it visibly pissed him off.

As the car turned into the driveway of 16 Happy Trails Road, Little Marty said, "It's about fuckin' time."

The gold 1968 Ford LTD Brougham with a vinyl roof the Pontis bought for Andy for his long stays at the cabin was parked in front of one of the garage doors, just to make it appear people were in the cabin. Sinatra was wafting through the open windows as Mike pulled the Catalina next to the Ford.

The four men exited and walked toward the cabin. Mike and Andy stood against the oak tree as Marty and Wayne approached the steps to the porch. But just before they got there, Enzo, with his arms at his side, breezed out of the front door, walked to the top of the steps and said, "Hi guys!"

Startled, they looked up to see another familiar face and his dangling large gold crucifix.

CC nervously barked, "Enzo! What the fuck are *you* doin' here?"

That was when Enzo raised his hands to show two Walther PPKs.

Little Marty's face went from being *tough shit* to *scared shit* as he cried, "Oh, *fuck!*" while his *and* CC's pants turned dark with urine.

"Bye guys!" Enzo said as he emptied the clips into them.

Mike looked at Andy and said, "I'll get the keys for their car. You get the backhoe." He looked up at Enzo and said, "Nice job," then shook his head and looked around. "After all these years I *still* can't get over how muffled the sound is when we shoot those things." Then he grinned and said, "Nature. It's a beautiful thing, ain't it?"

Once Salvucci's guys were buried and their wallets were tossed into the fire, the three men enjoyed dinner at *Carmine's* and spent the next few hours gambling with the two grand Little Marty and CC had in their pockets.

The next morning Mike and Enzo drove Andy to The Ramblin' Rose parking lot to claim the rented Chevy Bel Air as the property of the Ponti family. Hertz would have to track down Wayne Welstone and Martin McCarthy of East Paterson, New Jersey. Within three weeks, the car had a new paint job, new serial numbers and a new registration showing it was owned by The Ramblin' Rose, who used it to pick up the fish orders from Nick in South Lake Tahoe twice a week. The two guys then headed to Reno for the trip back home. With the holidays around the corner, they wanted to be with their families. By this time, the trip to Gabbs from New Jersey only took one day thanks to new airlines, modernized airports and additional flights, plus the guys were now flying in and out of north Jersey's Newark Airport.

After a few days, Little Calooch wondered where CC and Little Marty were. No one had seen them, and none of their pick-ups were being made, and that pissed off Luigi.

Joey Ponti, now the head of the family, had a Christmas party at Vechiarello's in Little Ferry for his *family* with kids. He was most proud as he watched his Godson, Chickie Santorella, who would be turning twelve in less than two months, playing with seven year old Bobby Battaglino and the other kids.

As he was becoming a teenager, there was one thing noticeable about Chickie. No matter where he was going or what the situation was, he was *always* the best dressed, and the cleanest. Diana's germophobia, as Mike would comically say, "…had infected my son."

Chickie had *many* of his father's traits, too. From an early age he was respectful and dedicated to his immediate family, and to his Uncle Joey's *family*. He was a gentleman to girls and women, yet flirtatious with them, too. He was a natural leader in whatever he did, and all the kids respected him…except little Richie Paldino.

Five year old Richie was the only undisciplined kid at the party as he would go up to any boy or girl near him, give a sick smile…then punch or kick them. As usual, Enzo and Christine were too busy arguing, smoking and drinking to notice or care.

From Tahoe, Joey flew in 56 year old Nick 'The Dick' Oliveri, his much younger wife Annette and six year old Donny, and put them up at The Gateway Motor Inn in Secaucus so they could see Nick's aged mother.

For the enjoyment of the parents, New Jersey's Italian legend Jimmy Roselli paid back an old favor to the Ponti family and sang for about an hour, then sat and had dinner with everyone.

A splendid time was had by all.

CHAPTER 8

The New Year brought in 1976 and a great time for America as it celebrated its Bi-Centennial. The Ponti family had no complaints either… except for Luigi Colucci, who was now allowing his men to stray outside their territory to strong-arm another family's business, forcing Don Giuseppe Ponti to step in and read the riot act *"one more fuckin' time"* to the perpetrator. Of course, each time Little Calooch pressed his luck, another earner or two would go missing.

Several months earlier, as Wayne McCoy & The Soul City Symphony's "The Hustle" played through the sound system, Don Antonio *'The Big Hand'* Agostini peacefully passed away somewhere between the antipasto and the entrée at his private table in the Little Italy restaurant where the Columbus Day Massacre took place seventeen years earlier. He was replaced by his son and longtime captain, Antonio Agostini Jr., known as *'The Little Hand,'* and the new don didn't like Luigi Colucci *or* his disrespect for the Ponti family.

In Gabbs, the casino and hotel were doing great, which Joey and Mike attributed to it never becoming too flashy or doing anything too high profile. There were never problems the local police and Sheriff's department weren't able to handle, and the casino *always* took care of them for their efforts. George Pipher was now 67 years old with no intentions of retiring, and as long as the cash kept coming in and the casino was being run the way Ponti wanted it run, no one was pushing him out. His managers made sure each department was running at the top of their game every day and every night.

Unfortunately, the New Year didn't start off well for the Dunay family. In early December, it was determined the mayor's heart gave out when he was found in the hotel's office, sitting in the high-back leather chair with his feet comfortably atop the desk and a Meerschaum pipe in his left hand resting on his chest. His right hand held that day's Nye County Gazette with the headline, GABBS CELEBRATES MAYOR WILLIAM DUNAY DAY!

Antoinette Goode not only lost her cousin Willie, but a few weeks earlier her grandfather, White Elk, passed away in his sleep. From that moment on, she became the Nye County Native American Historian and delved into everything she could find about the curse put on Shoshone land by the tribe's highest holy man. As a child she'd hear stories of what supposedly happened in Worley, Nevada in the mid-1920s, but no one had ever shown her proof. Nor did anyone openly speak about it. The best she was able to determine was that Worley was a worthless and poorly managed silver mining town incorporated in 1918, built on Shoshone land and named after Stan Worley, a wrinkled Texan whose personality and business sense ran the mine into the ground...literally.

Joey Ponti and Mike Santorella flew to Nevada and allowed no option for the Dunay family as the don paid for the wake and funeral. Vivian, Sheila and Willie Jr., who was unanimously named the town's mayor in an emergency election, said they had never known, "...such friendship from outsiders."

Apparently, another side of Sheila had surfaced during the thirteen years of doing business with the Ponti family. Since the mid-1960s, she would joke with Mike and say, "You take away my college diploma, and there must be a helluva lotta my great-granny in me." They'd laugh because besides being the mayor's daughter and a partner in The Ramblin' Rose's café and hotel, like her great-grandmother, Sheila operated Gabbs' legal brothel in a building on the outskirts of town, paid for with the money she earned being in a legitimate business with the New Jersey crime family.

But even with the passing of Don Agostini and Mayor Willie Dunay, the deals stayed in place and business went on as usual.

That also applied to the cabin.

As an excuse, an acre of forest was cleared for firewood and stacked neatly behind the three car garage. But the real reason for the newly opened land was to bury more contract jobs. The one-way visitors since Gary Gentile's inaugural demise never stopped, and neither did the growth of the oak tree as it exceeded the height of the cabin with thick limbs reaching toward the front bedroom windows above the porch.

The day before Valentine's Day, Mike brought Carmine 'Chickie' Santorella to the cabin for the first time to help take care of another wiseguy who needed to be shown it never pays to steal from *the family*, and to celebrate his 19th birthday.

For the last year, Chickie had been helping his now 47 year old dad with pick-ups and driving the occasional bound-and-gagged mobster or two to Enzo Paldino's basement for a little *straightening out* before being shot or sadistically beaten to death with little Richie's prized Louisville Slugger.

Chickie had grown to five-foot-nine with a strong body and the ability to use it, highlighted by the dark-skin, hair and eyes inherited from his Italian parents. He also had the aura of leadership and a talent for negotiating, just like his father. But the son *still* possessed his sense of style inherited from his mom…along with her germophobia.

Andy Cappomaggi moved back to New Jersey to care for his invalid father, so the cabin stayed empty except when Mike and Enzo would fly out to fulfill the contracted hits paid to Don Joey from families wanting to make their problems disappear.

The father and son arrived at 16 Happy Trails Road with Francesco Qualiano.

Qualiano was one of Mike's lower-level pick-up men who dreamed of building a condominium development in the Jersey swamps using Ponti family money, but without asking permission to use it, causing a couple of his pick-ups to be light. *Too* light.

He was told he was joining the Santorella's because Don Joey was thinking of building condos next to The Ramblin' Rose and wanted Francesco's opinion.

Mike knew how to appeal to a thieving mobster's desires and then watched it become their downfall.

With the AM signal just about gone during the final chorus of Paul Simon's "50 Ways To Leave Your Lover," Chickie drove the rented American Motors Ambassador toward the cabin with Francesco in the passenger seat holding two boxes of cold pizza. About 3 hours earlier Chickie said he was in the mood for, "…some *abeets!*" with the standard Jersey-Italian vocal flair and hand gesture. The only problem was that the closest place that made *any* kind of pizza was *Carmine's*, some forty-plus miles away. Chickie and Francesco took the drive and Mike said he'd have the oven warm by the time they returned, knowing the pizzas would need to be reheated. And with each mile, Chickie was reading the directions and getting more pissed off as Francesco repeated the same thing over and over.

"C'mon…it's your birthday, for Christ sake. Your old man should-a taken you to Vegas. Not to some joint in the middle of fuckin' nowhere."

No matter how many times Chickie said he didn't care where he was as long as he was with his dad, Francesco would wait another few miles and say it again.

Mike saw the car approaching the cabin through one of the kitchen windows, then walked out the rear door toward the wood pile.

Chickie parked so Francesco would have to exit facing the third garage door. But even as the complainer stepped out holding the boxes, he looked across the car at Chickie and kept it going.

"I mean, look how far you gotta go for a fuckin' *pizza!*"

As he walked to the other side of the car and took the pizza boxes from the thief's hands, Chickie shook his head to show nothing he was hearing mattered. That was when Mike stepped from the side of the garage and swung a long-handled axe into Francesco Qualiano's chest, causing blood to splatter all over Mike, the passenger side of the car, the pizza boxes… and Chickie.

"Ah *fuck*, Pop!" the germaphobe yelled, then dropped the boxes as his father continued to push the blade deeper into the horrified man who was collapsing to the ground into a puddle of his blood.

When Francesco finally stopped shaking, gurgling blood and breathing, they covered him with a tarp and let him lay there for about an hour with the axe still extending from the body while the father and son stripped off their clothes at the back door, tossed them into the washing machine and went upstairs to shower the blood from their hair and bodies. Chickie took longer, seeing as he had to scrub a layer or two of skin off before feeling clean.

Because of Chickie's summer job at construction sites, thanks to Uncle Joey's connections with the unions, the young man knew how to operate the backhoe. He was put to work lifting the axe-imbedded Francesco, digging the hole, dumping the body in and covering him. Mike stayed at the cabin to hose the blood off the car and shook his head in disgust as he took the perfectly-good-but-cold pizzas and threw them as far as he could into the woods for whatever animals would be lucky enough to enjoy them, then brought the blood splattered boxes into the cabin and watched them burn.

As usual, the victim's wallet went into the fireplace and the cash was enjoyed at the casino where they stayed until every dollar was lost. They weren't there to take the casino's money…only when it was in the filled briefcase George Pipher would send to Joey Ponti every three months.

Over the next few years, Chickie would come out with his dad or Enzo Paldino to do what needed to be done. But for the same reasons as everyone else, Chickie didn't like Enzo. Nobody except his own 19 year old son, Richie, liked Enzo. Christine despised him enough to get a divorce and move to Florida's Delray Beach, where she found the sleazy equivalent of the Transfer Station and rapidly drank, smoked and horrifically plastic surgery'd herself to death, leaving Enzo to raise his arrogant, disrespectful and viciously violent son. That meant Richie would grow up to be exactly like Enzo, although the son never took to the large gold crucifix his father constantly wore for all to see.

It was 1982 and a beautiful mid-June afternoon in the Shoshone Mountains of Nevada. Mike sat in the front of the 14-foot rowboat as his 25 year old son stopped rowing upon reaching the center of the cabin's tranquil lake.

"You know, Chickie, it's time for you to start thinking about the future," Mike said in a fatherly fashion. "The don loves you, and *I'm* already fifty-two. You know I ain't gonna be around forever. And not-for-nothin', but

I'm getting' tired of this shit. Me and your mother wanna travel. So I want you to think about takin' on some guys for a crew of your own, that way when I step down I can give you my territory and the business."

Chickie took out his Ray-Ban sunglasses, slid them on and looked at the water as he replied, "I got a few guys I trust. Good earners, too. But Bobby Battaglino, that fuckin' kid is amazing. I've taken him on pick-ups when I needed a two-hundred pound monster with me. Ever since his old man died, he's been unstoppable. Dedicated and loyal to me, you *and* the Ponti family."

"How old is he now?" Mike asked.

"Twenty-one."

"And already two-hundred pounds? Madone."

"Fuckin' guy loves spaghetti and sausage. And then bread for the gravy. A couple of meatballs. Soda. He'd eat the same thing every day if he could."

"You think he's ready to do things like *this?*" Mike asked as he nodded toward Randy Jones, a muscle-bound weed dealer sent to Gabbs by a mob family in Florida. He pissed them off by shorting them two bales before passing along what was supposed to be seven-hundred-and-eighty-nine pounds to one of their people, and now he was nervously and cautiously sitting on the edge of the rowboat. He was dressed like a nightclub bouncer in a crushed velvet suit. Even with his bulging arms, his hands were now bound behind him, a piece of duct-tape stretched across his mouth and his feet were encased in two small buckets of cement that had solidified about an hour earlier.

"Nah," Chickie answered. "I don't think he'd have a problem."

"You gonna go down to Seaside or Ortley next month?" Mike asked as if there was no one else with them. Before his son answered, Mike stood up, stepped over to Randy and ripped the tape from his mouth.

The weed dealer immediately screamed, "*Guys! I can't swim! I can't swim!*"

As Chickie lifted the buckets and turned Randy around, he looked at his father and nonchalantly answered, "Don't know yet. Probably Ortley."

Randy kept yelling over and over, "I can't swim! I can't swim," as Mike took out a pocketknife and said, "Not bein' able to swim is the *least* of your problems, asshole. But if you think you wanna try…" Then he cut the rope securing Randy's arms and gave just enough of a push so the dealer went cement-feet first into the water and sunk to the bottom.

"Yeah, Ortley's nice this time of year," Mike said as he looked over the side to see fish scatter and air bubbles rise to the surface. "Okay, start rowin'. I'm hungry."

The following day, Mike and Chickie held a charity event at *Carmine's* where the Ponti family donated $20,000 to Antoinette Goode and the Nye County Native American Heritage Foundation, which made the locals *and* Don Giuseppe Ponti *very* proud.

It was Tuesday, November 27th, 1990, when plans were made for the last hit at the cabin.

While wanting to keep the buried bodies a fair distance from the structure, and after clearing yet *another* acre for "firewood" deeper in the forest, the Ponti family felt things had slowed down enough to put a great and profitable business to sleep.

Don Giuseppe Ponti had personally invited one of the *family's* attorneys, Albert '*Pig Al*' Povich, to an all-expense paid weeklong trip to The Ramblin' Rose, complete with $500 in casino chips, three days of treatments at the new spa, and a seat to see Wayne Newton in the Dennis Dragona Theater.

Povich, 45 at the time, only needed one seat. Since those of his own profession felt he was the lowest form of scum, there wasn't a woman in the tri-state area who wanted to be near him because, it was said, "…his eating habits were atrocious. He cuts his food like a four year old and spills or drops everything on the table, the floor, himself and anyone around him." But the Ponti family used him for years because he was connected with the county judges and prosecutors who would take bribes. As long as Povich was paid enough, he knew how to spread the wealth…and usually got a free meal out of it.

He was *also* under investigation by the New Jersey Ethics Review Board due to incriminating information about numerous lawsuits he ineptly handled. Sure to lose his license and pay fines, Pig Al told the board to drop the investigation and just prior to the upcoming Jewish holidays, when he would be on vacation in Israel, he'd supply ample dirt on the Ponti family to the State Police, the IRS and the FBI.

Fortunately, Chickie Santorella, who was now 33, had a friend on the Review Board and got the information first-hand.

It was on that Tuesday when the don met with Albert Povich, 57 year old Enzo Paldino, 29 year old and 264 pound bulldog Bobby Battaglino, and Chickie. He told his men to travel with Povich the *next day* so they could, "…get him settled at the hotel, see that he's well taken care of in the casino, and make sure he has the lobster fra diavolo. Plus, I want him to have whatever the fuck he wants for Thanksgiving dinner. And tell the chef I said so!"

Being that his law office was closed that week for the national holiday, this made the corrupt, gluttonous attorney even happier knowing the don's own men would be driving him from the airport to the hotel, and would see to it he got the best of *everything*.

He never made it to the hotel.

Except for a couple of pee stops along the way, Chickie drove from Reno Airport directly to the cabin. Though this was his first encounter with Pig Al, during the flight and drive Chickie felt his skin crawl when he was around him. It was a feeling he never had with anyone before. Not even with Enzo.

Whenever Chickie drove, Bobby, now a veteran of several trips, sat in the front doing crossword puzzles or reading Time, Newsweek, Omni, Smithsonian or National Geographic magazines. He would bring them all.

"When do we eat, and when do we see some fuckin' broads?" came from a sweating Pig Al in the backseat, as he inhaled one cigarette after another.

Bobby turned to Povich and said, "You must be high on Don Ponti's list. He *never* invites people to see his place out here. We still have an hour-and-a-half, so enjoy the scenery, 'cause there ain't much else."

Enzo, also smoking and sitting in the back, grinned and answered, "As soon as we check out the cabin, *then* we'll go to the casino, get you registered, eat and do some gamblin'. You can count on *that*."

Chickie, Bobby and Enzo had a good laugh over what was just said. Povich didn't get it.

They pulled into 16 Happy Trails Road and cruised along the driveway. Once the car entered the clearing, Povich eyed the cabin and said, "Fuckin'

Ponti. He's got *this much?* You can bet my fees are gonna go up after I get back."

That's when *all four* men laughed, though Pig Al didn't know the real reason why *they* did.

With the Lincoln parked in front of the garage nearest the front door, they walked past the now forty-six foot tall oak tree, brought their luggage into the cabin and dropped everything in the living room, which now sported a four-and-a-half-by-nine-foot tournament pool table, all the necessary billiard accoutrements…and all new furniture with no plastic covers in sight. The only thing missing was the phone. With the advent of cell phones and Ponti's desire not to have documented records of calls from the cabin, or to have them tapped thanks to the RICO Act of October, 1970, the landline was removed. Chickie was given a Motorola MicroTAC 9800X, otherwise known as a flip-phone with an extendable antenna, registered to a sixty-four year old woman in Portland, Oregon.

Pig Al looked around the room and brazenly commented, "The joint's even nicer inside! Oh yeah. My fee just went up *again.*"

"Me and Enzo told Joey we'd check the furnace and basement for leaks when we got here," Chickie said to Povich, then looked at Bobby and ordered "Keep our friend company."

The guys were gone for less than ten minutes before returning to find Pig Al and Bobby playing Eight Ball.

"C'mon," said Enzo with an evil smile and his crucifix dangling. "You gotta see upstairs."

"Upstairs?" Chickie quickly questioned.

Enzo arrogantly replied, "Yeah. Upstairs."

As they entered the bedroom between the master suite and the front bedroom, Bobby opened the window to let in some fresh air and for Povich to view the scenery.

But when the rat attorney turned around, Enzo was sitting on the bed pointing a .32 Colt at him. Pig Al froze and freaked.

"What the fuck is *that* for?" were the first stunned words out of his mouth.

"C'mon, Enzo. Not in here. Stop fuckin' around," Chickie commanded from the other side of the room.

With his eyes and the gun still on the motionless Povich, Enzo growled, "First of all, don't *you* give me fuckin' orders, *kid*. You *or* your old man ain't the boss. Next, since this is the last hit in this place, and after doing this shit for the same fuckin' family for twenty-six fuckin' years, I think I can decide where to do what we gotta do. So shut the fuck up."

The hair on the back of Chickie's neck rose when he heard that. But this wasn't the time or place to deal with it.

Povich nervously asked, "Whatdya mean, '*do what we gotta do*'? What the fuck's *that* mean?"

Enzo, Chickie and Bobby looked at Povich and yelled, "Shut the fuck up!"

Chickie glared at Enzo, whose stare never moved from his target, and said, "I'm not givin' orders. But we *all* know the don don't want anyone killed in the cabin. That's been the rule since day-one."

Bobby humorously chimed in, "Yeah, Enzo, how about we just throw him out the window. He'll break a few bones, and you can bury him that way. Go out sayin' you did the last guy without firin' a shot."

Enzo looked at the younger men for only a second, gave his sick smile, then returned his gaze to the attorney and began taunting him.

"Entertain me, you piece-a-shit. *Dance!*"

The frightened and shaking man looked at Enzo as if he didn't understand what he had just been told.

"What-are-ya, deaf? I want you to *dance!*"

Enzo fired five bullets into the wood floor around the now-crying lawyer's feet as he feebly attempted to dance. And with each shot, Enzo's face became more insane and excited with the thought of killing this guy.

Povich pleaded through his tears, "I'm just a lawyer! What did *I* do? I'm *just a lawyer!*"

Chickie was getting frustrated, so he barked, "C'mon, Enzo! Don't make a fuckin' production outta this. Let's get this prick outside, whack him and go eat."

Pig Al looked like he was about to pass out from what he just heard. That's when Enzo said, "Ya know, kid…sometimes you just gotta have some fun and tell Joey Ponti to 'Go get fucked.' Know what I mean?" He eyed Chickie and Bobby to see their reaction, but the look on their faces showed they didn't agree.

Enzo turned his head to Albert Povich and said, "Fine." Then he pulled the trigger putting the sixth shot into the attorney's face. Blood and skull fragments splattered the wall and floor behind the lawyer's body as it flew back about four feet before landing in a wooden chair.

"I hope you know this is *your* bedroom tonight, wiseguy," Chickie sarcastically said.

Though they knew Enzo had just broken a rule set by Vincenzo Ponti a couple of decades earlier, they *all* laughed at Chickie's remark.

"Let's get this asshole into the ground. The sun's goin' down and I'm fuckin' hungry," Enzo said as he went through Povich's pockets for the wallet and cash. After checking everywhere on the corpse, he lifted the wallet up, looked in it and said, "You believe this guy? He gets a free trip to a casino and he brings sixty-one fuckin' dollars with him. Not only was he a rat, he was a *cheap* fuckin' rat, too."

Instead of carrying him through the cabin, they went with Bobby's idea of tossing the body out the window.

As the sun sank behind the horizon, they used the John Deere's headlights to show the way. Chickie carried Povich in the front shovel of the backhoe as Enzo and Bobby followed behind. They were going to put him in the most recent clearing, which was quite a distance from the cabin. A deeper-than-normal hole was dug, but Chickie began having a problem getting the long arm of the hoe to move in the direction of their victim so he could dump him in.

"*Motherfucker!*" Chickie hit the machine's controls. He shut off the engine, kept the lights on and yelled, "Just push the fuck in!"

Enzo was pissed off as he threw his half-smoked cigarette on the ground, and with his crucifix glittering in the headlights, pushed the dead attorney into the hole, then sarcastically looked at Chickie and said, "You know, kid, you and your old man have been comin' out here doin' Ponti's dirty work for years. Guess you ain't got no greater ambitions, huh?"

The younger man didn't respond. He just smiled, looked past Enzo and excitedly said, "Hey, look! It's Bobby!"

Bobby swiftly walked up behind Enzo, taking his right hand from inside his sport-jacket and raising it. Enzo, simply seeing his traveling companion, asked, "Hey, Bobby! What's that in your hand?"

It was an ice pick.

It all happened too fast for Enzo to react as Chickie grabbed him from behind and Bobby slammed the pick into Enzo's head. Blood sprayed and splattered *everywhere*…including on Chickie's face and hands. He flinched, yelled, "*Ah fuck!*" and dropped the convulsing Enzo into the grave already occupied by Pig Al.

As Bobby watched Enzo die, still with the ice pick embedded in his skull, Chickie pulled out a handkerchief, ran in front of a headlight and thoroughly wiped the blood from everywhere it hit his skin.

"Whatdya know. It looks' like *I'm* the last guy to kill somebody here, and without firin' a shot," Bobby laughed as he removed Paldino's wallet and cash while Chickie climbed onto the backhoe. Without a problem the machine's arm was used to cover and pat down the double-grave as Bobby said with confidence, "Fuckin' Enzo. I'm glad we ain't ever gonna see that ugly fuck again. *Nobody's* ever gonna see him."

Chickie agreed. Then they went into the cabin to burn Enzo's and Pig Al's wallets, cleaned up, dressed in the fashion guys these guys dressed, and got in the Lincoln.

There were no cell signals until they were about 10 miles from the center of Gabbs. That was when Chickie called his boss to say, "Yeah, everything's fine out here. The two of us are on our way to dinner."

Don Joey knew that meant the ratting lawyer would no longer be a problem for the Ponti family, *and* he'd never have to tolerate Enzo Paldino again.

The guys now had to stay an extra couple of days to burn and replace the bloodstained chair, then paint the wall and ceiling where parts of Pig Al had splattered.

But they did it. And that was that.

CHAPTER 9

1999 didn't start off well for the Ponti family.

The Salvucci crew started skirmishes up and down the Jersey shoreline. For more than a decade, while still considered *the renegade crew* of all the Jersey families, Luigi '*Little Calooch*' Colucci used his Uncle Allie lessons about bringing in new men to earn, grow and impress the boss, who was now Little Calooch. Over the last couple of years, he felt the Ponti and Agostini families no longer had the strength and respect they previously held, and he wanted to expand the Salvucci family's territory, wealth and power.

Though no attacks were made on Ponti's territories of Hudson and Bergen Counties, there were murders, kidnappings, fires and explosions along the Salvucci borderlines, and the other families were fed up with Colucci's attempt at expansion. And as usual, Joey Ponti would have to preside over the complaint hearings between the conflicting territorial bosses.

But at 74, Joey was getting tired of it.

On Sunday, January 31st, in the comfort of their Englewood Cliffs home, 69 year old Mike Santorella had just finished watching the Denver Broncos beat the shit out of the Atlanta Falcons in the thirty-third Super Bowl. His wife Diana was already in bed and practically asleep when she heard Mike go into the kitchen to make tea. Then she heard him call her name as he had never called her before.

By the time she got to him, Mike was on the floor…and gone.

The stroke was a massive blow to Diana, Chickie and every level of the Ponti family. And as usual, only the Salvucci crew was absent from the wake and funeral, which made Carmine 'Chickie' Santorella dedicate his life to wiping out the entire Salvucci family.

Less than a month later, Chickie was taken to Don Joey's home and went through the same ritual as his father four decades earlier and was named a *man of honor*...a made man.

Tony Bennett's "Swinging On A Star" played in the background on the warm, breezeless evening of Wednesday, June 9th, in the living room of Don Joey Ponti. He had maintained his image as a strong leader and a man of respect, but carrying the weight of the Ponti family on his shoulders was showing...and he knew it, too.

Joey knew he had no heir to leave the family and its businesses to. He only had his loyal Godson Chickie, who was standing on the other side of the hand-carved wooden bar. Chickie was told to come to the house because his Godfather had something to tell him, and that was all that needed to be said.

Chickie Santorella was now 42 and had grown into an old-school mafioso devoted to the life of his father and grandfather, and to its codes of respect, honor, loyalty, and a man's word.

"Two things, Chickie. The first is...I need you to go to Nevada."

"Sure, Don Joey. What's up?"

"The casino. I got word from our partner out there...we been takin' a hit."

Chickie knew "our partner" referred to Sheila Dunay, who the Ponti family shared a close relationship with for decades. The loss of casino money could only come down to one person.

"No shit? *The Dick's* kid?"

In the mid-to-late 1980s, as Native Americans began opening casinos on tribal land, laws across the country were put into effect to ensure they were operated according to the approved standards, and those employed in upper-management positions had to be no less than one-quarter Native American.

Because The Ramblin' Rose was grandfathered in, the owner, Giuseppe Ponti, didn't have to be Native American, but he *had to* install a new casino manager within a certain period of time.

Nick The Dick's son, Donatello '*Donny*' Oliveri, was half Native American thanks to his full-blooded Shoshone mother Annette, and had graduated with a Bachelor Degree in business from UCLA in 1984...an education paid for by Don Joey in honor of his father, Vincenzo Donatello Ponti, Donny's namesake. Besides being athletic with a model's face, Donny excelled at his career. He was a genius when it came to casino calculations, odds, and managing a business.

Nick The Dick passed away two years later at 74, but was always indebted to the Ponti family for what they did for him, his wife and son. Annette, only 52, took over *Nick's Seafood Restaurant* and as the fish supplier to The Ramblin' Rose.

In 1987, because he was smart, because he had a solid connection with the Ponti family, because he was fifty percent Native American, and because Casino Manager George Pipher was now 78, Donny Oliveri was named Assistant Casino Manager while he learned the business...and how much of it went to the Ponti family every three months.

A few months later, George was in bed with a beautiful 64 year old former blackjack dealer, who was his lover for more than two decades, when her husband shot and killed them. That put Donny in the casino's driver seat *and* made the Ponti-owned business one-hundred percent up to code. The 25 year old even got along with Sheila Dunay, who, at 49, still ran The Ramblin' Rose's hotel and café, plus moved her brothel to a 22 acre ranch ten miles out in the desert, *and* became the mayor once Willie Jr. decided he was happier running The Gabbs Hotel with his 70 year old mother, Vivian.

After Chickie and Bobby's last trip to the cabin in 1990, every three months one of the don's lieutenants would fly to Reno and check into one of The Ramblin' Rose's rooms. Donny would visit the room with a briefcase filled with Ponti's money, and the next evening the cash would be on the don's desk in New Jersey.

Ever since then, things ran perfectly...until now.

As Joey took a bottle of anisette from a shelf and placed three aperitif glasses on the bar, he said, "That motherfucker's been skimmin' two to three hundred grand a month, maybe more, and for a year or more."

The bathroom door next to the bar opened. Bobby Battaglino, still 264 pounds, still a loyal bulldog, but now 38, walked out and immediately asked, "Skimmin'? Who's skimmin'?"

As Bobby stood next to his best friend, their boss unscrewed the top off the bottle.

"Pop opened the joint in the early-sixties and it's been problem-free ever since. We put money into the town, left them alone, didn't do anything to bring federal heat around. You two know. You been there. Then back in the eighties the government passed this law saying casino managers had to be part Indian."

Chickie turned to Bobby and asked, "Remember Nick The Dick?"

"He had the restaurant in Tahoe. Made the lobster fra diavolo. Got the fish for *Carmine's*," Bobby answered in detail.

Joey started to fill the glasses as he continued, "He had a kid with some Indian broad he met out there."

Accidently, a drop of the thick, sticky liqueur fell on the bar. The conversation stopped as Chickie took a small paper bar napkin, neatly wiped up the drop and meticulously folded it. Joey and Bobby watched, but said nothing. They knew what Chickie was like.

The don picked up where he left off.

"His name's Donny Oliveri. We paid for his fuckin' education and he turned out pretty smart. He grew up knowing who the fuck we were and what we'd done for his family. So it made sense to give this half-breed-guinea cocksucker the job, right?"

Bobby shook his head in disgust as he asked, "And now he's stealin' from ya? What the fuck? And what the fuck *is it* with these friggin' kids?"

"They're not made from the same mold *we* came from, paisan. You know that," Chickie shook his head and answered.

Joey raised his glass and before putting it to his lips he looked into Chickie's eyes and said, "I want you two to talk to him. Take him to the cabin...and get my money back."

Chickie respectfully raised *his* glass. Bobby smiled, raised his glass and comically said, "Nice. We haven't been there since that thing with Enzo Paldino, that big-crucifix-wearin' prick. *Jesus!* Remember that?"

The men laughed, tipped their glasses toward each other and downed their anisette.

Once they placed the empties on the bar, Joey continued, "And since we're talkin' about old Enzo, I want you to take his kid Richie and *his* guy Sammy Trombino with ya's."

Chickie interjected, "Frick and Frack? Why *them?* Richie's a disrespectful-fuckin'-whack-job just like his old man. Don't worry, Don Joey. Me and Bobby can handle it."

The boss once again poured anisette into the glasses, making sure not to drip any while letting his reason be known.

"You're my Number One guy, Chickie. You know that. But I know how you like to keep things, ya know, neat and clean. This? This is a job for someone who don't mind gettin' a little messy. And Richie loves gettin' up-close and personal," then he winked.

And that was that.

They raised their glasses, saluted each other and drank.

Once the empty glasses were again on the bar, Joey shook his head in disgust and said, "Just be careful. Unlike you guys, Richie Paldino don't give-a-shit about loyalty. But he'll get Donny outta that office one-way-or-the-other, and then he'll find out where my money is. I guarantee *that.*"

Chickie remembered something.

"You said you had *two* things you wanted to tell me."

The head of the Ponti family filled the glasses one more time, made sure each man had them in his hand and said, "When you come back, I'm retiring…and you're gonna take control of the Ponti *family.*"

Nothing was said as they again respectfully tilted their glasses of anisette toward each other and drank.

Chickie Santorella walked behind the bar, said, "Whatever you wish, Godfather," then they hugged and kissed each other as only Italian mob men do.

It was around 11:30 that night in a ninth floor Edgewater, New Jersey hotel suite living room that faced the Hudson River and Manhattan skyline where a few well-to-do men and women sat on sofas and chairs watching the dealer and five gamblers play poker. The players were all men with their sleeves rolled up, smoking cigarettes and cigars. With several thousand dollars in each pot, these people were serious about the game.

Tattoos adorned what was visible on the neck and arms of a very large, long-haired and intimidating gambler. His presence alone threatened a couple of players and spectators.

That's when the bedroom door opened and 36 year old, muscular, well-dressed and better-looking than his father Richie Paldino walked in with a cigarette in his lips. It was obvious the only thing bigger than his ego was the chip on his shoulder.

He circled the table and came to a standstill behind the tattooed gambler, whose shifty eyes started to show some nervousness. Without warning, Richie grabbed his hair, viciously yanked him off the chair and threw him to the carpeted floor.

The frightened gambler began yelling in pain, causing the others to slide their chairs back from the table.

Still holding the gambler's hair, and with a sick, sinister smile, Richie viciously punched him twice in the face, then reached down into his shirt pocket, pulled out two aces and held them in front of the bleeding gambler.

"Please Richie! Please! Lemme go. I'll leave the cash. Just please, lemme go!" he pleaded.

"Yeah, I'll letcha go, scumbag," the now insane Richie responded as he dragged the gambler by his locks into the bedroom and slammed the door behind him.

Within a few seconds the card game resumed.

Sammy Trombino, 30 years old, was upset and pacing the bedroom. He had a kind side, but was as dumb as a bag of hammers, strong…and very loyal to Richie Paldino.

"We got a problem, Richie. A *big* fuckin' problem."

Richie yanked on the gambler's hair lifting him off the carpet and angrily said, "Not as big as the one this motherfucker's got."

"Yeah, well, that's the thing. We're outta the big trash bags. All we got are these," Sammy said as he held up a plastic sandwich bag. "We can't fit a big fuck like *that* into *this*. How we gonna get him outta here?"

"How many we got?"

"Forty-five? Fifty?"

Richie looked down, and with his cold eyes never leaving his victim, he said to Sammy, "Okay. Get the *big* knife outta the bathroom. He's gonna have to *rest in pieces*. A *shitload* of pieces."

As ordered and without question, Sammy walked into the bathroom as the gambler looked up at Richie. His eyes glazed over and he fainted.

Paldino released his hair and the body fell like a stone. That's when Richie's cell phone rang.

He looked at the Caller ID and rolled his eyes before answering it.

"Hey, Chickie. How you doin'? What can I do for ya?"

It was Saturday, June 12th, 1999, nine years since Chickie and Bobby had taken their last trip…and things had changed. Reno Airport had substantially grown and it took longer to get from the plane to the baggage carousel, but once they got there, Chickie stood to the side with Bobby and watched.

Their luggage rode along the conveyor as Richie and Sammy grabbed only theirs. Sammy was about to pick up Chickie's and Bobby's, but Richie stopped him.

Chickie saw their bags continue on the carousel, so just before the two subordinates stepped away, he said, "Richie, the bags."

"I ain't your fuckin' bellboy," was the response, and a little too loud.

Chickie raised an eyebrow, then he stared at Richie. Richie stared back.

Quietly, Chickie simply said, "Bobby."

All 264 pounds of Bobby Battaglino, with an icy intense gaze, stepped in front of the taller Richie. Not to cause a scene, Chickie's right-hand-man spoke sternly-yet-softly.

"Richie, let me tell you this once. Don Joey put Chickie in charge. So when Chickie tells you to get the bags, that's like Don Joey sayin', 'Pick up the fuckin' bags before I put my foot up your stupid-fuckin' ass.' Capisce?"

Richie didn't reply. He glared down. Bobby looked up with a sarcastic smile. While still facing the disrespectful hood, he loudly asked, "What about *you*, Sammy? Problem?"

Sammy, not wanting to be on the shitlist of *any* of these guys, quietly answered, "No Bobby. No problem."

Frank Temple had long retired as the Hertz manager. Chickie found that out when he expected to rent a Cadillac or Lincoln.

The two younger men struggled with everyone's luggage in the nearly empty rental lot. As Chickie approached holding a set of keys, the other Jersey guys stood among three red VW Beetles and a white 4-door Toyota Prius.

A pissed off Richie bellowed, "What the fuck is *this?* They ain't got a bigger car?"

Chickie opened the trunk and said, "This is all they had that could fit us *and* the luggage."

All four looked into the tiny space. But it was when Sammy seriously asked, "How we gonna put somebody in there?" that made them break out laughing.

Then they howled when Chickie answered with, "Fuck it. We'll tie him to the roof."

Sammy and Richie stuffed the luggage in the trunk, but it pissed Richie off that he had to do grunt work. Like his father, he felt he deserved to be treated better. He was, after all, a killer.

Chickie tossed the keys to Sammy and said, "Let's go. By the time we get to Gabbs it's gonna be a long day. We'll go visit the thievin' fuck tomorrow after breakfast."

The Prius pulled out of the parking lot with the four beefy guys comically stuffed inside. Sammy was behind the wheel with Richie in the front passenger seat. Chickie was behind Richie and Bobby sat behind Sammy.

As Bobby took out a pen and crossword book, Chickie removed a folded piece of paper from his jacket, tossed it over the seat to Richie and said, "The directions. Follow 'em."

Just as the first time Vincenzo Ponti, Mike Santorella and Enzo Paldino made the drive, it still took about four-and-a-half hours to reach Gabbs. Chickie and Bobby thought it was best not to stop in South Lake Tahoe to eat at *Nick's Seafood Restaurant*. After all, Annette was Donny's mother, and knowing they came to Nevada to beat the shit out of her son until he told them where Ponti's money was and then kill him…it would've been a hard meal to get down.

Because it was a Saturday and they knew Donny wouldn't be there, the guys stopped at The Ramblin' Rose and had an early dinner at *Carmine's*, then headed to the cabin.

Donny always took Fridays and Saturdays off, but he was accessible if the casino needed him because he'd be at Sheila Dunay's ranch spending cash on the girls. There was no need to let him know the guys were in town.

Chickie felt good about going to 16 Happy Trails Road. He was returning to a familiar place. A place he and his father spent many days and nights doing the things a father and son enjoyed doing together. Granted, what they did was kill people for money. But still, they were together and enjoyed their time as father and son.

Chickie also noticed things hadn't changed much since he was last there. It still took an hour on the mountainous two lane highway that was more dirt than blacktop before the Prius made a left onto Old Shoshone Road, where it was *still* a one lane dirt road. Only now that the sun was going down and the New Moon was one day away, it was darker than normal.

Just like decades earlier, the mobsters cruised along the desolate road while remarking on everything from the scenery, to the need for paved roads, to having to take a leak. Then Sammy slowed the car as they approached the large wooden sign that read, "Entering Historic Shoshone Tribal Territory."

It was an old landmark for the guys in the backseat. But the two in the front stared at it like it was a prehistoric relic.

"Look at *that*. This is fuckin' Injun land," came from the big-mouthed Richie. And just like Mike and Vincenzo said in unison back in May of 1962, Chickie and Bobby said, "It was *all* their land, you dumb fuck."

And just like 37 years earlier, the guys in the back turned to one another and broke out laughing because they said it together. Paldino wasn't as happy about it.

The Prius continued for the next 12.2 miles before turning right onto Happy Trails Road for the last two-and-a-half miles.

A radio station playing David Lee Roth's 1985 cover of Louis Prima's "Just A Gigolo/I Ain't Got Nobody" was the last song they heard before the signal disappeared. Nothing much changed when it came to getting radio or cell phone signals once they left the center of Gabbs. But none of that mattered to these guys. They were only planning to be there for a few days before going back to New Jersey to do what they did best.

There was *still* nothing around as far as they could see. No homes. No cars. No people. Just tall pine trees, the unpaved road they were driving on and the occasional screeches from birds of prey.

Sammy stopped the car as they came upon the wooden post bearing the address that had been there since Chickie's father first saw it. Richie looked up the long dirt driveway bordered on each side by the thick forest and asked, "Any chance you wanna tell me what's up there?"

Bobby answered, "The cabin."

Sammy asked, "*What* cabin?"

Richie excitedly spoke up, "The *cabin!* Yeah, my old man told me about this place."

"He *told* you about it?" Bobby asked, knowing he was the one who killed Enzo and buried him with an ice pick in his head and on top of *Pig Al* Povich.

"He tell you what he was doin' out here?" Chickie cautiously asked.

As Sammy turned into the driveway, Richie answered, "Yeah. He used to come out here to pick up Ponti's casino money and to hit some local broad's whorehouse."

Bobby and Chickie looked at one another and decided to keep quiet as Richie continued, "I always figured he ran off and went MIA with some hooker from out here after my old lady left. Who knows? Maybe he's still out here. It's been a long time. I don't give a fuck about him anymore anyway. He's history."

Again, the guys in the back didn't respond.

After a minute, Sammy looked into the darkness and said, "I *still* don't see no cabin."

"It's up-a-ways. Far enough so nobody can hear or see anything," Bobby answered.

The sun was just about down when the car parked in front of the garage. As the guys got out, Richie and Sammy, having never seen anything as tranquil and serene, scanned the surrounding trees and acreage. Chickie and Bobby stood in the clearing and faced the cabin, remembering the good times, but saying nothing about them.

"Look at that fuckin' tree, Bobby. And I thought it was big when my old man took me here. It's gotta be fifty feet or more by now. And look at the thickness of that fuckin' trunk. Madone," Chickie said as if wishing his father were alive to see it with him.

Sammy and Richie struggled with the luggage as Chickie went to the front door and took out the keys Don Joey presented him in New Jersey. The same keys his father used.

Once inside, the guys opened the windows on both floors to air out the place. No one had been there in nineteen months since Joey came out with a couple of his lieutenants while Chickie and Bobby were in Jersey paying back Luigi Colucci for a destroyed delicatessen in Paulie Schielzo's territory. It was a senseless act that killed three workers and two civilian bystanders.

By that time, Schielzo had been promoted to a captain in the Ponti family.

While Don Joey Ponti was at The Ramblin' Rose having dinner in *Carmine's* with Mayor Sheila Dunay, Chickie's and Schielzo's crews spent the evening sweeping six Salvucci hangouts and Luigi's biggest seaside pizzeria, killing nine hitmen, plus destroying Little Calooch's most profitable and legitimate business for the remainder of the summer. They were specifically looking for Little Calooch, but he chose to spend that night taking his cut in trade at one of the Chinese massage parlors he had under his thumb in Paterson.

The local police spokesman told the news media, "At this time, we have no leads as to who these perpetrators are, but law enforcement officials stated they couldn't have done a better job of removing the criminal element from our streets and neighborhoods."

"That's twice we tried to get rid of that little scumbag. Third time's gonna be the charm," Chickie told Joey upon his return from Nevada.

"He's gonna be expecting something," Joey said. "We've waited decades to get rid of these fuckin' roaches. Another couple of years ain't gonna matter. Don't worry, he'll fuck up again."

And with that, Chickie waited.

Chickie took the master suite. Bobby claimed the middle bedroom and had a laugh with his old friend when they saw Enzo's bullet holes in the floor from making Pig Al dance. They also reminisced about replacing the bloodied wooden chair and painting the blood-splattered wall before leaving back in 1990. Richie took the front bedroom, and Sammy was left with one of the large sofas in the living room, but not before complaining about no TV, no radio…just peace and quiet, something unheard of where they came from.

As they lay in their respective beds, Chickie and Bobby were looking forward to getting back so the Ponti scepter could be passed along…and Luigi Colucci and the Salvucci family could speedily be eradicated. Richie couldn't wait for the following morning so he could eat breakfast, get the casino manager, bring him to the cabin, viciously beat the shit out of him, find out where Ponti's cash was, get it and, "…get the fuck outta this place and back to makin' money in Jersey." Sammy was happy to be anywhere, but would've preferred a bed.

At the same time, historian Antoinette Goode, now 70 and widowed for the past few years, had recently found information she thought was enthralling and dug as deep as possible to learn more. It first came from folded pieces of paper she found in a 1923 book on 19th Century Native American mysticism that was sitting untouched in the basement of the Gabbs Public Library since 1928. What made *these* papers important was that they were dated August 29th, 1925, about five weeks after the Worley event.

According to what she read, one of the last true Shoshone braves, known as Quishindemi, which translated to 'Bobtail Horse,' was around 60 years old when he told a young Worley resident named Lou Rittberg about the forced removal of the Shoshone tribes from their homeland by the white invaders in the mid-to-late 1870s. Though they left peacefully, U.S. Army soldiers killed old men and women unable to keep up, raped squaws without fear of official reprisal, took young children from their families and sold them to work on the farms and ranches owned by settlers, and countless braves were taken to large fields and slaughtered with Gatling guns. And, of course, there were the smallpox-infested blankets given to the rest, causing what came to be known by the Shoshone as "the great sickness."

Bobtail Horse's story went on to say the chiefs and their councils from the converging Shoshone tribes sought out Tenupah Dome-up, '*Man From*

The Sky,' the most powerful and respected of all the *Not-tsoo-Dainnahpeh,* a word best known to the invaders as a *medicine man.*

The pages Rittberg wrote to the best of his uneducated ability went on to say that as the tribes passed through certain parts of their hills and valleys during the forced exodus, Man From The Sky put a curse on the land, saying, "...for eternity, those killed upon the ground our ancestors lived and hunted will rise should Shoshone blood touch the ground in anger, hatred or war. Chanting their last words, *the risen* will seek and kill those causing the fallen blood, and those who stop *the risen* from their task."

Antoinette was having a hard time believing what she was reading. It brought back memories of hearing similar stories from the tribe's elders when she was a child, though they were *always* told in whispers. The killings in Worley was only one such story, but it was the only one where someone claimed to have actually seen them...*the risen.*

Antoinette used whatever research technology was available, but even that was sparse for such an in-depth project. Getting up in years, she didn't like to drive far distances anymore. Then one day her daughter and son drove her to what was left of Worley, where they dug through a dozen boxes of newspapers and books from the mid-to-late 1920s. That's when she found several articles spread out over four weeks that would be the missing piece of an unbelievable legend...and could prove that legend to be true. All *too* true.

On Saturday afternoon, July 4th, 1925, in the middle of Prohibition, two local 18 year old boys and their 16 year old girlfriends went for a ride to celebrate the holiday with their guns and fireworks, which were nothing more than short sticks of dynamite. One of the boys was Stan Worley Jr., so it was easy for him to obtain a few bottles of whiskey from the local pharmacy. Having that last name also allowed young Stan to often get away with murder...literally.

With his friends jammed into the front cab, Stan drove his father's 1923 flatbed Ford along a deserted road that meandered through the valley where they came upon 17 year old Pete Johnson, whose Shoshone name translated to *Swift Wind,* walking home as he carried a heavy load of supplies from town for his family.

The guys offered Pete a lift to the reservation and said they would sit on the back bed with him as Stan's girlfriend got into the driver's seat. It was a very hot day and though Pete wouldn't normally accept the offer, he still had more than an hour to go before getting home, probably longer because of the load he was carrying.

It wasn't long before the whiskey made brave men out of Worley and his friend, Kent Dooley, causing the insults and slurs to come out. Pete read the situation, cordially thanked them and asked to stop the truck so he could walk the rest of the way. That was when the driver turned off the road and pulled into a wooded area.

Pete knew this was a bad sign and hopped off the slow moving vehicle, but Stan was fast with raising his rifle, and though being drunk and on a moving flatbed he aimed for his target's back, but hit Pete in his left leg, causing the innocent boy to drop to the ground.

With the truck stopped, Stan and Kent took their rifles and a long piece of heavy rope to the fallen and bleeding Swift Wind who was nervously trying to stop his blood from hitting the ground. The teenagers grabbed Pete's arms, put them behind his back and as Kent hovered over the Indian with a rifle, Stan tied their catch to a tree. That's when the young Shoshone's blood ran onto the dirt, then was sucked into it.

As the teenagers ran to the truck, they never saw the wave of energy burst from under their prisoner, expanding in every direction through the ground. That was when Swift Wind heard the faint sound of a Shoshone war song.

It was said the people in the area saw a bolt of lightning and heard the crack of thunder that afternoon…though the sky was clear.

When they returned to their captive, Worley Jr. took four small dynamite sticks, placed them firmly between the strands of rope and ran each fuse into a long one. Once back at the truck, Kent took another swig of whiskey as he lit the fuse from his cigarette, and then they drove away.

About a quarter of a mile away they heard the sound of the blast, which meant nothing to them. What it *did* mean was that they had viciously and hatefully killed Pete 'Swift Wind' Johnson. A full-blooded Shoshone. On sacred land.

It wasn't until sunrise on Monday that Julie, Kent Dooley's girlfriend was found covered in dried blood and walking along the center of Worley's

Main Street. She spent the next four days in bed with a doctor and the town's minister at her side before she was able to speak.

Julie said she snuck out of her bedroom to meet Kent in the barn on Sunday night after her parents had gone to sleep. While they were in the hayloft, they heard people climbing up the two ladders. It was dark and neither could make out who it was. They only heard the mumbling of words no one could understand. Thinking it was Stan and his girlfriend, Kent called out, "C'mon, asshole! Get out of here!" Then Julie heard skin being torn apart and Kent screaming for only a second before he went silent. She cried hysterically as she told the elders, "The tearing…it seemed to go on forever. Then they left. They left…still mumbling." The young girl said she huddled in a corner of the hayloft, shaking and afraid to move for hours until the sun rose. That was when she saw what little was left of Kent…and went into shock as she walked into town.

When asked why she was untouched, she said she had no idea.

That same morning, Stan Worley and his wife, along with the parents of Stan's girlfriend, discovered someone had come through their children's open bedroom windows. Each teenager's pillow was covered in blood as if their skulls were crushed with a rock while they slept before they were taken away. A short time later, a search party found what was left of the bodies about fifty yards from their homes.

It was also determined Stan Jr. and his friends had something to do with Pete's disappearance because the Johnson family's supplies were discovered in the back of Worley's Ford truck.

After reading the articles and putting all the facts together, Antoinette knew she would never be the same. She was the only person alive who knew this dark secret about her ancestors…and she hoped no one would ever know again.

CHAPTER 10

Though it started just like any other day, Sunday, June 13th, 1999, would turn out to be like no other.

The coffee beans Don Joey left in the freezer were still good, so Bobby ground them in preparation for the coffeemaker. The noise woke Sammy as he stretched out on one of the sofas, but it was already 9:15AM and the rest of the guys were up and showered.

"As long as you like it black or with sugar, that's the best we're gonna get until we go food shoppin'," Bobby said as Chickie poured a cup of coffee.

He took a mouthful of the hot black liquid, then said to Bobby, "See if you can get a signal."

Bobby whipped out a Nokia from his sport jacket, looked at the bars and shook his head in disappointment. Sammy, coffee in hand, was walking upstairs to take a shower as Richie entered the kitchen, all ready to go. Before he could say a word, Chickie said, "You got a phone signal?"

Richie reached into his sport jacket, took out a Samsung, looked at the bars, then held it up for the others to see. Nothing.

"So, when do we leave?" Richie asked as he lit his second cigarette of the day and poured a cup of coffee. "It's a fuckin' hour to town and I'm starvin'. I wanna eat, do what we gotta do with this casino fuck and get back home as soon as we can."

Chickie preferred not to answer Richie, so Bobby took the lead.

"There's no milk, and we'll leave as soon as your guy gets his ass down here."

Richie didn't respond or react. He just turned and went outside to finish his cigarette and coffee.

Once the front door was closed, Chickie said, under his breath but loud enough for Bobby to hear, "I *hate* that motherfucker. Like to do to *him* what we did to his old man."

"Yeah, well, that's not what this trip's about. Let's just get the missing money, put Frick and Frack in a casino limo and send 'em back to the airport. You and me stay here for a couple of days to make sure Donny's assistant has a smooth transition taking over the operation, and *then* we go home so you can take the don's place."

Chickie said nothing. He finished his coffee while gazing out of the kitchen windows remembering the times he was here with his father.

Sammy drove the Prius to the employee lot behind The Ramblin' Rose and parked next to Donny's private space and his new gold Cadillac Seville. When they finished breakfast at *Sheila's*, the three men waited while Chickie made a quick call on a house phone. Once he hung up, they followed him through the casino and down the hallway to the business offices. It was Sunday and fairly empty of employees.

Donny's secretary was about forty and could have been one of the showgirls, waitresses or dealers a decade or two earlier…and was startled when the guys brazenly walked in.

"May I help you?" she asked from behind her desk, more nervous than cordial.

Chickie took control as he stepped close and replied, "Yeah, sweetheart. Is Donny in? And don't say he's not, 'cause his car's outside."

"Yes, he's in. How may I help you?"

He moved a little closer and softly-but-*very*-sternly said, "Tell your boss Chickie Santorella is here."

She looked at an appointment book, then lifted her head, swallowed hard and said, "I'm sorry, but Mr. Oliveri is in a closed-door conference and left strict orders not to be disturbed."

"Yeah, well, when he gave you those orders he didn't know I was comin'," Chickie said as he backed away, went to the casino manager's door, listened to the silence inside and turned the knob. It was locked.

The secretary freaked and loudly said, "I'll call Security!"

Chickie turned to her and said, "I'll tell you what, go get 'em."

She saw that as an excuse to grab her purse and run out of the room.

Chickie looked at the locked wooden door and said, "Bobby."

Inside the casino manager's office, 36 year old Donatello Oliveri, with cheekbones and reddish-brown skin that showed off his half-Indian heritage, was sleeping on the plush leather couch. He couldn't have looked more comfortable and peaceful.

That was when Bobby Battaglino's body came crashing through the door, showering wood and splinters everywhere. Donny jerked awake in a panic…unsure of what just happened. He instantly sat up and tried to get his bearings when Chickie, Richie and Sammy walked in.

"What *the fuck?* Who the fuck are *you* guys?"

Chickie looked down and said, "Donny…stand up. Ya look like you were up late bangin' hookers."

"What?" he arrogantly answered. "Why you want me to stand up?"

"You know who I am, right?"

Donny focused on the man talking and said, "You're…Chickie. Chickie Santorella from years ago. You work for Mr. Ponti. Who are *these* guys? What are you doing here? I gave your guy Mr. Ponti's money a couple-a weeks ago."

Suddenly, Donny felt safer as two armed Security Guards stuck their heads and guns through the destroyed doorway and looked around the room. The one with sergeant stripes looked at Chickie and asked, "Mr. Santorella?"

Chickie made no facial gesture. He just nodded his head.

The sergeant looked at his partner and said, "We're good here. Let's go."

The look on Oliveri's face changed to fear.

"Donny. When I walked in I told you to stand up," Chickie quietly said.

"*Fuck that!* I wanna know what's going on?"

Chickie sadly shook his head and simply replied with, "Richie."

Richie walked from the far side of the room to the couch, grabbed Donny's shoulders, stood him up and stepped away. Without saying a word, Chickie pulled his left arm back and wailed a punch directly into the casino manager's face, throwing him against the wall and onto the couch, then stepped away and calmly stood next to Bobby and Sammy as Richie, with his sick and sinister smile, pummeled Donny's face. Something made Chickie look down at the large colorful tribal Indian rug in the center of the room and said, "Ya know, Donny…this is a real nice rug." And with that, Richie gave Donny one more punch that knocked the assumed-skimmer unconscious.

A few minutes later, the Prius pulled out of the parking lot weighed down as low as a Prius can get without scraping the road.

Sammy drove. Richie was in the passenger seat. Chickie sat behind Richie and Bobby, already deep into his crossword puzzle book, was next to him. Tied to the roof was Donny's rug, rolled up with a large bulge in the middle.

Richie bitched, "I don't understand why we have-ta jam ourselves in this friggin' thing when we could-a taken his Caddie."

"It's leased by the business and the new manager gets it." With his left hand Chickie pointed to the roof and continued, "'Cause the prick up there ain't ever gonna use it again."

As he pulled his hand back he noticed dried blood on his knuckles. Pissed off, he said, "Fuck," then reached over, tapped Sammy's shoulder and barked, "Find me someplace to wash my hands. *Now.*"

Richie scowled at someone giving orders to his man.

Sammy parked the car alongside the old Sinclair gas station on Brucite Street which had fallen into disrepair over the years. As everyone got out, Chickie rubbed his left hand with a handkerchief, but that wasn't good enough. He needed to wash with soap and hot water.

That was when Donny woke up in his woolen cocoon and started writhing around and yelling, "*Help! Help! Where am I?*"

Though the rug was tied on tightly, it thrashed as Donny tried to get loose and escape. So Richie walked over and began punching the shit out of the spot where Donny's head was until the rug stopped moving.

Once everything was under control, Chickie said, "I'm goin' in here." He looked at Bobby and said, "Make sure the rug stays quiet." Then he pointed to the two underlings and said, "Since me and Bobby gotta stay for a few days, we're gonna need some supplies." He focused on Richie as he continued, "There's a store a couple-a blocks back. You two take a walk and get what we need."

Richie wasted no time responding with, "Fuck that."

Chickie ignored Richie, then looked at Sammy.

"Get coffee, milk, eggs, bacon, plenty of toilet paper and some paper towels…"

As Chickie kept speaking, he pulled a pen from his sport jacket and handed it to Sammy, who started writing on his palm. Again, the look on Richie Paldino's face changed to *pissed off* because he didn't want Sammy taking orders from anyone other than him.

"Bobby, you want some sausage?" Chickie asked. Bobby nodded, so the list continued. "Hot and sweet sausage, orange juice, wine, butter, bread, garlic…*fresh* garlic, cold cuts, spaghetti and everything we're gonna need to make gravy. You two got that?"

Only Sammy answered.

"Got it."

Richie replied with, "You gonna pick us up?"

"With this stroonze kickin' and screamin' on the roof? What do you think?" came the response.

Richie just sneered and started walking away. Sammy, wanting to appease everyone, gave Chickie a respectful nod, then obediently followed his boss.

As they walked away, Chickie decided to bust Richie's balls and called out, "We're gonna need a couple of frozen pizzas!"

So Bobby added, "And get me some of that hot cocoa mix. The one with the little marshmallows!"

As they walked, Sammy continued to write on his hand, making Richie even angrier.

"You even *think* of getting' that cocoa-shit for that fat fuck, I'll blow your fuckin' head off."

Sammy stopped writing.

Chickie walked in and then out of the gas station. He yelled to Bobby, "It's in the back. Gimme a few," as he walked to the side of the station. It pissed him off to tread where there was mud and puddles of water from a recent rain, especially since he was wearing an expensive pair of Italian loafers.

As he turned the corner to the rear of the property he saw a crudely written *Out Of Order* sign on the Men's Room door, and standing in front of the Lady's Room were two tough-looking hicks in their late 20s, wearing well-worn cowboy boots and hats, smoking cigarettes and sharing a bottle in a paper bag.

Something made Chickie cover his bloodstained hand with the handkerchief.

The slightly taller and more sober of the hicks looked the older man over, snickered at his appearance and said, "Waitin' on a friend. Be a minute."

Chickie responded with an appreciative nod of the head. That was when he heard the gentle voice behind him.

"Excuse me. Are you in line?" asked Jenny, a 22 year old whose Midwest accent showed she wasn't a local. At five-foot-seven, with her clean scrubbed face and shoulder length natural blonde hair, she was the proverbial Girl Next Door.

Chickie simply smiled, gestured for her to cut in front of him and said, "Ladies first."

The young woman smiled and was taken by his manners as she replied, "Thank you. You must not be from around here."

He smiled and winked, thinking it best to keep the conversation and his Jersey accent to a minimum.

The bathroom door swung open and *another* local stepped out rubbing his left boot on the ground, yelling, "Motherfucker! Stepped in somebody's shit!" as the door slammed shut behind him.

Chickie could barely hide his disgust. Jenny ignored them as she walked toward the bathroom and reached for the door handle.

That was when the taller hick grabbed her arm and said, "Where you goin', whore?"

Not wanting to have any problems, she answered, "I thought you guys were done."

"The girl goes next."

The words and the way Chickie said them caused everything to stop. Jenny *and* the three shitkickers looked at the lone Italian from New Jersey only a few feet from them.

The cowboy with shit on his boot puffed up his chest and asked, "You her father or her pimp?"

Chickie didn't give a shit that he was up against three stout and younger men. His eyes went dead…and they saw it.

"No. I'm the guy sayin' she goes *next*. You got a problem with that?"

There was silence.

The shit-scraper tried to laugh off what Chickie said, but it turned into more of a scared and nervous twitch. His chest rapidly deflated.

Chickie waited for them to step up or step away.

They stepped away, making them look like the bullying morons they were. Not surprisingly, Jenny was thoroughly charmed by Chickie's chivalry.

Trying to avoid the mud, Chickie walked to the bathroom door and used his handkerchief to hold it open for her. She saw the blood on his hand, but showed no reaction. Nor did she comment about it. She simply gave him a respectful smile and said, "Thank you. I'll only be a minute," and walked inside, avoiding the shit on the floor.

By the time Richie and Sammy left the market, Chickie and his clean hands were back in the car listening to some station playing Willie Nelson's "Stardust," while Bobby was doing a crossword puzzle.

Sammy carried three overloaded bags as he and his empty-handed boss walked along Brucite Street toward the Sinclair station. But of course, Richie bitched every step of the way.

"Fuckin' Chickie. Thinks he's the don or somethin'."

"The don *did* put him in charge, Richie."

"When this job's over, I'm tellin' Ponti I wanna start my own crew."

Almost afraid to ask, Sammy went for it anyway.

"What if he says 'No'?"

"Then Don Giuseppe Ponti, Chickie Santorella, Bobby Battaglino and everybody else in that fuckin' family can go fuck themselves. Luigi Colucci will let me start one with the Salvuccis in a heartbeat…in a fuckin' *heartbeat*."

That's when Sammy shot his boss a worried glance because he *knew* what the next question would be. And it was.

"You with me?"

As if there could be another answer, he said, "Sure, Richie."

Making their way to the end of the first block, Richie raised his head and said, "*Ah!* Things are lookin' up," as he watched the cute and happy

Jenny, having recently left the filthy bathroom, casually walking on the sidewalk in their direction.

Just like his father, and ever classless, Richie said, "Hey, sweetheart! C'mere."

Don Giuseppe 'Joey' Ponti and *his* boss, Don Antonio '*The Little Hand*' Agostini, had some plans of their own while Chickie was finding the casino's lost money. The two family heads knew the incoming boss of the Ponti family would meet resistance from Luigi '*Little Calooch*' Colucci, and Joey wanted to make sure there would *be* a family and business to leave behind, and in the hands of someone his father would be proud of.

Told that Don Ponti was tired of the ongoing problems caused by the Salvucci family over territorial rights, Luigi agreed to a sit-down in a Manhattan attorney's office. He was guaranteed to get more Jersey territory in return for an end to the violence his family had been causing throughout the years, but he would also have to agree to an increase in the tribute to the Ponti and Agostini families, *and* include the monthly money that was supposed to go to Ponti.

The meeting, set for 3:30PM on Sunday, June 13th, would include the captains of Salvucci's crews so they would hear the agreement directly from Don Agostini, thus avoiding any possibility of things going askew in the future.

Everyone showed up on time and were led to the law firm's conference room. In the center was a table that sat ten on each side, with food and drinks set up by three waiters who served everyone and kept everything replenished. What made the dons even happier was that all the men were getting along.

Everyone except Little Calooch.

Even though he agreed to the terms set prior to the meeting, he now demanded more territory and let the dons know it as soon as he walked in. They were miffed by his attitude, but wanting to keep the peace, they agreed it would be discussed and worked out during the meeting.

Even with that assurance, Colucci *still* had a puss on his face as everyone took their seats. Don Ponti and Don Agostini sat in the center on one side with a couple of their captains next to them. Luigi Colucci and his

Consiglieri sat in the center opposite the bosses, with four of their captains on each side.

Joey turned to one of the waiters and politely said, "Bring in some fresh coffee and sandwiches. We'll let you know if we need anything after that. Thanks."

The waiter respectfully bowed his head and the servers left the room.

Things started as they normally would with Don Agostini thanking everyone for attending, then introduced the men on his side of the table.

When the waiters rolled in two carts with a fresh urn of coffee and sandwiches, the don stopped talking and patiently waited.

After placing everything on the table, the waiters pulled three Uzi's with silencers from behind the carts and faced the barrels toward Colucci's side of the table. He and his men froze.

Realizing he let his greed, ambition and disrespect get the better of him by agreeing to a meeting to get something he didn't deserve, Luigi stared angrily at Giuseppe Ponti.

Emotionless, Ponti looked at Little Calooch and simply said, "Whatever."

That's when the barrage of silent bullets riddled the Salvucci family captains, their Consiglieri and their boss.

At the same time across the river in New Jersey, Paulie Schielzo's crew, as part of a planned attack by the heads of the other Jersey families being tormented by Colucci, hit every Salvucci lieutenant so there would be no one to replace the now-slaughtered captains. Only a few were killed on the spot. The rest simply disappeared and were never heard from again.

Within days, the Salvucci territory was divided peacefully and satisfactorily between Ponti and the rest of the Jersey families.

There was no Luigi 'Little' Calooch' Colucci to deal with any longer.

This would be Don Ponti's and Don Agostini's gift to Carmine 'Chickie' Santorella upon his return to New Jersey.

The weather conditions and temperature were perfect that afternoon in Nevada's Shoshone Mountains when the Prius pulled in front of the cabin. They weren't out of the car for five seconds before Chickie bolted up the steps and unlocked the front door to get to a sink with *real* soap and hot water. Bobby pointed to the rug and told Richie and Sammy to, "Bring that asshole inside."

Again, it pissed Richie off that he was now being given orders from Chickie's man.

Donny woke up screaming during the drive and tried to get out of the rolled up and tightly bound rug, but to no avail. By the time they got to the cabin, most of the fight had been taken out of the casino manager. But now that the car had come to a stop and all four doors had opened and closed, he knew they arrived at their destination, so he started screaming and writhing again. Sammy expertly released the knot and let the still-securely tied rug roll and fall to the ground with a thud.

Once again, things were quiet.

As the two carried it toward the porch, Sammy said, "You know, this *is* a nice rug."

Richie responded with, "I just hope this fuck didn't bleed on it too much."

A couple of minutes later they unrolled the rug across the living room floor, sending the semi-conscious Donny, his face bloodied and bruised, crashing into the far wall.

"That's why I put him into the rug's underside, so he didn't bleed on the good side," the experienced Bobby said, leaving Donny on the floor while they turned the rug over and admired its quality.

Chickie told Bobby to put everything from the market into the kitchen cabinets and refrigerator, and for Richie and Sammy to bring their victim upstairs and tie him to a chair using the rope from the rug.

"Once that's done, we'll clean up, have a talk with this thievin' prick, then mangia."

It was nearing 7PM. The sun started its descent behind the trees, though it would still be a while before it sank below the horizon. It was going to be a New Moon, so it would be a dark night.

Bobby and Chickie thought it was funny Richie picked the middle bedroom to do that evening's torture session, since this was the one his father used to kill Albert 'Pig Al' Povich. This time it was Donatello Oliveri in the wooden chair that replaced the blood-splattered one, and Sammy had done a quality job tying him to it.

The four men walked in to find Donny bloodied, bound and hoarse from yelling for help out the open window on the side of the cabin.

As they surrounded their prisoner, Chickie stood about five feet in front of him and calmly said, "Donny, because I have respect for your dead old man, I'm gonna give you one chance."

Still trying to struggle out of the tight ropes, Donny pleaded, "One chance for *what?* Who *are* these guys?"

"They're friends of Mr. Ponti's. Now, tell me about the cash."

Donny swallowed hard, then lowered his voice and said, "Chickie. Mr. Santorella. I have no idea what you're talking about. If you think I stole somethin', you're wrong. I'd never rob *anything* from Mr. Ponti. What his family did for mine, do you *really* think I'd take his *money?*"

Chickie gave him a hard, cold stare as Donny kept trying to prove his innocence.

"Chickie, I swear to Jesus Christ and those twelve *other* Jews he had dinner with, I have no idea what money you're talking about."

"Oh, you *don't?* See, Mr. Ponti was told differently, and his source is pretty reliable."

As the sunlight disappeared, the lack of any moonlight caused Richie to walk to the lamp atop the night-table and turn it on.

Chickie looked at the two men standing on each side of him and asked, "Bobby, Sammy, whatdya think? Think this is some kinda misunderstanding?"

They each innocently shrugged their shoulders. Oddly, their actions relaxed Donny.

Chickie took out his Ericsson cell phone and waved it around while saying to Donny, "Ya know, if I could get a signal I'd be able to get Mr. Ponti on the phone to tell him what you said, but I can't get nothin' up here." Then he lowered the phone, looked at the casino manager and said, "Richie."

That's all that had to be said as the most vicious of the four walked in front of Donny and...*whack!* Richie punched Donny's face so hard that fresh blood splattered from his newly gashed lip.

Bobby and Sammy took out their cell phones to check the bars. Nothing.

Sammy commented, "These mountains, they must be blockin' everything."

"They put men on the moon and a fuckin' rovin'-thing on Mars and communicate with 'em, but you can't make a fuckin' call from Nevada to Jersey," Chickie angrily said.

Whack! Richie punched Donny's face again, and said, "That's for making me come all the way out here, you motherfuckin' half-breed!"

With blood flowing from above his eye, Donny mustered enough energy to yell, "*I didn't take any money! When are you greaseballs gonna get it?*"

That was it. The words set Richie off.

"*Greaseballs?* Hey, Dances-With-Scumbags, who the fuck said you could talk to me like that?"

Richie's sick, sinister smile intensified as he swung a vicious elbow into his victim's face, cracking the bones in his nose so everyone could hear it. Donny screamed as blood ran down his face and onto his shirt and the rope. It was obvious Richie Paldino enjoyed what he was doing just a little too much. Just like his father.

In a full rage, Richie yelled, "Now, you Injun cocksucker, you're goin' out the window!"

Donny continued to struggle as he was being dragged to the window, but there was no way he was escaping Sammy's handiwork.

"*No! Please! No!*"

With an adrenaline-rush of strength, Richie picked up the chair with its now-upside down human attachment and dangled Donny outside. As he wailed into the dark empty acres, the blood emanating from his beaten face ran across his forehead and fell…as if in slow motion…spattering on the ground. And then *into* the ground as the dirt consumed the red drops.

Within a few seconds, and above the screams of the half-Shoshone, a bolt of lightning flashed and thunder clapped as if they were only a few miles away.

"Fuck, sounds like it's gonna rain." Chickie said, thinking of the mess it would be to bury Donny in the mud. "Pull him in. I'll let you beat the shit out of him after we eat."

As Richie hoisted Donny and the chair into the room, no one saw the wave of energy burst from where the blood dripped as it traveled through the ground in every direction.

Only Donny heard the Indians chanting their war song in the distance, though he didn't know why.

Once things settled down, the prisoner pleaded with the men, "I'm telling you! Please! I don't *have his money!*"

Richie responded with, "Wrong answer," and *another* punch to the side of Donny's head.

Chickie said, "Let him think about it for a while. He's smart. He'll make the right decision." Then he looked at the casino manager's badly beaten and bloodied face and asked, "Won'tcha, Donny?" While still looking at him, Chickie changed the subject. "I'm hungry. You hungry, Donny?

The casino manager was afraid to answer, so Chickie looked at the guys and said, "C'mon. He ain't goin' nowhere." The boss returned his eyes to Donny and continued, "As soon as you tell me where the shkadole is, you can join us and mangia."

Bobby closed the window and commented to Donny, "Ya know, it's gonna be tough to take a leak while you're tied to that chair, and those look like nice pants."

Before leaving the room, Richie gave Donny one more punch for the road. Then he leaned close to the beaten man's ear and whispered, "You're gonna tell *me* where that money is, scumbag, or I'll kill ya." Then Richie flashed his demented smile and walked out.

About an hour later and seventy-five yards or so away from the rear of the cabin, several sections of dirt began to move as if being dug from underneath. Slowly, a left hand of rotted flesh and exposed bone broke through, and then…the right hand, this one wearing a dirt encrusted diamond pinky ring. The clear polish on the long curled nails was now caked with dirt.

In the lake, bubbles popped to the surface about 40 feet from shore.

In a cleared section of the 225 acres, two dead mobsters wearing dark, Italian suits and silk ties rotted from years being buried, crawled from their graves with aimless stares on their eroded faces.

Over the next several minutes *more* dead mobsters, hookers, loansharks, politicians, extortionists, drug dealers, second-rate crooks, insurance salesmen and attorneys crawled from the ground in various stages of decomposition, and all baring the signs of their demise. Hands bound together. Bullet holes in various body parts. Garrotes around their necks. Ice picks and knives sticking from their chests and skulls. Each of their dry, crusty lips were moving and softly mumbling.

Oblivious to their surroundings, they slowly shuffled and wandered around the large acreage in the darkness of the New Moon.

These were not Shoshone warriors.

Bobby was in the kitchen, happily smoking a cigar and putting together four sandwiches...Jersey style. Richie, smoking a cigarette, and Sammy were at the dining room table drinking sodas and reading the Nye County Gazette's sport section.

Chickie walked into the kitchen, looked at the food and smiled.

"Get yourself something to drink. These'll be ready in a minute," Bobby told his friend.

The boss grabbed a bottle of water, then walked to the entrance of the dining room and asked, "Get the pizzas?"

The arrogant Paldino didn't lift his head from the newspaper as he sarcastically answered, "Havin' 'em delivered."

Chickie returned to the kitchen shaking his head and softly said to Bobby, "Disrespectful wise-ass. What was that reason we don't do to him what we did to his old man again? Oh yeah. He's supposed to know how to get the money outta that prick upstairs."

They both laughed loud enough for Richie to hear, and that pissed him off.

Chickie watched Bobby sprinkle pepper over the open sandwiches, then flicked cigar ashes onto one and covered each with a slice of bread. He picked up a large coffee mug and they carried the four plates into the dining room.

Chickie put two plates in front of Richie and Sammy, making sure the sandwich with the ashes went to the wise-ass.

"Thanks, Chickie," came from the respectful Sammy as the older guys sat down.

When Bobby put his mug on the table, Richie glanced over and saw marshmallows floating on top. It was hot cocoa. The pissed off tough guy leaned close to Sammy and arrogantly grunted, "You pussy fuck." His man shrugged apologetically, then started eating as Richie shook his head in disgust and bit into his sandwich.

This time Bobby and Chickie held back their laughter. But it was hard.

It was nearly 8:45PM when the guys, each carrying a plastic bottle of water, stepped into Bobby's bedroom to find Donny's face, neck and shirt smeared in blood. He was barely conscious, still bound to the chair and his crotch soaked with urine. The smell immediately hit them.

"I *told ya* you were gonna fuck up those pants. A shame, too," Bobby said as he rushed to the window, opened it and took a breath of fresh air.

Richie casually stepped in front of Donny and threw a hard fist into his chest, knocking *all* the air from his lungs.

"*Ughhhhh!*"

Chickie came close to Donny's face and said, "Now, Donny, you don't look like you can take much more of this. So the sooner you give up where the cash is, the sooner we can all go home. You're a smart guy. Think about it." Then the boss backed up and said, "Richie."

Richie wailed another punch into Donny's gut.

"*Ughhhhh!*"

Chickie returned to Donny's face and said, "You sure you don't wanna talk?"

Donny's head tilted to the side, too exhausted to respond.

Chickie shook his head, turned to the others and said, "Bobby, Sammy, let Richie spend a little *quality time* with our friend here." Then he whispered to Richie, who already had that psychotic smile on his face, "Take it easy until he talks. He's no good to us dead. After that, I don't give a fuck what you do to him. But *call me* if he starts talkin'."

Richie couldn't be happier as the other three left the room.

Bubbles of air continued to break the surface of the lake, now only 25 feet from shore. Two dozen *mob-zombies* continued to aimlessly shuffle as if listening for a sound, looking for a human, while softly murmuring to themselves. Every fifteen-to-twenty minutes another decayed corpse would dig and crawl its way out of one of the countless graves around the property. Their tattered and worm-eaten clothes showed many of them had been well-dressed, manicured and bejeweled at the time of their demise and burial. The only thing missing was their identification and cash... which was always reinvested into the Ponti family's casino.

Meanwhile, in the second floor bedroom of the cabin, Richie looked Donny over. He was a mess. His face was swollen from the multiple punches. Dried and fresh blood surrounded his eyes, ears, nose and lips. Even Richie knew Donny would never be able to take any more hits. That was when he looked at the lamp on the night-table near the open window, and then back at his victim.

The sadistic mobster grabbed Donny's bloody collar and ripped the shirt open, exposing his shoulders and upper-back. Not knowing what was about to happen, Donny started to tussle in the chair, making a racket loud enough for Chickie, Bobby and Sammy to hear in the living room.

Richie gave Donny his sadistic grin as he walked to the night-table, removed the lampshade, picked up the lamp and strolled toward the wide-eyed Donny as he cried, "What are you gonna *do? No!* Please *don't!*"

Suddenly the room went dark. The cord wasn't long enough and had popped out of the wall outlet.

"*Shit!*" Richie angrily yelled.

Because of the lack of moonlight, Richie had to use his Bic lighter to put the plug back into outlet. He returned the lamp to the night-table, then dragged Donny's chair next to the window and slowly put the hot bulb on Donny's back.

Flesh sizzled and Donny screamed wildly.

The screams of pain caused zombies between the cabin and forest to turn in the direction of the open window, but then return to wandering aimlessly once the sound disappeared.

Smoke rose from Donny's back, then he fainted. That pissed Richie off even more as he returned the lamp to the night-table and said, "You think passin' out's gonna make you miss this?" Then viciously said, "No fuckin' way."

Chickie was sitting comfortably in a living room chair with his feet up, relaxing for the first time in a few days. Sammy was prone on a sofa, waving his cell phone around trying to find a signal. Bobby sat on the other sofa with the newspaper, expertly attacking the crossword puzzle. They had nothing else to do until the casino manager cracked.

The beautiful rug from Donny's office now covered the floor in the middle of the room.

Richie picked up his bottle of water and poured it over Donny.

"Let's go, fuck-o. Wake up."

Donny stirred and was able to open his swollen eyes just enough to see Richie with his fist raised and ready to use it again. His eyes went as wide as they could in fear, though he was barely able to open them at all.

"No more. *Please. No more*," he barely had the energy and breath to say.

"Then talk to me, you fuckin' weasel, or I'll cut your balls off."

Knowing his torturer would do it, Donny took a deep breath and held back pain and tears as he hoarsely said, "Please, I'll give it back. I'll tell Mr. Ponti I'm sorry. *Very* sorry."

Richie's eyes widened with greed.

"How much?"

"Three-and-a-half million. Maybe more." Then Donny sorrowfully looked at Richie and begged, "Please don't hit me anymore. Please." The thief began weeping, "I buried it. The cash. Behind my house. Under the lilies."

Richie's sick smile came through as he said, "Yeah, motherfucker. No problem. I won't hit ya," then put his arm around Donny's throat and with a quick jerk, broke his neck.

Donny's body, still tightly secured to the chair, convulsed, then stopped moving.

Mobster zombies trickled through the edge of the clearing in the dark, listening for a sound to guide them. Searching for prey.

At the lake, a pair of decayed, wet hands broke the surface 12 feet from the shore.

The guys in the living room were enjoying the quiet and solitude. Bobby and Sammy were happy to see Chickie content. That was when they heard three very slow, loud knocks on the front door that echoed through the cabin.

Knock. Knock. Knock.

Bobby and Chickie turned toward the door, then toward each other. Sammy rose his head off the sofa.

"Want me to get it?" Bobby asked.

Chickie, *very* pissed off, shook his head, got up and said, "Just hope the two upstairs don't make any noise."

Sammy sat up and watched with interest as the boss walked to the door.

Knock. Knock.

"Take it easy. I'm comin'," Chickie said as he flipped the switch to turn on the porch light.

Knock.

Chickie quickly swung the heavy door open. The men's eyes went wide.

Standing there were three young women. Three *very* hot young women carrying beer and pizza.

Just as quickly as he opened the door, he shut it, stomped into the living room, angrily looked at his men and asked, "Who the fuck *are they?*"

Sammy, knowing he was going to be in trouble, nervously replied, "The hookers."

"What hookers?"

Knock. Knock. Knock.

"Richie figured Donny would-a cracked by now. So on the way back from the store he arranged for a few of 'em to come by for a couple-a hours." Then, as if remembering something *important*, he asked, "They bring the pizzas?"

Chickie couldn't get any madder. If he had a gun on him, he'd go upstairs and shoot Richie right-fuckin'-now. Seething, he said, "Great. With everything else going on, now I gotta get rid of these puttanas."

Sammy responded with, "C'mon, Chickie! We're in the middle-a nowhere. We ain't even got cable. What the fuck *else* we gonna do?"

Chickie shot Sammy a look that could kill and quietly said, "You're a good kid, Sammy, but don't push me."

Knock. Knock. Knock.

Bobby knew to keep his mouth shut.

Chickie returned to the door and opened it. From the living room, Bobby and Sammy craned their necks to see the girls.

Dallas, in her mid-20s, a natural brunette beauty in tight shorts, made it obvious she was the hooker-in-charge. China was also in her mid-20s, Asian, buxom and in the smallest of mini-skirts. They each carried a purse, a pizza box and a 6-pack. Standing behind them was 22 year old Jenny, the girl Chickie helped at the gas station. Along with her purse, pizza and beer, she wore shorts and struggled with a mini-boom box.

She recognized Chickie and, embarrassed, moved behind China.

"It's about time, handsome!" came from Dallas, in nothing that sounded like a Texas accent. "We hear there's a party goin' on. I'm Dallas, and this is China and Jenny," she continued as she pointed to her girls.

That was when Chickie saw his friend.

"You're the girl from the--"

She interrupted, "Yeah. Thanks again for that."

There was an awkward moment of silence broken by a loud thud from upstairs.

Chickie took control, "Sammy! Get over here and take care of this. I gotta see what that was."

As Chickie stepped away, the girls entered the foyer and closed the door behind them just as five shuffling zombies turned the corner of the cabin and came around the thick trunk of the oak tree to see the empty porch and the light go out.

With his hands still raised, the skeletal and wet head of Randy Jones, the muscle-bound weed dealer from Florida who was pushed overboard wearing cement buckets back in 1982, rose from the lake. A small fish flopped out of the water draining from his open mouth as he began saying, "...can't...swim. I can't...swim..."

The wooden chair was on its side with Donny's body still tied to it. Through the rope, Richie pulled out Donny's wallet, took the driver's license, read the address, then looked at the dead body and said, "Behind your house under some lilies, huh?"

Richie heard someone coming up the steps, so he jammed the license in his pocket and tossed the wallet out the window, whacking a bewildered, wandering zombie in the head.

Knowing someone would be walking in within seconds, Richie stood over the corpse yelling, "Look what you did, you dumb motherfucker!"

Chickie entered, looked at the scene in front of him and angrily questioned Richie.

"What the fuck happened?"

With the straightest of lying faces, Richie answered, "He woke up and started talkin', so I went into the hallway to call you. Next thing, I heard the chair fall over. I came back and he's dead. He must-a tried to get out, fell over and broke his fuckin' neck."

Chickie, already angry about the hookers, was super-pissed off now.

"Are you tellin' me we came out here and didn't get the information about Don Giuseppe's money, Paldino? Are you sayin' I gotta tell the boss he got fucked out of his money? I've *never* let the boss down."

As if Chickie's words and anger meant nothing, Richie lit a cigarette and calmly responded, "Relax, asshole. He told me about the cash. So instead of blowin' your fuckin' top, why don'tcha shut the fuck up and listen."

Chickie was stunned by Paldino's blatant lack of respect, but he wanted to hear about the money, he figured *then* he'd kill him.

"Okay, let's hear it. But keep it low. Your hookers are downstairs."

"No shit? Perfect timing."

"Not if you plan on bangin' one of 'em in *this* room with *him* here," Chickie responded sarcastically.

Richie's face got serious as he told the dead casino manager's bullshit story.

"Donny flipped and went over to the Salvucci family. Believe that shit? He said the Salvuccis are plannin' to whack Ponti in a week or so, take over the family, the territory *and* The Ramblin' Rose. They were gonna make this dead prick a partner, but he had-ta *buy in*, so he used the don's own money. Fuckin' cocksuckers…all of 'em."

Chickie listened and believed what he heard. It was possible. It was logical. And in the world they lived in, it could be all too real. He sat on the edge of the bed and said, "Fuck. I was hopin' he just got greedy. But this? This is bad. *Real* bad. Things are gonna get ugly back in Jersey. First thing tomorrow we gotta get to town so I can call Joey with this." Then he looked at Richie and grudgingly said, "Good work."

Without breaking his act, the liar replied, "Yeah, well, looks like we ain't gonna have-ta worry about this prick makin' any noise. Let's go see these hookers. Are they hot? I ordered *hot*."

Chickie didn't answer. He just looked down at Donny. Richie was right. There was no need to worry about the dead guy anymore.

"Untie him. Check his pants," the boss ordered. "Get his wallet. Maybe we can find somethin' we can use. A name, a phone number or somethin'."

Richie already knew the back pockets were accessible without untying Donny, plus he already knew what he needed to know, but he figured this would appease Chickie. As he untied the knots and loosened the chair from the body, Richie sarcastically said, "I'll check his wallet, but there's no way I'm puttin' my hands in the front pockets of these pissed-in pants," knowing Chickie's germophobia would keep him from doing it, too.

Richie checked both rear pockets, then looked at Chickie and said, "Look at *that*. This prick didn't even carry a wallet. It's probably back at his office."

That pissed Chickie off a little more.

As they left the corpse on the floor and were closing the door behind them, Richie asked, "These hookers…they bring the pizzas?"

"Yeah, wiseguy. They brought the pizzas," Chickie responded as they made their way down the steps.

"*See*. I *told ya* I was havin' 'em delivered."

CHAPTER 11

It was about thirty minutes later, and whatever music was blaring from the boom box wasn't close to *anything* Bobby or Chickie enjoyed as they sat in the comfortable living room chairs off to the side. Pizza boxes and empty beer cans covered half the dining table and Chickie *definitely* wasn't appreciating the mess.

Dallas and Jenny seductively danced barefoot atop the pool table, rubbing and kissing one another, and occasionally teasing Richie and Sammy with flashes of nipple as they sat on the sofa facing the girls.

The boss wasn't in the mood for a party. He had *other* things on his mind, like how he was going to eliminate Luigi Colucci for getting Donny to steal Ponti's money. It was time to get rid of the Salvucci family once and for all, and the new boss wanted to do it the day after he returned to New Jersey.

As Chickie read a Time magazine, Bobby was finishing his fourth crossword puzzle of the day.

From time-to-time, Jenny would shyly glance at Chickie, feeling embarrassed to be stripping in front of him.

China walked behind Sammy and started massaging his shoulders, so it only took a few seconds before the big man swept the 105 pound Asian in his arms, walked into the dining room and spread her out on the table, knocking some of the beer cans to the floor, which caused Bobby to yell, "Don't look at *me* when this party's over, kid! You're gonna clean that mess up yourself if you know what's good for you!"

China was writhing enticingly as Sammy, still dressed, mounted her. Instinctively, she wrapped her legs around his hips.

Bobby, with his chair conveniently facing the pool table, looked at Dallas. He licked his lips and smiled. He wanted to join the fun, but not while his boss was pissed off, or without his permission. So he quietly took a shot.

"So, uh…Chickie…"

The boss's head rose from the magazine.

"Ya know, there's, uh…there's three of *them*, and only the two *pazzi* brothers. So I was thinkin', since we gotta pay for *all* of 'em whether we use 'em or not…"

Chickie raised an eyebrow and said, "Bobby."

"Yeah, Chickie?"

"Fuck one if you want. Fuck 'em *all*. I don't *give* a fuck. Just shut up about it."

Bobby respectfully replied, "Thanks, boss," then got off the chair and happily walked in the direction of the girls dancing on the pool table. As he sat on the sofa next to Richie, he jokingly said, "Hey, Dallas, got any Italian in ya?" Before she could answer, he finished with, "Want some?"

Since good hookers always have to play the game, she smiled, laughed and blew him a kiss.

In the dining room, China still had her legs around Sammy and was grinding against his crotch. He returned the gesture, then ran his hands up her body and cupped her breasts. Not being the classiest guy in the place, he said, "You are absolutely the hottest Chink I ever seen."

She didn't allow herself to get pissed off at the racial slur. She was only in it for the money, not the class of people she knew she'd be fucking in Gabbs, Nevada. Upon giving him a sexy smile, she sucked on one of his fingers and said in a Chinese accent, "Ooooh, Sammy. Me love you loooong time."

She put the bullshit-level on "high" as she pressed her chest against him to close the deal, then said in perfect English, "Want to go outside? I have a really cool constellation to show you."

"A constellation, huh? We got a Prius, but it's a rental."

China laughed at Sammy's stupidity, but he didn't get it. She grabbed his ass and pulled him closer, making her intentions clear. He climbed off the table, then walked into the living room and looked at *his* boss. Richie was busy ogling Dallas and Jenny, who were now dancing topless. Then he looked at Chickie, the *real* boss, reading in his chair.

He returned to China and quietly said, "Let's get outta here."

She hopped off the table, grabbed his hand and led him to the door, but just before they opened it they heard Chickie.

"Sammy."

Sammy's faced changed He was sure he was about to be admonished as he returned to the living room and knelt next to Chickie.

"You got the car keys, right?" the boss asked quietly. The younger man quickly responded by nodding his head as Chickie continued, "I put an envelope with some extra cash in the glove compartment. When you finish doin' whatever the fuck you're gonna do out there, bring it in so I can pay the girls. I want 'em outta here as soon as Bobby and your paisan are done. Capisce?"

There was only one answer to give.

"Sure, Chickie."

Once outside, China grabbed Sammy's crotch and tried to get him into the woods, then playfully taunted him by lifting her shirt and squeezing her sizeable breasts together.

"Think you can catch me?" she asked before turning and sprinting into the darkness toward the trees…slowly, because she was in hooker-heels.

The foolish mobster yelled, "Hey! I thought you were gonna show me your car!" as he looked at the only two vehicles parked there. The Prius and Dallas's BMW. He was visibly confused as he shrugged, then loped after her.

The lights of the cabin faded as China scampered into the forest, giggling and staying ahead of Sammy. Then she stopped and hid behind a tree, waiting for him to catch up. She called out in an innocent-but-sexy voice, "It's so dark and I'm *all alone* here in these woods. You won't hurt me, will you?"

There was nothing but silence and darkness.

"Sammy?"

A hand slowly came up behind her head.

Her voice lost its sexiness as she called out, "Hey Sammy! A city boy like you could get lost out here. Where are you?"

The hand grabbed the back of her neck.

With trained fighting precision, China took the hand, spun its owner around to find she had Sammy pinned against the tree with her fist ready to strike. Apparently, this girl knew how to fight.

She looked him in the eye and sternly said, "Don't you *ever* do that again."

"Holy *shit!* Where'd you learn *that?*"

She didn't answer, but got back to business as she rubbed his pants along the zipper and asked, "So, you want to *fuck me*, big boy?"

He started clawing at his belt buckle and answered, "That's the plan, sweetheart."

China took a condom wrapper from her skirt, knelt on the ground and slowly pulled down Sammy's zipper as he looked at her.

She dropped his creased dress pants and boxer shorts to the ground and rubbed his dick to make him hard as she returned to her sexy Asian-hooker voice and asked, "Want to know what *I'm* thinking, Sammy?"

Still looking down, he arrogantly replied, "If it ain't got nothin' to do with fuckin', I don't give a fuck." Then he closed his eyes once she slid him into her mouth.

After a few oral strokes, she looked up and teasingly said, "I'm thinking I'd like you to make me scream. Think you can make me scream, big boy?"

It was only minutes later that China was naked, leaning against a tree and balancing on her heels. Sammy stood behind her, his pants and shorts still at his feet, pounding away as she screamed like a banshee to a sky glowing with a million stars.

"Yeah!" Sammy howled. "*More!*" He spanked her ass, causing her to scream again. "You fuckin'…" he spanked harder and she screamed louder. "…whore!"

"Yes! C'mon, give it to me! Slap me! Slap me *hard!* I *love* it! Harder! *Harder!*"

At the lake, the decayed-but-muscular corpse of Randy Jones struggled to trudge left…right…left…right as he tried to get closer to shore. He looked frustrated as he ever-so-slowly moved forward.

China's screams got louder. She wasn't kidding. She really loved getting slapped and pounded. It was only a minute later before Sammy's face contorted and savage grunts came from each of them as they climaxed. Well, at least *he* did.

After regaining their composure, Sammy flung the filled condom into the woods, hitting a wandering zombie on the head, right next to the bullet hole that caused his death. It didn't faze him as he quietly mumbled, "...taking me in...the woods...why you taking me..."

As Sammy pulled up his shorts and pants, he gave China one more slap on the ass and said, "Get cleaned up. I'll see you back inside."

She winked and blew him a kiss. He didn't acknowledge it as he zipped up and headed in the direction of the cabin. As soon as he walked into the darkness, China dropped her Asian-hooker act and loudly said, "Guido schmuck," then picked up her top and skirt and slipped them on. Unable to locate her panties in the dark, she walked to where Sammy threw them.

With the music still playing, Jenny, wearing her shorts, uncomfortably danced between Richie's legs. Dallas, dressed the same, was on Bobby's lap, facing him, running her hands over his shoulders and brushing her nipples across his face.

Chickie would have been asleep in the chair if it weren't for the boom box, so he continued reading his Time magazine.

Sammy could hear the boom box from the open living room window as he exited the passenger door of the Prius, holding the envelope. While idly fingering the hundred dollar bills and putting the car keys in his pants pocket, his eyes rose to see he was face-to-face with a wandering skinny little zombie that had been shot several times in the back of the head, leaving a large gaping hole where his mouth used to be. Sammy dropped the envelope, causing the cash to fall out, as he freaked out at what was in front of him, and yelled, "What the fuck happened to *you?*"

The zombie inaudibly stuttered through the hole that used to be his mouth as it tried to step away, but the frightened Sammy instinctively reacted and punched the zombie in the mouth, getting his hand stuck in the head's gaping hole and leaving the door to the Prius ajar.

China found her panties on the ground near a bush. Teetering on her heels, she bent over to pick them up as a dirty shoe stepped behind her. She felt a crotch slide against her ass, so without turning, she switched on the Asian-hooker charm and said, "Sammy, I *told* you not to do that, didn't I?" She rubbed her ass into his crotch and continued, "Hmmmmm…you want more? It'll *cost* you more. You know that, right?"

She spun around to see a fat zombie standing before her. A garrote hung from his neck with the wire embedded into rotting flesh, dried blood covered his shirt, two dead fish were stuffed into his muddy suit jacket pockets, and he grumbled, "…came…to make…a deal…a deal…I came…"

China's scream was enough to cause all the undead in the area to look up, but none shuffled in her direction. As the fat zombie raised his arms to balance himself, she saw he had a knife sticking through his right hand.

"*Help!*" the Asian girl screamed at the top of her lungs, but her voice was deadened by the forest around her.

Suddenly, the fat zombie turned and began walking toward the clearing. Seeing more of them, she ripped off her heels and ran in the direction of the cabin, a good 75 yards away. She passed the frustrated weed dealer who had finally dragged himself out of the water and still rambling, "…can't… swim…I…can't…swim…" Behind him, the cement buckets were leaving a trail of scraped dirt as he made a feeble attempt to reach for China, but didn't come close. Other slow-moving zombies easily shuffled past him, and it was pissing him off.

Once she entered the clearing, she came within a foot of running into three ambling corpses. Again China screamed, causing them to look at her as she bolted away, not realizing they weren't interested in her. She could see the side of the cabin and kitchen lights in the distance. Doing everything to sidestep and stay away from the dead mobsters, fear overcame her as she called out as loud as she could, "*Help! Help me!*" and ran blindly into the darkness, only to come face-to-face with *another* zombie whose throat had been cut from ear-to-ear, with clothes covered in blood, dirt and maggots. She went into a fighting stance and with a loud yell of adrenaline, kicked him.

She was now fair game.

As he fell backward, *all* the visible reanimated dead turned toward her. Seeing them, she retreated and backed right into the big, fat zombie.

"…to make…a deal…I came to…"

He grabbed her head from behind, causing the knife sticking through his hand to gash her face. She turned, grabbed his left wrist and pulled it to flip him around like she did to Sammy. Instead, the bones loudly cracked and his hand broke off, followed by a stream of thick, black goo running out of his stump. Unaffected, he continued to grab at her with his bladed-hand.

"*Heeelllppp!*" she screamed again.

Inside the cabin, a Rod Stewart CD was blaring as Jenny and Dallas continued their playful act. Always thinking about business, Dallas had told Jenny not to go any further with the guys until the money arrived.

China was now in the midst of a full-scale fight with the fat zombie. Having a clear shot, she kicked him in the balls, but was stunned when there was no reaction. He grabbed her left shoulder, causing the knife to cut into her, so she kicked him in the balls again.

Nothing.

She raised her right foot, put it against his gut, pushed away and broke his hold, causing her to cry out in pain as the knife ripped across her shoulder. Another zombie leaned in to grab her, but in a flash she was heading toward the cabin's lights as more closed in and blocked her way.

One of the undead came out of the darkness and grabbed her from behind. He resembled a very-well-dressed guinea hood from Queens, complete with a pointy-collared once-white shirt. With a bullet hole through the back of his head and the front part of his skull blown away, he repeatedly uttered, "...oh no...oh...no..." Using her right arm, China expertly elbowed his face, causing him to release her as he fell backward.

On the verge of hysteria, she just wanted to stay alive. To do that, China knew she'd have to get to the cabin, but she was losing steam.

Bobby and Richie weren't paying attention to anything other than the hookers dancing before them.

Chickie looked up from the magazine and eyed the open living room window, then pointed to the boom box and ordered, "Paldino! Shut that off."

The girls stopped dancing. Bobby looked at his boss. With an evil stare, Richie loudly answered, "I'm *busy*."

Chickie shook his head in disgust and said, "Bobby."

Without hesitation, Bobby rose from the sofa and hit the Off button. Then Chickie listened closer for a sound he thought he had heard. It was faint, but they all heard it.

"*Hey! Help me! Richie, help me!*"

Richie quickly stood up and said, "Sammy. *That's Sammy!*"

The girls looked at each other, now concerned about China. Chickie sprung up and turned on the porch light as the others rushed to the front windows to see Sammy fighting several shambling zombies. He may have been quicker and stronger than they were, but Sammy was handicapped by the fact that his hand was stuck in the face of the skinny little zombie. He was punching them furiously with his left hand, which was now covered in black goo, while swinging the little zombie around and using him as a shield with his right.

From inside, the three mobsters and two hookers couldn't understand *what* they were seeing as Chickie said to Bobby and Richie, "Who the fuck *are* they?"

Richie angrily responded with, "Fuck *that*. *What* the fuck are they?" Then he turned to Chickie and Bobby and said, "C'mon. We gotta help him!"

As Dallas and Jenny gazed in horror, the guys ran to the heavy door and swung it open to find six decomposed bodies on the front porch, reaching, murmuring, and giving the Jersey guys a chance to see what they were up against.

Standing in the doorway, Chickie yelled, "Jesus-Fuckin'-Christ, Bobby! Look at 'em!"

Bobby pulled Chickie and Richie back inside, slammed the door and bolted the lock. The two mobsters didn't argue with him as they ran back to the windows.

Jenny squinted to see something in the distance, then yelled, "Look! China!"

With zombies closing in on her, China was faintly visible by the light emanating from the porch, and nearly exhausted as she closed in on the cabin.

Suddenly, a hooker-zombie with a large butcher knife sticking in her chest, stepped in front of the frightened China and grabbed her. A quick punch to the zombie's face broke the grip. China backpedaled to get away, only to wind up surrounded. Ducking under an oncoming pair of hands, she pushed one zombie who fell into another, who fell into another.

Gasping for breath, China tried to run through the crowd of murdered mobsters, hookers, lawyers and stoolies. Tears of terror streamed down her face, but now…she was only forty feet from the front porch and could see those inside at the windows.

"*Richie! Get the fuck out here and help me!*" China heard Sammy scream as he beat away zombie after lumbering zombie, still with the skinny zombie attached to his fist.

Shocked at what she was witnessing, China paused to take a closer look, and for several much needed breaths. That was her mistake. Four zombies surrounded her. A fifth came from behind and wrapped his arms around her. Before she could react, and as those inside watched, they dragged her to the oak tree and stood her against the trunk. Two zombies grabbed each of her arms from behind and yanked on them, causing the Asian hooker to scream in pain as no one had ever heard a scream before. More zombies began tearing at her. Suddenly, China's arms simultaneously ripped off at the shoulders, causing blood to eject in each direction. Her eyes rolled back as she slid to the bottom of the tree…dead.

Jenny and Dallas were crying hysterically as Richie yelled, "Holy fuck! Did you *see that?*" Bobby and Chickie stared at each other, not knowing *what* to think.

Richie ran toward the front door. Bobby, though heavier, was faster and blocked his way, then said, "Don't do it, kid. You open that door and you'll get us *all* killed."

Richie, showing no regard for anyone, looked viciously at Bobby and said, "Get outta my way, you fat fuck. That's Sammy out there!" Angrily shoving Bobby aside, Richie unlocked the door, swung it open and barreled through the zombies on the porch and down the steps. Decayed hands grabbed at his clothes, but his rage gave him strength.

Bobby watched in horror as the girls ran over and slammed the door shut, then locked it.

From the foyer, Bobby looked at Chickie and asked, "Fuck him, right?"

Chickie had to force himself to stop and think about it.

Richie made it through most of the crowd, but there were now too many once-well-dressed zombies between the cabin and Sammy. Hands were grabbing from every direction. Like a madman, Richie shoved, elbowed and punched every *thing* that passed in front of him while trying not to look at their horrific faces. But no matter how many he hit, they didn't react. As those in the cabin watched from the windows, it seemed Richie was about to go down fighting.

The cabin door suddenly swung open. Chickie and Bobby came out armed with pool cues…and they were swinging them. As they cleaned off the porch, Jenny slammed the door and locked it.

Once on the ground, the guys smashed a couple of zombies in the knees. The cracking of bones was followed by the dead attackers dropping to the ground, causing them to crawl toward their prey. It seemed as if nothing would stop them from achieving their sacred goal.

Sammy, exhausted from fighting off the never-ending onslaught of creatures, and with his right fist in the skinny little zombie's face, saw re-enforcements on the way and screamed, "About fuckin' time!"

The guys were still a distance from Sammy. Bobby and Chickie, expertly using their pool cues, made their way to Richie. The impact of the wood to the zombies' heads knocked them back and loosened their hold on Richie, but several more were approaching.

"Inside! *Now!*" Bobby yelled as Chickie grabbed Richie and pulled him toward the cabin.

"I gotta help Sammy!" Richie defiantly screamed back.

As they got closer to the porch, putting a little distance between them and the pawing hands, Chickie told Richie, "C'mon, kid. These things almost killed ya. And you're no good to anybody dead."

Sammy saw the guys retreating and yelled, "Hey! *Hey!* Where the fuck you goin'? Help me! *Richie! Help me!*"

Chickie looked at the oak tree and yelled, "Sammy! Get up the tree! Get in through the window!" Then he ordered Bobby and Richie, "Go!"

Once the guys were back on the porch, Jenny, now dressed, opened the door as they backed in, keeping the zombies at bay.

Dallas was also dressed and standing in the foyer holding a cue in one hand and the kitchen cleaver in the other.

Once the guys were in, Richie tried to close the door, but a large decayed arm reached in and grabbed him. Bobby grabbed the cleaver from Dallas, and in one blow chopped the arm from the zombie, causing black blood to ooze from his shoulder and its severed arm lying on the floor. Richie pushed the door shut and bolted the lock as Chickie, disgusted by the mess, looked at the arm reaching for Richie's ankle.

Bobby got on a knee and uttered every English and Italian curse in the book as he hacked away again and again, until it was nothing more than chopped meat in a thick black goo.

Chickie, forever the germaphobe, looked at him and said, "You're gonna clean that up, right?"

Bobby Battaglino respectfully smiled at his boss and winked.

"Shit!" Dallas screamed, as she saw a zombie trying to get into an open living room window.

Bobby and Richie easily pushed the intruder back with pool cues as the girls and Chickie raced through the first floor, locking the windows and the back door.

Suddenly, Chickie remembered what he told Sammy, and yelled, "Richie! Sammy!"

Richie shot up the stairs, headed to the front bedroom, turned on the light, opened the window and looked at the tree's sturdiest limb that had grown to be only a few feet away.

In the front porch's light he could see Sammy still fighting, exhausted, but getting closer to the tree. As he backed up to step away from the crowd, the skinny little zombie tripped and fell to the ground. Sammy saw this as an opportunity to step on the zombie's chest and pull his hand out with all of his might. The head, still wrapped around Sammy's fist, popped off the skinny body as black goo flowed from its neck. Dazzled at the result, Sammy lifted his hand to see the face of the attached head blinking at him.

"Motherfucker!"

A zombie grabbed Sammy's shirt from behind. Instinctively, he spun around and swung the attached head like a club, smashing it into the zombie's chest, causing him to crash to the ground. Sammy proudly looked at the blinking appendage on his hand.

From above, he heard Richie's voice, "Sammy! Up here! Climb the tree!"

Sammy yelled with every ounce of strength he had left, "Fuck you! I'm beat! And I got these zambonies all over me!"

"C'mon, get up here! You can do it!"

As Chickie, Bobby, Jenny and Dallas watched from the living room windows, Sammy staggered to the tree and jumped for the lowest limb, but his exhaustion prevented him from attaining the extra inches needed, and more zombies were heading his way. He looked around for something to step on to gain the distance he lacked. Seeing China's lifeless body against the trunk, he backed up to within inches of the oncoming crew, then ran a few steps and with his right foot landing atop her head, pushed off and was able to grab the first limb he could reach. Then he wedged the zombie head into the cleft between two branches and pulled himself higher.

Everyone in the cabin was relieved to see Sammy out of harm's way.

Richie, leaning out the front window looked at the head attached to Sammy's right hand and loudly asked, "Who the fuck is *that?*"

"I'll introduce ya's when I get there!"

Zombies stretched and pawed to grab Sammy, but he kicked them away as he climbed up to a higher branch and out of their reach.

"C'mon, Sammy! A few more and you'll be here." Richie called down.

Sammy looked at the crowd gathering below. Stopping to take a breath, he yanked the head from his black goo covered hand. The face blinked just before Sammy angrily threw it to the ground, yelling and pointing to those below, "Fuck you...and fuck *you*...and *fuck...you...too!*"

Just then, Sammy and Richie heard the sound of wood cracking. The branch the young mobster was on couldn't take his weight or movements. Sammy's eyes rose to his boss as he cried out, *"Richie! Help!"* The branch snapped, causing him to fall with a thud a few feet from China's armless body.

From the living room they watched as hands grabbed and ripped at Sammy as he lay sprawled on his back. Throughout the cabin they heard Richie scream out, *"Saaammmmyyy!"*

There were too many of them as Sammy kicked and punched at whatever he could. Hands ripped his skin, mouth and eyes as one of the zombies pulled a claw hammer from its own head and whacked it into Sammy's skull, causing his screams to turn into gurgles, and then...silence. Sammy's body jerked a few times, then went limp.

It was too much for Richie. He stood in silent shock and paralyzed with fear.

Dallas and Jenny were horrified as they held each other and wept. Chickie sorrowfully shook his head as Bobby backed away and walked into the kitchen. Chickie saw him and followed.

Standing at one of the windows, Bobby stared outside. Chickie went to the sink and washed his hands as Bobby spoke to his boss's reflection in the glass.

"Jesus, Chickie, what the fuck do you think they *are?*"

"Think about it, Bobby. When we were outside, didja notice anything?"

"Besides them tryin' to rip us apart and ya can't kill 'em?" Bobby thought for a second and continued, "They're the best-dressed zombie-things I ever saw, I can tell you *that.*"

Chickie came back with, "And you, me, my dad, Richie's old man and a few other guys from Jersey whacked and buried these fucks a long time ago."

Bobby peered outside. This time his eyes went wide. *Very* wide.

"Remember that insurance guy we brought out here? The one who was supposed to okay the money for that arson job in Jersey City, and then reneged?"

"That Irish guy? What's his name?"

"Yeah, him," Chickie revealed. "He's out there. I'm *sure* I saw him."

"Get the fuck outta here."

"And I *know* I saw that fat prick attorney who was gonna rat on Don Joey."

"Pig Al?" Bobby asked in disbelief.

Chickie nodded, but was still confused as to what was actually happening. Then he thought of something and chuckled, "That means old man Paldino's out there with your ice pick stuck in his head." They laughed as he followed it up with, "What if Richie sees him?"

It got quiet. The two men thought about that for a few seconds and said nothing. They returned their gaze to the mob-affiliated zombies shuffling past the window, visible because of the fluorescent light coming through the panes of glass. Suddenly, Bobby nudged Chickie's shoulder and pointed at something outside.

Chickie couldn't believe that walking amongst the grotesque corpses was a dark, headless horse meandering by.

Amazed, Chickie said, "I always *wondered* what they did with the rest of that thing."

Bobby, mouth agape, nodded in agreement. But his look changed once he saw a reflection in the glass. He tapped Chickie's arm and cocked his head, indicating the boss should turn around.

Jenny was standing in the archway between the foyer and the kitchen. She walked over to them and softly asked, "You guys are gangsters, right? Like in the Mafia."

The men laughed as Chickie answered, "What are ya talkin' about? There's no such thing as the Mafia."

Bobby followed it with, "Everybody knows that, honey."

She rapidly came back with, "C'mon, guys. I might've grown up on a farm, but I'm not stupid." Chickie and Bobby eyed one another and shrugged, as if admitting the jig was up. She asked Chickie, "How's your hand?" He eyed her, not readily knowing what she meant, so she continued, "This afternoon at the gas station. It looked a little banged up and bloody."

He nonchalantly responded, "The blood?" then held up his left hand to show it was fine as he finished with, "Wasn't mine. It was somebody else's." Jenny stopped cold and stared at Chickie as he continued, "Just had-ta wash it off. Thanks for the concern. But right now, all we should be thinkin' about is gettin' the fuck outta here in one piece."

CHAPTER 12

Chickie, Bobby and Jenny entered the living room to find Dallas nervously handling the cleaver as she paced and watched each window.

"Relax," Chickie said, hoping to calm her down. "All the windows are locked."

"But how long before they break in?" she asked frantically. "We have to get out of here and into those cars!"

Bobby backed Chickie's words up with, "Nothin's gonna get through that door *or* these windows, honey."

Jenny jumped in and asked, "How do you know *that?*"

"Let's just say the people who built this place figured they'd have to defend it one day," Chickie answered.

"Yeah, but against the Feds. Not *these* friggin' things," Bobby added.

Richie solemnly walked down the stairs as everyone sympathetically looked at him. He didn't stop until he was face-to-face with Chickie. Bobby's radar switched on as he closely watched. Richie grabbed Chickie's sport jacket lapels and was just about to yell at him when Bobby sprang into action. An instant before Paldino was grabbed and pummeled, the boss, without taking his eyes off the disrespectful, younger and taller wise-ass, raised his hand, causing Bobby to stop on a dime, but ready to attack if he needed to.

"What's goin' on, Chickie? Who *are* they? *What* are they? Where'd the fuck they come from?" Paldino angrily asked, in a tone one wouldn't normally use when speaking to someone in Chickie Santorella's position.

Chickie was silent, unsure if he wanted to tell him what was outside, *or* about the cabin's history.

Richie looked at Bobby, who was just itching to pounce on Paldino, then released his grip, but growled in Chickie's face, "You're in charge. Whatdya gonna *do* about 'em?"

Dallas and Jenny looked at Chickie, wanting to hear words that would give them hope they'd be getting out of there alive.

After a few seconds of thought, Chickie walked to the window, looked outside and said, "If we're gonna do something about these pricks, we're gonna need the right..." he smiled, turned to Bobby and finished with, "...tools."

At the base of the oak tree, sitting in a pool of her own blood and black zombie-goo, China's eyes opened. Having no arms, it took a while for her to clumsily stand, then wobbled a bit as she took one step after another, with, "...heelllppp...heelllppp..." repeating from her dead lips.

Shuffling awkwardly away from the tree, she tripped over Sammy's body just as *his* eyes opened. It took him a minute or so to lift himself up and take a few steps, now with a claw hammer protruding from the top of his skull and crying, "...Richie...help...Richie..."

Dallas, Bobby, Richie and Jenny stood in the doorway atop the staircase and looked down into the darkness as Chickie hit the switch, lighting the cavernous basement.

"What's down there?" asked Richie?

"You'll find out when we get there. Now shut up and let's go," barked Chickie, once again pissing off his subordinate who didn't want to be spoken to that way in front of anyone...even hookers.

What no one expected was for Dallas to freak out and start yelling, "*No! No way!* I've seen those movies! I *know* what'll happen when we go down there. They're *waiting for us!* Or they'll break in and we'll be trapped with no water, no food, and they'll *kill us! They'll kill us!*"

Chickie shook his head, having never dealt with a screaming woman *or* zombies before and was trying to decide which was worse. He said to Dallas, "Tell you what. Stay up here and keep your eyes open. *We'll* go down. That way, if they start to break in--"

"Which they won't," Bobby interjected with a laugh.

"You let us know," Chickie continued. "Alright?"

Dallas nodded and nervously caressed the cleaver. Chickie turned to Jenny and asked, "What about you?"

She moved next to him and said, "I'm stickin' with *you*," trying to imitate a north Jersey accent.

As the four headed down, Dallas went into the living room and perched herself on one of the sofas to stare at the windows and front door. A few zombies were now scratching at it in an attempt to claw through to get to their prey.

Once in the empty basement, Chickie reached into his dress pants to pull out his father's keyring and the special key, then led them to the large steel room in the corner. Bobby knew what the others were about to see, so he stepped aside as Chickie unlocked and opened the door, then hit the light switch and announced, "Behold. The Ponti Collection."

Seeing it all gave Richie Paldino an erection as he let out a "Jesus-Fuckin'-Christ" that echoed out of the armory and into the concrete room.

Over the years, additional and newer weapons were brought in. Pistols, rifles, machine guns and shotguns of various sizes and makes still hung on three walls, along with crates of ammunition stacked against the other.

Dallas sat on the edge of the sofa staring at the door and windows, nervously jiggling the cleaver and listening to the constant scratching. She didn't hear the door to the upstairs bedroom open as the reanimated corpse of Donny' Oliveri, complete with a horribly twisted neck, shuffled into the hallway.

The men descended on the weaponry.

Richie grabbed two Glocks and a handful of empty clips.

The scratching was making Dallas antsier than she already was, so she went to the kitchen, stood at the top of the stairs and called down, "Is everything okay down there?"

Jenny stuck her head out of the steel room and yelled back, "Yeah, honey! We'll be up in a few minutes."

That was enough to pacify Dallas. She returned to the sofa to continue her vigil, but the scratching was driving her crazy. To cover the incessant noise she hit the boom box's Play button. Rod Stewart's "Do You Think I'm Sexy" came on, just loud enough to cover the sound and calm the near-frantic hooker.

Chickie went to the far wall and opened a specific crate. Unseen by the others, he smiled as he put his hands in and came out with four grenades, slipping two into each jacket pocket. He re-closed the crate, returned to the others and picked up a 9mm Beretta.

Bobby zeroed in on two silver .45 automatics in a double-sided holster complete with slots for extra clips. He strapped it onto his large torso, smiling at the fit and ease of access to each pistol.

Chickie looked at Jenny and asked, "What about you, kid? See anything you like?"

She shook her head, making it obvious she didn't want a weapon.

"You sure? You don't know, you might need it," he pressed.

"It's a long story," she replied.

Bobby threw in, "Ya got a short version?"

She liked Bobby and felt comfortable around him, so she smiled and gave in.

"My dad was kinda…religious. More of a psychotic zealot, really."

Dead Donny was halfway down the staircase, mumbling and looking for his intended victims. Dallas was feeling a little better as she swayed and sang along with Rod.

Jenny continued her tale as the three men filled their clips and listened.

"He thought we'd be fighting in some Thousand Year War, you know, *after* the Apocalypse."

As she went on about her father's arsenal that included dozens of guns, bazookas, single-shot anti-personnel missile launchers and a few hundred land mines, Chickie slid the Beretta in his waistband, then put the filled clips in his pants and sport jacket pockets. Richie loaded his pockets with as many clips as they could hold, and Bobby made sure each slot on his dual-holster was filled.

Standing in the middle of the room full of weapons, Jenny finished with, "So we had guns stashed *everywhere* around the farm. I *hate* guns. I hate 'em."

Bobby jokingly asked, "That doesn't mean you can't carry some ammo, right?"

She laughed as Chickie and Bobby loaded a few boxes into her arms.

Donny made it to the bottom and stepped into the living room without being heard by Dallas. She continued to move to the music while watching the zombies in the light of the locked windows.

Chickie and Bobby picked up shotguns with bandoliers holding two dozen shells and slung them over their shoulders. Richie grabbed a gun-cleaning kit and put it on top of Jenny's armload of ammo as they walked out of the armory. Then Chickie locked the door.

Paying no attention to her, Donny ambled behind Dallas, repeating, "…my house…under lilies…cash…under…" as he headed to the basement.

Dallas looked up. She thought she heard something and sprang from the sofa to the kitchen, unknowingly walking only a few feet in front of Donny.

Bobby led the way up the stairs as he loaded his shotgun and joked with the others. He lifted his head to see Dallas at the landing…and Donny-zombie right behind her. "Holy *Shit!*" he yelled, then leveled the shotgun in their direction.

Thinking Bobby was going to shoot her, Dallas screamed, dropped the cleaver and turned to run…right into Donny, freaking her out even more. The zombie pushed Dallas away as Bobby ran up the steps to help her. Donny went to grab Bobby, who easily stepped away from the reaching arms. Seeing Dallas on the floor, unhurt but screaming, he trotted into the living room with Donny following him. Chickie barreled up the steps to assess the commotion.

Seeing his boss, Bobby yelled out, "Chickie! You see who this is?" as he evaded another sloth-like grab.

Taking in the unbelievable sight, Chickie called back in amazement, "Get the fuck outta here!"

Bobby and the mumbling zombie were making their second pass around the sofa as Rod Stewart started singing "Young Turks." As Bobby passed the boom box, he hit the Off button.

"Thank you," Chickie laughed.

"No problem," Bobby laughed back.

Jenny put the boxes of ammo on the kitchen counter and tried to calm Dallas as Bobby yelled to Chickie, "Get ready to open the door!" He tossed his shotgun onto the sofa and dove at the zombie. They crashed to the floor as Bobby wrestled Donny onto the tribal rug from his office.

Richie rushed into the living room, stopping short when he saw Bobby fighting with the guy he had killed just hours earlier, and exclaimed, "What the *fuck?*"

Chickie, now *very* pissed off, bellowed, "I thought you said he was *dead!*"

Still in the kitchen, Jenny's ears pricked up when she heard Chickie's words.

As Bobby secured Donny's hands from doing any damage, he heard the words, "...my house...behind...under lilies..."

Richie, confused, yelled back, "He *was* dead!" Then he looked at Donny and foolishly yelled, "Shut the fuck up, asshole!"

Chickie wasn't listening to what the zombie was saying. He was more concerned about his best friend as he ordered Richie to, "Help him."

Dallas stopped screaming long enough to loudly proclaim, "I *told you* they'd get in! There must be more upstairs! We gotta get out of here!"

Richie got on the floor and started punching Donny's face to prevent him from speaking as Chickie called to the girls, "It's alright, it's alright! He was the only one up there."

"How do *you* know?" Jenny shot back.

There was no response.

Donny struggled as Richie and Bobby rolled him tightly in the rug for the *second* time that day. Though the zombie's arms were pinned, he continued with, "...cash...behind..." To shut him up, Richie pulled a handkerchief from his pocket and stuffed it in Donny's mouth. Then the men dragged the dead casino manager toward the front door.

"Wait a minute," Chickie said, as Jenny and Dallas came in to watch the zombie be thrown outside. "I wanna look at this fuck," he said as Bobby and Richie stood their victim up. They pulled away enough of the rug to see the twisted vertebrae under Donny's jagged skin at the base of his skull, and his growling blue face.

Bobby's sense of humor kicked in as he said, "This fucker's as dead as Hoffa. He's just too stupid to know it yet."

Seeing the zombie's face, Dallas shouted, "That's Donny!"

Chickie turned and asked, "You know this guy?"

"That's Donny Oliveri. He runs The Ramblin' Rose. I know him from the ranch."

"What ranch?"

"The *ranch*," she replied. "The mayor's place outside of town. *All* the working girls there know him. He's a regular." Then she looked at Donny again and said, "Well, he won't be any*more*."

Richie still wanted answers. He wanted to know what was happening and why zombies killed his friend. He spoke up as Donny growled with the handkerchief in his mouth and his body writhing, trying to break free.

"So why we got dead guys tryin' to tear us apart?"

Other than the grunts coming from the rug, the room was silent, until Jenny slowly raised her hand like a frightened schoolgirl, and shyly said, "I think I might know. But it's just a story." Everyone turned toward her as she kept going. "It's some old story about Indian curses and the Shoshones from this area. For thousands of years and for hundreds of miles this was all their territory. They say this shaman put a curse on--"

"A what?" Richie interrupted.

"A shaman. A holy man," Bobby offhandedly answered as Donny tried gnawing through the handkerchief. "He was right up there with the chief. Maybe even higher. He was supposed to have magic powers and shit."

Everyone turned and looked at Bobby as he nonchalantly stood next to the zombie-filled rug. He eyed each of them and said, "What the fuck you want from me? I *read*." Then he turned to Jenny and said, "G'head, honey. Keep goin'."

As all eyes returned to Jenny, Chickie proudly smiled and winked at his friend.

"So, as the Shoshone were being wiped out, this shaman put a curse on their land."

"Get the fuck outta here," Richie sarcastically laughed.

Chickie glared at the arrogant Paldino and barked, "Shut up and listen."

That was it. Richie took his last order from Chickie and flipped him the finger. Bobby let go of the rug to go beat Richie's ass, but it started to fall. He grabbed it, straightened it out, and angrily barked to Richie, "If I wasn't holdin' onto this prick, I'd break that finger off and shove up your fuckin' ass, wiseguy." Then he thought a second and arrogantly added, "But you might like that."

Chickie ignored Paldino, then asked Jenny, "The curse. What was it?"

She thought for a couple of seconds and said, "Something about if any Indian's blood fell on the ground, the Indians buried in it were supposed to crawl out and avenge them as long as they were on Shoshone land. Something like that."

Dallas started to get frantic again as she said, "That's crazy! Donny didn't look buried, and not *one* of those things out there were Indians. *None of them*. And what Indian's blood hit the ground out here?"

Chickie and Bobby shared a glance and a sick chuckle. They knew where the bodies came from, and whose blood hit the ground.

"That's the dumbest bullshit I've ever heard," Richie barked.

Again, Chickie glared at Paldino and barked louder, "I said shut...the fuck...*up*."

Richie went ballistic. He rushed to the pool table, picked up a cue and headed toward Chickie. Bobby let go of the rug, pulled out a silver .45, pointed it at Richie's head before he got close to the boss and cocked the hammer back.

Richie Paldino froze and dropped the cue to the floor. He knew Bobby would shoot him.

The girls froze. They had never seen anything like this go down, and were now fearful for their own lives if bullets started flying.

Nobody seemed to notice or care as the rug fell with a hard thud onto the floor, with Donny still wriggling and gnawing.

Chickie looked at the frozen Richie as if nothing had happened and asked, "You got a better story, tough guy?"

Seeing he had been given a reprieve, the disrespectful thug took a breath, sat on a sofa and said, "Fuckin' *zombies*, Chickie? Really? You wanna tell old man Ponti some hooker and Sammy got killed by *zombies?*"

As Bobby uncocked and reholstered the pistol, he asked, "Like he said, you got a better story?" Richie went silent. "Then shut your fuckin' mouth and keep it that way until you do." Bobby started to lift the rug, and ordered, "Now get your guinea-ass over here and gimme a hand. I wanna get rid of this garbage."

Gritting his teeth in anger at being bossed around by *both* men, Richie grabbed dead Donny's feet and Bobby lifted the head. Chickie unlocked and prepared to open the door as the guys carried the rolled up zombie closer. Jenny picked up the pool cue from the floor, and Dallas hurriedly found her fallen cleaver and kept it close.

"Ready?" Chickie asked. The men nodded. Then he swung the door open.

Several zombies were on the front porch murmuring their final words. One had the side of his skull blown away and was straightening his rotted tie as he repeated, "...get the paper...get the paper...I'm...gonna get..." A machine gun riddled mafioso was carrying a camelhair coat, was saying, "...my...coat...gotta go back...lucky coat..." A well-attired-but-decayed mob boss slurred, "...told the...kid...never sit...in...the back..."

Unbeknownst to Chickie, his father's first official "cabin kill," Gary Gentile, was among them, still cracking the same joke, "...your day in... the barrel...today's your..."

It was a surreal scene for the guys from Jersey.

"C'mon, let's get this over with," Bobby said as he and Richie stepped onto the porch. He looked at his helper and asked, "What the fuck are they sayin', Richie?"

"Fuck if I know, and I ain't stickin' around to find out," he snapped back.

Like bouncers ejecting a drunk, they tossed the rug, knocking down a few zombies on its way to the dirt.

"Damn shame," Bobby said with a laugh. "That *was* a nice rug."

Chickie started to close the door as the men turned to come back, but Bobby wasn't quick enough as black-nailed hands grabbed his clothes and arms before Richie and Chickie could react.

"Get the fuck off me!" Bobby yelled, but to no avail. More zombies closed in on him, dragging him farther from the door, then down the steps onto the ground.

With the door still open, Chickie looked at his friend and cried out, "*Bobby!*"

Chickie unslung his shotgun and blasted at everything that was already dead, splattering black sludge and body parts in every direction, but there were too many of them...and too close to Bobby to shoot.

Bobby struggled with every ounce of his strength as he was dragged farther from the porch, while other zombies reached for Chickie. He fired the shotgun until it was empty, then dead hands sizzled as they grabbed the hot barrel and yanked it away. All Chickie could see were zombies surrounding the downed, screaming Bobby as they began ripping into him.

The girls stood at the window, too shocked to react. Richie pulled Chickie into the foyer and slammed the door.

Chickie, shocked by what he had just seen, *still* needed to save his childhood friend.

"Bobby's out there!" he yelled.

"Now you know how it feels," Richie uncaringly returned.

Chickie, with tears and rage in his eyes, pulled the Beretta from his waistband and pointed it at the man he had wanted to kill since they arrived in Nevada. Richie once again froze, backed up, pointed to the door and said, "You wanna go out there? Knock yourself out."

Without saying a word, Chickie unlocked the door, took a step onto the porch and blew the knees off those near him, then aimed and fired at the zombies around Bobby. The bullets knocked them back a few steps, but didn't stop them, and then the gun was empty.

With Bobby's cries of, "*Chickie! Chickie! Get 'em off-a me! I can't move!*" filling the air, Chickie popped in another clip and continued to shoot the attackers, but he knew it was useless.

Seeing and hearing his friend's belly being torn open and his organs pulled out, Chickie took careful aim, said, "You...mother..." then fired one shot and cried, "*Fuckers!*" as a chunk of Bobby's head exploded and his screaming stopped.

Chickie went back inside and locked the door. He had just killed his best friend.

Overtaken by sadness, everyone stood silent and still. The scratching at the door once again started. Dallas, with cleaver in-hand, walked to the liquor cabinet on the far end of the living room, opened a bottle of Dewar's, slid to the floor and took a mouthful from the bottle.

Richie started pacing the long room. He was itching for a fight…either with Chickie or the zombies. He didn't give a fuck. He just wanted to kill some *one* or some *thing*.

Jenny was sitting on the sofa, staring wide-eyed at the front door.

Chickie walked from the foyer, picked up Bobby's shotgun and with a sullen expression announced, "I'm gonna make some spaghetti and sausages. Bobby's favorite. Who wants some?"

Richie and Dallas looked at him like he was crazy. Jenny didn't respond. She recognized the pain and confusion on his face.

Chickie entered the kitchen, looking over his shoulder to make sure no one was following him, then took a few deep breaths in an attempt to keep his emotions under control. Putting the shotgun on the counter, he went to the cabinets and refrigerator to get what was needed to prepare the meal. As he knelt to reach for a couple of pots in a lower cupboard, his emotions took over and tears streamed down his face. He almost sobbed, but stayed silent through a sheer force of will.

Dallas had knocked back a few more slugs of scotch when Richie walked over and extended his hand. Without looking, she put the bottle in it. He took a few swallows before saying, "Looks like we're gonna have-ta wait 'til that old-school guinea fuck comes up with a plan to get us outta here."

She lifted her head and asked, "You gonna keep me alive until then?"

"Depends. What's in it for me?"

Jenny watched from the sofa as Dallas put her hand out and said to Richie, "I'll show you." He pulled her up and they made their way up the stairs.

The young hooker curled her legs to her chest and quietly began to cry, not knowing if she would ever get out of 16 Happy Trails alive.

Chickie stood at the stove frying sausage, boiling water and heating the sauce. He seemed to have regained control of himself as he drank red wine from a half-full glass. As with everything in his life, he was immaculate in preparing each ingredient before slipping them into the pots. If anything spilled, it was rapidly and thoroughly cleaned up and the area was disinfected.

Unbeknownst to him, Jenny watched from the archway, but ready to leave if he wanted to be left alone.

"Can I help?" she asked.

He cleared his throat and answered, "Sure, kid. You wanna cut up some garlic and onions for the gravy?"

She contorted her face, "Gravy? With pasta?"

He was glad for the conversation as he laughed and replied, "I guess you people call it *sauce*. In north Jersey where *I* come from, it's *gravy*."

She stepped next to him, grabbed a knife and began dicing onions on the cutting board. Unseen by them as they spoke, Bobby's reanimated corpse, with a chunk of his head blown away by Chickie's well-aimed bullet, wandered past the kitchen window.

"He was a good friend of yours, wasn't he?"

"Bobby?" he answered as his eyes teared up again. "Yeah. Since we were kids." Then he raised his head and wiped his eyes as Jenny scraped the onions into the pot of sauce. He tried to blame them, saying, "Fucking onions." But she knew better.

With the sauce simmering and the pasta boiling, they prepared the small kitchen table. Chickie sprayed it with disinfectant and wiped it down, then Jenny arranged two place settings.

"So, tell me *your* story. How long you been hookin'?" he asked, returning to the stove to stir the pasta.

"Almost five months," she answered as she followed him, took a wooden spoon and stirred the sauce.

"I *thought* you looked pretty green, compared to your friends."

As they stirred their respective pots, she continued, "I'm not really into it. I just wanted to make enough to get back home, pay for college classes, then I'm done."

"Good for you. Where's home?"

"Ohio. Solon. A town outside of Cleveland."

He pulled out a strand of spaghetti, tasted it and expertly said, "A couple of more minutes."

Jenny kept going, "I'm pretty much a walking cliché. I went to Los Angeles to be in movies, got jerked around for a couple of years, then landed a dancing job in Vegas."

She lifted the spoon from the pot of sauce, put her hand under it and brought it to Chickie's mouth for a taste. It made him smile and relax a little more.

"After that dried up, I started stripping, which led to hooking, which led to meeting Dallas," she said, taking the spoon from the pot to try some herself, unknowingly getting some on her chin. "She knew Vickie. That was China's real name. Vickie lived in Gabbs and said we could make good money at the mayor's ranch without giving sixty-percent to some pimp like we did in Vegas. And now, I'm here with you."

That made Chickie smile.

Like an old team, they worked smoothly together as they prepared everything for their plates of spaghetti, sausage and *gravy*.

"You know, it was Vickie who told me that Indian legend. I don't know where *she* heard it, but *shit*, it looks like it was true, huh?" Before they sat, Jenny teared up and sobbed, "Vickie was a good friend. I really owed her for getting me out of Las Vegas. This town was my last stop before going home."

Chickie leaned close to Jenny, looked at her in a big brother-sort-of-way, then took his paper towel and wiped the sauce from her chin as he said, "Loyalty. I like that."

They sat and toasted each other with their wine.

"Don't worry, kid. I'll make sure you get home."

Like a kid-sister, she respectfully said, "That'll be *twice* you've come to my rescue, Chickie. Grazie."

He lifted his glass, saluted her again and replied, "Prego, bella. Now mangia."

And they did.

The sounds of Dallas and Richie fucking like minks emerged through the closed front bedroom door. Dallas was moaning and working it like the hooker she was.

"Oh, yeah! C'mon, Richie. Fuck me. Fuck me. Fuck me so *good!*"

Knowing he was about to blow, she let out an Oscar-worthy, but fake, orgasm, complete with head turning, arms twirling and screams of, "Ohhhhh…mother*fucker! Yes! Ahhhhhh*…oh my…fucking…god!"

A wallet, two pistols, a pack of American Spirit cigarettes, a Bic lighter and the quarter-full bottle of Dewar's were on the night-table. Clothes were scattered around the room. Richie was lying on the bed with Dallas, naked, straddled on top of him, both sweaty and spent.

She reached over, took the lighter and two cigarettes from the pack, then handed them to Richie. He lit them as she asked, "So, like, that guy Chickie…he's your boss?"

Insulted and more than a little drunk, he snapped back, "No. He's some guinea fuck who thinks he should be treated better than anybody else. Fuck 'im." He handed her a cigarette, took a drag on his and was getting full of himself as he kept going. "They had me come here to handle somethin' the clean-freak motherfucker couldn't do alone."

"What do you mean? Handle what?"

He drunkenly shook his head, not wanting to show his hand, and said, "Don't worry about it. All you gotta know is that it's done, and in a few days things are gonna be different back in New-Fuckin'-Jersey."

She wiggled her ass and rubbed her breasts as she cooed, "You gonna bring me to New Jersey? To that town?"

"Lyndhurst?"

"Yeah, Lyndhurst. Is it nice?"

"It's a fuckin' paradise on Earth." Then he pointed to the night-table and told her to, "Get my wallet and the bottle. I'll show ya somethin'."

Dallas stretched over, making sure her breasts brushed his face. He nibbled. She giggled. Still straddling him, she handed over the wallet and bottle. He took a couple of swigs from the scotch, then handed it to her as he opened the wallet and slid out Donny's driver's license.

"See this?"

She looked at the photo and replied, "That's not you. That's the guy in the rug, or it *used* to be."

He drunkenly responded, "There's a few million bucks buried under some lilies in this prick's backyard, and it's all mine. He gave it to me."

All of a sudden, Dallas became *very* attracted to the guy beneath her. She watched as he returned the license to his wallet, then handed it to her. She replaced it on the night-table as he took another long swallow of scotch, then played with her nipples as she placed the bottle next to his wallet.

"Well, I've gotta clean up." Then her voice went *very* sexual as she wiggled her ass and cooed, "…if you plan on fucking *this* again."

Richie raised an eyebrow as she slid off of him, picked up her clothes and headed for the door. As she grabbed the doorknob, he slurred, "And bring me back somethin' to eat," then his head knocked back against the headboard. He passed out, exhausted and drunk.

Dallas gave Richie the finger as she closed the door behind her. Stepping into the hallway, she followed it up with, "Go fuck yourself, asshole."

In the living room, music from the 1960s played from a CD to drown out the non-stop door scratching.

In the kitchen, except for the shotgun propped on a chair and zombies outside the window, Chickie's and Jenny's meal looked homey and comfortable.

Dallas exited the upstairs bathroom and made her way down the steps. Without being noticed, she heard the two in the kitchen laughing, talking and enjoying their meal. With the music covering her steps, Dallas approached the archway and leaned against the wall, keeping out-of-sight to eavesdrop.

"Yeah, the girls never liked music from the sixties. But it's what I remember my mom listening to when she'd be cleaning the house. So I always keep some with me. Glad you like it," Jenny said to her dinner partner.

Chickie took a drink and said, "You know, Donny didn't seem too interested in Dallas when he was standing behind her. But he sure as shit wanted a piece of Bobby and Richie."

"I was thinking about that, too. The way I heard it, they're only supposed to go after the person who caused the pain or death, and anyone who tried to stop them. I don't recall China saying anything about people being in the wrong place at the wrong time."

"So why'd they go after *her?*"

"She was fighting with them. I'm sure that counted as 'trying to stop them.'"

"And once she did that, all bets were off," was Chickie's correct conclusion.

Dallas listened intensely, putting the pieces together.

"So what you're sayin' is…if you don't fuck with 'em, you can just walk outta here?" Chickie asked.

Dallas's eyes lit up.

Jenny answered, "It sure sounds that way," then she finished her glass of wine.

Dallas looked back at the staircase. A plot was formulating in her mind.

She turned and quietly went upstairs as she heard the chairs move back from the table and Chickie say, "Let's not put it to the test yet. Get some sleep." Then with determination he continued, "Lemme see what I can come up with to get us all outta here."

The clock in the kitchen showed 3:37AM. The scratching at the front door continued, but now as nothing more than background noise while Chickie patrolled the cabin.

Jenny, not wanting to be trapped in any of the bedrooms if zombies actually did break in, was fully dressed and asleep on one of the living room sofas. As he passed by, Chickie pulled up her blanket to cover her shoulders, then walked upstairs and made the rounds checking each room.

Sticking his head in the front bedroom, from the hallway light he saw Richie, naked and with one of the pistols in his hand, and Dallas, fully dressed and sleeping. The other gun, the wallet and an empty Dewar's bottle were on the night-table. As Chickie shut the door, Dallas's eyes opened.

He returned to the living room and the incessant scratching. Taking a deep breath, Chickie dusted off the other sofa's cushions, sat, laid the shotgun next to him and after a *very* long day, put his head back to rest.

Dallas slid out of bed, knowing Richie was still in his alcohol-induced coma. She took the cash and Donny's license from the wallet, then grabbed the gun and slipped them into her purse. Opening the door, she stepped into the hall and silently made her way down to the back door, unlocked and opened it…though ready to close and lock it if anything came near her.

Zombies wandered around, but not nearly as many as were in the front of the cabin, and none approached her.

Swallowing nervously, Dallas walked out, leaving the door ajar in the event they changed course. It was readily apparent they didn't care about her. With a sigh of relief, she moved slowly, trying not to look at their rotted faces or touch them, but she was close enough to hear *Little Marty* McCarthy whining, "…fuck…oh…fuck…" Passing the wood pile, she turned the corner to the side of the garages and didn't notice two zombies in the rear of the cabin meander near the open door.

As she rounded the corner to the front, Donny-zombie came close and mumbled, "…buried…cash…behind house…" She looked at his face as he continued, "….under lilies…"

"Not for long, asshole," she laughed, looking at her BMW only a dozen yards away and ready to take her to a fortune and her ticket out of Gabbs.

Dallas slid into the driver's seat, then started and revved the engine. Knowing she was only seconds from getting away alive, her delayed tension reared its head and she began crying hysterically.

The sound of the revving through the bedroom's open window stirred Richie. He reached for the sleeping hooker he thought was next to him… but wasn't, causing him to rapidly and painfully lift his hungover head.

Chickie, *also* awakened by the sound, sprung up. He instinctively picked up the shotgun and went to the front window. Squinting into the darkness, he called out, "Jenny! Wake up! Your friend. She got out. She's in her car."

Jenny jumped at the sound of his voice, but didn't comprehend what he had said as she groggily asked, "What? Are we okay?"

"Dallas. She's in her car."

Jenny excitedly ran to the window and yelled, "She's going for help!"

"You sure about that? I noticed she didn't come lookin' for *you*."

Jenny didn't reply, but the look on her face remained hopeful.

Struggling to get herself under control, Dallas put the car in Reverse and slammed on the gas, but the abrupt acceleration crushed one zombie and knocked two others into the air. Clearing the cabin and the Prius, she shifted into Drive and sped down the long driveway, spraying zombies with dirt and pebbles.

Watching the BMW's taillights disappear, Chickie thought, "How'd she get out?"

Dallas wiped her eyes and concentrated on driving. About halfway down the driveway she realized she was safely away, causing her crying to turn into laughter from relief. What she didn't see rising in the backseat, wearing a large, dirty gold crucifix while sporting an ice pick in its head, was the corpse of Enzo Paldino, grunting, "...Bobby...what's in...your hand..."

Hearing the voice, she looked in the rearview mirror to see the decayed skin and bones of Richie's father. She turned her head and screamed, causing her to lose control of the fast moving vehicle. Enzo pulled the pick out of his head, leaned forward and began stabbing at her while repeating, "...in your...hand...Bobby..."

The car slammed hard into a tree. If the crash didn't kill Dallas, the multiple stabs she endured in her head, face and neck surely did.

Wearing only his dress pants, Richie came down the stairs into the living room holding his open wallet, and he was pissed. "Where the fuck is Dallas?" he yelled.

Chickie continued to stare at the zombies in front of the cabin and answered, "Well, if there's three of us here, and her car just drove away... figure it out yourself, moron."

"She'll be back. She's going to get help. She won't leave us here," Jenny said, trying to believe her own words.

Richie went to the closest window, looked at his empty wallet and under his breath said, "Don't count on it."

CHAPTER 13

While Chickie, Richie and Jenny stared out the front windows, two zombies trudged unhurriedly through the open rear door…breaching their defenses. A scattering of others in the distance saw them and headed that way.

Certain if he were able to get into town he'd be able to find out where Donny lived, a very pissed off Richie confronted his boss, yelling, "What *the fuck* we gonna do about getting outta here?"

Chickie didn't have a clue, but had to keep up the mob boss persona, not just to Richie, but to himself. It was the only way he knew he'd be able to stay in control.

"I don't know yet. I just know I never had-ta deal with shit like this before." Then he glared at his subordinate and growled, "Anything like this ever come *your* way, genius?" Knowing he wasn't going to get an answer, Chickie calmed himself for an instant and continued, "Besides, I *gotta* get to town to call the don and let him know what you found out about Colucci's plan. So if you got any ideas on how to get outta here, let's hear 'em."

Jenny's ears pricked up again when she heard Chickie say, "the don."

"Well, fuck-o, I got nothin'. Joey put you in charge, so *you* come up with a plan," Richie bristled.

Shaking his head at the disrespect, Chickie returned his gaze to the creatures outside.

Jenny decided to have her say. Furrowing her brow, she got in Richie's face and barked, "What the fuck is your problem? You're not doing anything to make it any better in here. We're *safe*. Maybe all we have to do is wait until morning. Maybe these things only come out at night. As long as we keep them out of *here*, we'll be okay."

Richie angrily grabbed the shotgun off the sofa and said, "Yeah, maybe, and maybe not. Maybe all you gotta do is blow their heads off."

Chickie spun from the window to look at him just in time to see the two zombies entering from the kitchen, through the foyer and into the living room. The clothes on the one in front weren't old and rotted, just torn and bloody. With the handle of a claw hammer coming from his head, he grumbled, "…*ahhhh*…Richie…fuck you…and fuck…you…too…"

Richie freaked out at seeing his dead friend, and screamed, "It's Sammy! It's motherfuckin' *Sammy!*"

Chickie didn't waste any time as he yelled, "Jenny! Upstairs! *Now!*" then grabbed his pistol as she bolted up the steps two-at-a-time.

Sammy, only a few feet away and with his arms outstretched, approached his stunned partner, saying, "…Richie…fuck you…"

Crazed, Richie looked Sammy in the eyes, raised the shotgun and said, "This is for buying that fat fuck his motherfuckin' *cocoa!*"

BAM.

Sammy's head exploded, throwing the body back into the others coming into the room. Zombie sludge sprayed the walls…and Chickie. The headless body stood up and, walking aimlessly, slammed into a wall, then turned and ambled in another direction as it reached for a victim.

Chickie wiped the goo off his face and said, "So much for *that* theory, huh, wiseguy?"

Richie sneered, showing how badly he wanted to kill Chickie. The feeling was mutual, but there were gory *things* just a few feet away that wanted to kill both of *them*, a priority that needed to be dealt with first.

Chickie shot them in the knees. Hitting some. Missing some. But with each blast, he advanced toward them.

Richie unloaded the shotgun into the three closest zombies. Throwing it aside, he pulled out a Glock and emptied it into two more. Once it was empty, he threw it at one, hitting him in the head. It did nothing but cause the intruder to reach for Richie, resulting in the Jersey mobster going into *attack mode*. Richie lunged at the oncoming zombie and gouged out its eyes with his thumbs. Black slush blew out of the zombie's ears and sprayed Chickie, to his scream of, "Motherfucker!"

More zombies found their way into the room, causing Chickie to select his targets and shoot anything that got too close, adding more sludge onto the walls and himself.

Chickie's Beretta fired its last round as Richie spun and kicked the knee of another zombie, snapping its leg and sending it to the ground.

Popping out the clip, Chickie reached into his jacket for another as he ducked under a zombie's reach and came up swinging his elbow to the back of its neck. The strength of the blow broke the zombie's spine. Chickie reloaded and went back to shooting more knees. It didn't stop them, but they were left crawling and moving much slower.

Richie, his trademark sick smile on his goo covered face, stopped to proudly survey the downed creatures. Turning to boast to Chickie, he unknowingly slammed into his father's last kill, the decayed Pig Al Povich, ranting, "…I'm just…a lawyer…what…did I do…"

"Holy Shit!" Richie yelled, going insane and tackling Povich. He rained down punches on the attorney's decomposed face until it was just glop and bits of bone.

More entered the room. Chickie wiped black goo from his face, looked over the situation and yelled, "There's more of them than we got bullets. We're better off fightin' 'em from upstairs."

Chickie continued shooting every approaching zombie. Richie came back to his senses, scanned the room, got to his feet and headed up the steps leaving Chickie behind. Chickie grabbed the empty shotgun and backed up the stairs, shooting his Beretta at anything that followed, until the clip was empty.

On the second floor, Jenny struggled with a heavy armchair as the guys reached the landing. They grabbed the chair, took it to the top of the staircase and sent it tumbling down, crushing a zombie and partially blocking the way up.

Richie and Chickie looked at one another, immediately knowing what they had to do. Barreling into the bedrooms, they grabbed large pieces of furniture and pushed them down the stairs, crushing an advancing zombie or two and building a barricade.

But now they were stuck upstairs.

Chickie was disgusted as he looked at his hands and clothes. Wiping black gunk off the face of his watch, he said, "It's almost four o'clock. The kid may *have* somethin' about these things only comin' out at night." He handed Richie the shotgun. "I gotta take a shower. There's a couple-a boxes of shells in my bedroom. Make sure nothin' comes up these stairs."

Chickie headed toward the master bedroom as Richie eyed the clogged staircase. Nothing was going to climb through…for now.

It was just before 5:30AM when the sun's first rays broke the horizon.

The two mobsters had showered and changed clothes. Jenny showered and wore one of Chickie's clean dress shirts, along with the shorts she arrived in.

Richie sat on the top step using his Glock to blast anything that dared crawl over the goo-covered wall of furniture.

Jenny and Chickie were at the front bedroom window appraising the situation.

She excitedly said, "Watch! The sun's going to hit them any minute."

Hearing that, Richie went into the bedroom to watch.

Seconds slowly and agonizingly clicked by as the sunshine crept closer to the shambling zombies in the clearing.

A path leading toward the cabin that trailed back to the thick tree-line, led to the drowned muscleman Randy Jones. For having been submerged for 17 years, what was left of his face looked tired from dragging the cement-filled buckets. *Extremely* tired.

The sunlight cleared the treetops and covered Randy's weary face. As if feeling the heat, he looked up dumbly and continued to ramble, "…can't swim…I can't…swim…"

Randy lowered his head and kept pulling himself forward, inch-by-frustrating-inch.

The sunlight had no effect on them.

Jenny and Chickie slumped in disappointment.

Richie sneered and sarcastically repeated Chickie's words, "So much for *that* theory, huh, wiseguy?" then stalked away to shoot zombies in the stairway.

It was 8:43AM.

Chickie and Jenny looked out the window at the Prius. So close, yet so far.

BAM.

"Fuck you!" came from the hallway as Richie, continuing his watch, shot the occasional zombie that managed to make its way over the furniture barrier.

BAM. BAM.

"How you like *that*, you fuckers?" yelled the enraged Jersey boy.

BAM. BAM. BAM.

Another grotesque, decayed mobster took a couple of bullets to the head, then Paldino reloaded his gun and walked into the bedroom to confront Chickie.

"You just gonna stare at these things? Scared of gettin' your hands dirty, faggot?"

That was it. Chickie had enough. He turned from the window and was about to charge the guy he had been waiting to kill, but Jenny immediately stepped between them and faced Richie.

"Who are you to talk to him like that?"

He looked down at her and arrogantly asked, "You wanna get outta here?" Before she could answer, he continued, "Then you'd better start kissin' *my* ass. Otherwise, you can stay here with this guy and let those things rip ya apart."

Jenny tried to make her point.

"Dallas got out. I'm sure she told someone what happened. She's my friend. She'll get help."

Richie shook his head unsympathetically and told her, "You think that whore's worried about you? She left your ass behind hours ago. Where the fuck's the re-enforcements?"

Chickie broke his silence.

"Its *Jenny's* ass we should *both* be kissin', moron. She--" then he stopped himself.

"She *what?*" Jenny asked.

"Nothin'. Forget it."

Jenny frowned. What was he not saying? Then…she got it.

"I'm *safe.*"

"I told you, we don't know that for sure."

"Dallas got away. I haven't touched any of them yet, so maybe--"

"No! Forget about it," Chickie commanded.

"*Don't* forget about it," Richie interjected, then asked, "Are you sayin' this puttana's got a free pass?"

Jenny ignored Richie's insult, took Chickie's hand and bravely said, "I can do this."

Chickie frowned, not wanting to admit she *was* their last hope. He grit his teeth and reluctantly said, "We're gonna need the car key." They all remembered where it was. "I saw some headless fuck walking around outside about an hour ago. Hopefully that means Sammy found his way outta the living room. How? I don't have a *fuckin'* clue."

A short time later, the trio stood near the window looking at the oak tree's branches and limbs closest to the cabin.

Chickie was still trying to talk her out of it.

"You really don't have to do this," he said with almost fatherly emotion.

"You saved my ass a couple of times since I met you. And *that* was less than twenty-four hours ago. Now…" she fondly looked at Chickie and continued, "…it's my turn."

It touched Chickie's heart and burned Richie's ass that *he* didn't get any recognition.

Jenny climbed out the window as Chickie unnecessarily reminded her, "Remember, don't touch 'em or piss 'em off. Just find Sammy…" He looked at Richie, "…or what's left of him," then returned his eyes to Jenny and continued, "As soon as you get to the car, we'll be right behind you."

Uncaringly, Richie threw in, "Just move your ass."

Jenny leaned back into the bedroom, gave Chickie a kiss on the cheek and the finger to Richie, then took a deep breath and leapt onto the tree.

She climbed down like a girl raised on a farm, then jumped to the ground amid several walking corpses milling around. They ignored her, though she still cautiously made her way through the throng, searching for the headless Sammy. Slowly moving through them, she was able to hear the words coming from their rotted mouths.

"…why are you…taking me…in…the woods…" came from one. "…how'd…you know…how'd…" came from another.

By turning to avoid the zombie holding a camelhair coat and moving like a sloth as he continued to mutter, "...gotta go back...lucky coat..." Jenny came face-to-neck with Sammy.

In the scariest moment of her life, Jenny approached him as he continued to blindly step around. Gingerly feeling the outside of his pockets for the key, she tried not to look at the bloody stump where his head used to be. She became *more* terrified when she felt the piece of metal and had to reach into his pants to get it. Slowly, and while trying to follow his aimless stepping, she slipped her hand into his pocket. Unfortunately, it was a deep pocket. Down...down...until she reached it, then *very* carefully slipped her hand out. Sammy stumbled away as Jenny proudly held up the key for Chickie to see from the window, then headed toward the Prius.

The guys watched their only hope as a zombie stumbled over the stairway's stacked furniture, causing a couple of chairs to fall away, creating a gap large enough for them to pass through...and no one was there to shoot them as they made their way up.

The horde of dead mobsters were now on the landing. Chickie and Richie were busy making sure their remaining weapons were loaded, unaware zombies were approaching from the hallway. Upon hearing the shuffling and mumbling, they turned to see several walking into the room. It only took a millisecond for their guns to be cocked and start blasting.

The room lit up from the eruption of gunfire, catching Jenny's attention, but she was on a mission and needed to get into the car.

Seeing more zombies than they could handle, without saying a word, Richie pocketed his Glock and abandoned Chickie by diving through the window onto the thickest limb and began a slow descent.

Chickie realized he was the only non-dead person in the room, then looked at the window.

"Fuckin' cocksucker. Just like his old man."

Two zombies grabbed Chickie's arm, but were too close to shoot with the shotgun. He pulled out the Beretta and held it to the side of one of their heads. Pulling the trigger five times, the bullets went in one side of its skull, out the other and into his friend's head, knocking them back and spraying goo all over, including onto Chickie.

"*Motherfucker!*" he yelled, knowing he wouldn't get to a shower until they got to Gabbs.

He continued shooting anything that got close as he shouldered the shotgun and climbed out the window. He knew he was past his prime tree-climbing age, but he refused to let his body fail him as he reached for the limb and swung his body securely onto it.

Almost to the ground, he found Richie clinging to the lowest strong limb, seemingly afraid to go any lower.

"Thanks for bailin' on me, prick."

"Fuck you," Richie retorted. "I'm surprised you made it *this* far."

Chickie rubbed his pistol and seriously considered shooting Richie there and then, but he knew he'd need as many guns and fists as possible to get to the car and away from 16 Happy Trails Road.

Jenny reached the Prius. Once inside, she turned the key to the sound of a drone. The gauges barely registered, only to show the battery was as dead as those now walking toward their victims in the tree.

"C'mon, you sonofabitch!" Jenny yelled at the car.

She tried starting it again. It droned just as it had the first time, only weaker.

Looking to the right, she saw the slightly ajar passenger door and realized it was open all night.

She had to let Chickie know right away. She jumped out of the car to see the guys had dropped to the ground and were making their way in her direction. She waved her arms, but they had a few other things to take care of as zombies rapidly approached. Chickie swung the shotgun from his shoulder, aimed it and blew the legs out from an oncoming threat, dropping him to the dirt.

Moving fast, Chickie headed toward the car shooting anything coming at him. Richie was a few feet behind, blasting at zombies following them.

Chickie saw Jenny frantically waving and yelling, but couldn't hear her over the blasting of their guns.

When they reached the car, Jenny was hysterical. Richie shot at a few approaching zombies and put in a new clip as Chickie tried to get Jenny under control.

"The battery!" she got out. "It's dead! It's dead!"

"Fuck!"

Richie heard him and asked, "What's the matter?"

Chickie put his back to the car and methodically shot oncoming zombies as he said to Richie, "The battery's *mooshat!*"

Richie angrily turned to Jenny and screamed, "You motherfucking whore!" as if she had something to do with it.

With a grimace of hate, Chickie shouldered the shotgun and pointed his Beretta at Richie's face. This had been a long time coming. Richie's eyes went wide with fear.

"I'm tired of your fuckin' mouth. I should-a let Bobby pop ya, just like we whacked your pain-in-the-ass cocksucker of an old man."

As the meaning of Chickie's words sank in, Richie's fear was replaced with an old simmering rage.

"Stop it!" yelled Jenny. "We've got bigger problems!"

Chickie looked at her, turned and shot the bullet meant for Richie smack into a nearby zombie's throat, causing a geyser of black blood to fountain into the air. Richie glared at his adversary and growled, "If we get outta this…"

Chickie knew what Richie was inferring, so he grinned and responded, "You got it, scumbag."

They each turned and shot the closest zombie. Richie moved to the passenger side of the car and kept shooting until the pistol ran out of ammo. He smoothly ejected the magazine, slapped in another and continued blasting away.

Still on the driver's side, Chickie swung the shotgun off his shoulder and fired away.

The flow of the murdered underworld from the cleared sections kept streaming through the woods, and they were closing in. Chickie's shotgun was the first to run out of ammo, so he dropped it, pulled a grenade from his jacket, looked at Jenny and said, "Cover up, sweetheart. There's gonna be a big noise."

They knelt behind the car as he pulled the pin and tossed it at a group thirty-five feet away. Among them was the "…I can't swim…can't swim…" weed dealer who eyed the grenade. Desperately, though comically, he tried to hop away but was too exhausted. The look on his decayed face simply said, "Oh fuck," as the small device exploded into a cloud of shrapnel, shredding everything near it into bits. The unsuspecting Richie Paldino was knocked to the ground by the concussion, and the cement-filled buckets of Randy Jones were still there…with stumps of legs protruding from each.

"What the fuck was *that?*" Richie yelled.

Chickie smiled and answered, "Artillery, asshole!"

The smile rapidly disappeared once he saw how many zombies were left, so he called out, "Paldino! I think we can outrun these fucks if we get a good start. How's it look on your side?" as he ejected an empty clip and reached in his pocket for a full one.

Suddenly, Richie was on their side of the car with his Glock pointed at Chickie's head. The boss looked at Richie and realized his time had come.

Richie knew he only had a few seconds before he'd be surrounded again, so he cocked his gun and said, "I want you to know something before I fuckin' kill you. That was bullshit about Donny and the Salvucci family."

Accepting what was about to happen, Chickie sarcastically grinned and said, "Ya know, Paldino, you're a piece-a shit…just like your old man."

"When you get to hell, let him know I was the one who sent you there," Richie growled back.

A zombie's hand grabbed Richie's right arm just as he squeezed the trigger. Chickie took the bullet to his left shoulder. His blood shot out as he was blown to the ground. Jenny screamed and ran to his crumpled body.

Richie spun to shoot the zombie and came face-to-face with a large dirt-encrusted gold crucifix on the reanimated corpse of his long-dead father. Richie frowned, not believing his eyes.

"…what's that in your…hand…hey Bobby what's…that…"

"Poppa? Is that *you?* Poppa?" Richie stepped toward the zombie, his tough-guy composure cracking. From the ground, a stunned Chickie and Jenny watched the bizarre father-and-son reunion.

"It's me, Pop. It's Richie. It's your Richie!" the younger Paldino said, bursting into tears, losing the macho façade he had been carrying since Enzo's disappearance. Then he leapt forward to hug his father.

For a second, the murmuring zombie appeared to return the hug, but was actually raising the ice pick in his hand. Enzo held his son tightly, then brought his arm down over and over and over, each time stabbing Richie with the pick, then dragged him away with several zombies in tow.

That was the last thing Chickie saw before he passed out. Jenny screamed and pressed on the wound hoping to stop the bleeding.

"Chickie! Chickie! *No!* Chickie!"

He opened his eyes, looked at her and weakly said, "C'mon kid. We gotta get outta here."

Smiling through her tears, she helped him to his feet. Once he was up, he painfully put a new clip into his gun and fired at the knees of approaching zombies, but his aim was off.

He pushed her away and yelled, "Get goin'! I'll be right behind you!"

They headed toward the driveway, but Chickie stumbled. Jenny didn't see him fall and kept running. Suddenly, she came upon Bobby Battaglino wailing, "Chickie…get 'em…off-a me…can't move…"

He paid her no mind. As he ambled past her, she saw the two silver .45 automatics and clips in his dual-sided holster.

A score of zombies had honed in on Chickie. He was alone and shooting as many as he could, but there were still too many. Two zombies came up behind the unaware Chickie. One was *Little Marty* McCarthy, and still whining, "…fuck…oh…fuck…"

Unable to get to another clip in time, he was certain he was going to die.

BAM. BAM.

The knees of the approaching zombies were blown out, dropping them to the ground.

Chickie spun his head to see Jenny holding Bobby's pistols…and they were smoking.

She continued to fire, with every bullet hitting its mark, knocking zombies back several steps or having their knees blown to hell. Chickie looked at her, shocked.

"I said I *hate* guns. Never said I don't know how to use 'em."

Even with the impending doom around them, he smiled and said, "Glad to hear that. I'd say we're even," as he started to stand up.

But now, Jenny was fair game. Zombies headed toward her. She ran, leading the bulk of them away from Chickie. While looking at those behind her, she slammed right into the mumbling Donny.

"…cash…buried…under…lilies…behind…my house…"

He scared the shit out of her and she fell on her ass, dropping her pistols. Chickie was too far away for Jenny to see if they had gotten to him. Zombies closed in. Picking up one of the pistols, she fired away until the clip was empty. Expertly popping in a new one, she fired off a couple of shots that momentarily stopped those around her, but she knew the inevitable. She popped out the clip to count the remaining rounds, then looked at the oncoming horde and under her breath said, "Five for you, one for me." Tears streamed her face as she slapped the clip home. As they approached, she took aim at their knees.

She fired. A zombie dropped.

"One."

She aimed and fired, dropping another.

"Two."

Sobbing didn't spoil her aim. Another one got close. She fired. It fell.

"Three."

Two walked next to one another, heading directly for her. She fired twice. They dropped.

"Four and five."

But several more remained. Jenny knew she'd rather be dead than alive when they'd be ripping her apart as she put the barrel of the.45 to her temple and closed her eyes.

Zombies surrounded Jenny, her finger tightened on the trigger…and BAM.

Her eyes flew open. The shot came from somewhere else.

Chickie was back on his feet with his Beretta blasting at everything around Jenny. With each shot, he made his way to her. Five shots in a row caused his five targets to drop to the ground. He checked the clip and called to Jenny, "That was it for me. How about you?" Just as she was about to answer, she raised her weapon, pointed it in Chickie's direction and fired, hitting the knee of an approaching zombie and dropping it.

She yelled back, "That was it!"

Suddenly…there was stillness in the chaos. Their guns empty, Jenny looked at Chickie with gratitude. He smiled back, his chest heaving with exertion and his wound pumping out blood.

Dropping the pistols, Chickie helped her to her feet, then reached down and pulled the long-handled axe from the chest of the kneeless Francesco

Qualiano, who was weakly trying to grab Chickie's leg. It was the same axe Chickie's father had used to kill the thief decades ago. Since Chickie was the one to bury him, he recognized the axe and looked at Francesco and said, "Hey, buddy! How you doin'?"

His reply was, "…look…how far you…gotta go for…a fuckin'…pizza…"

"Same old story, huh?" Chickie laughed, then turned to Jenny and ordered, "C'mon, we're gettin' outta here." He used the goo-covered axe for support as they headed for the driveway, but more dead avengers appeared from both sides.

"Jesus! The Pontis must-a killed more wiseguys than Scorsese and Coppola put-together," he half-jokingly said as zombies got closer and closer.

Chickie knew he had to do the right thing.

"You go ahead, kid. I'll keep 'em busy as long as I can," he said, pushing her forward, knowing he wasn't moving fast enough.

"No, Chickie!" Jenny cried as she came back to help him.

He pushed her away, and yelled, "Go! But ya gotta tell Don Giuseppe Ponti I tried. You gotta get to Jersey. He's gotta know I tried."

Confused, she asked, "Tried what?"

He was near tears as he told her, "I never let him or the family down. I can't believe it's gonna be like this."

With only seconds before they would be surrounded again, Jenny pleaded, "What? You tried to do *what?*"

"To find the money Donny stole. The boss's money. You gotta tell Don Ponti." He pushed her away again, "Get outta here. It's time for me to get my hands dirty." Then he weakly whacked a zombie with the axe.

Jenny looked at Chickie and the oncoming zombies. Crying, she headed to the mile long driveway.

Chickie yelled to the zombies to lure them away from her.

"Yo! Wiseguys! Let's go, motherfuckers!"

As he hoped, they surrounded him as he swung the axe wildly, using the blade, the back and the handle to hold them off. Jenny stopped and watched in horror as a pack of zombies engulfed Chickie, making her too grief-stricken to speak.

Chickie put the axe into a zombie, getting it stuck in its chest. Others grabbed at Chickie as he desperately tried to get free. From behind a chef's knife went into his right shoulder. Knowing it was over, he took a deep breath and reached into his pockets. Pulling out the three grenades, he pulled the pins and hugged them against his chest with the trigger levers tightly in his fists.

He lifted his head just enough to see Jenny watching in the distance and yelled, "Get outta here!"

Following his orders, she turned and ran.

Black fingernails tore at Chickie's skin. He smiled to himself as he let the levers fly off of the grenades. It would be five seconds to oblivion. Humorously, he looked at the closest zombie and said, "They'd *never* believe this shit back in Jersey."

The explosion was massive.

Jenny cried for the man who heroically died for her…and for taking a dozen zombies with him as she ran along the driveway.

Stumbling to a stop when she saw the BMW smashed into the tree, Jenny ran to it, then looked in horror at the inside. It was covered in blood. Hearing a rustling behind her, she nervously spun around to see Dallas emerge from the woods covered in multiple ice pick punctures and heading right for her. Jenny ran to the driver's side of the car, got in, slammed the door and hit the automatic door locks. She saw the keys in the ignition, with Dallas' purse, Richie's gun and Donny's license on the passenger seat. With Dallas pounding on the windows wanting to attack Jenny, the frightened girl reached for the ignition and, almost in prayer, said, "Please, please, please…"

The car started. Breathing a sigh of relief, she cautiously backed the car from the tree and sped away, leaving Dallas in her dust.

Jenny looked in the rearview mirror. Other than Dallas in the distance, nothing was following her, and it didn't appear there were any *things* in front, either.

Exhausted, traumatized and free, she was able to concentrate on driving as the BMW sped past a sign on the mountainous one lane road that read, "Leaving Historic Shoshone Tribal Territory."

With their last target off Shoshone land, the zombies, who now included Bobby, an armless China, a headless Sammy, and a perforated Richie and Dallas, crawled into shallow graves and pulled dirt over themselves...to rest until once again called by the shaman's curse.

EPILOGUE

By Friday, June 18th, Don Giuseppe Ponti expected to be relaxing on a beach somewhere, while Carmine '*Chickie*' Santorella ran the family. But no one had heard from Chickie since the four Jersey guys arrived in Nevada on Saturday, June 12th.

CP's Riverside Restaurant in Hoboken, though a fine eatery, was void of customers that early afternoon, yet the standard array of luxury cars were parked in front.

Three well-dressed lieutenants and four bodyguards lingered outside, waiting and whispering to each other.

In the dining area, Stefano, the don's husky bodyguard, stood to the side of Don Ponti's booth. The boss was sitting with longtime family captain, Paul Schielzo, and sipping espresso.

"So," said Don Joey, "What did you find out?"

Schielzo seemed reluctant to speak, and it was readily apparent to his boss.

"Let's hear it. Where's Chickie? Bobby? *My fuckin' money?*"

The captain put his hands in front of him in an Italian gesture to express how strange what he was about to say would sound.

"I got the call from Lenny Flora about an hour ago." Joey leaned closer as Paul continued. "He said the new casino manager confirmed Chickie took Donny out of the place last Sunday, so we know *that* happened. When Lenny got to the cabin he said it looked like a fuckin' war-zone. Bombed out craters. Shell casing and body parts all over the place, a couple of cement buckets with bones stickin' out of 'em, but not one full body… and there was some dried black shit all over the ground."

Joey couldn't believe what he was hearing as he barked, "What about inside?"

"The front door was locked, but the back door was open…furniture, bullet holes and that dried black shit was *everywhere*, like there was a big gun fight happenin' on both floors. Oh, there was a Prius parked in front with a few grand on the ground next to it, and the room downstairs was locked."

"A Prius?" Joey said with confusion. "Chickie? In a Prius? No way. What else?"

"Sheila said around the same time Donny, Chickie and everyone else went missin', so did three of her girls. I doubt there's a connection, but who knows?"

The men sat, deep in thought and bewildered.

Don Ponti raised his aged, tired face, looked at Paul and somewhat reluctantly said, "We're gonna have to go out there right away with some of our people to see what needs to be done. Get the fuckin' place cleaned up. Maybe sell it. Sell the fuckin' casino, too. I'm too old and tired for this shit."

Then he thought about his Godson, and in front of his two men, the don wept.

The bodyguard and captain said nothing.

After a moment, the boss shook his head, looked at Stefano and commanded him to, "Try Chickie again."

Stefano pulled out his cell phone, tapped a programmed number, then handed it to the don to hear, "The subscriber you have dialed is out of the service area. Please try your call again later."

"Bah fungool, these friggin' things," growled the angry mob boss.

Outside, the lieutenants and bodyguards turned their attention to an attractive, smartly dressed blonde woman who had rounded the corner and was heading their way. It was Jenny…carrying a heavy, dirty duffel bag.

Instinctively, the men reached into their jackets as she neared.

Don Joey and Paul Schielzo continued sipping their espresso and discussing other business when Stefano saw two people enter the empty restaurant. His hand went into his jacket, just in case. One of the lieutenants held up the duffel bag as he and Jenny approached the dining room. Motioning to Stefano that he had checked her and the bag for weapons, the bodyguard handed it back to Jenny, then pointed toward the don's table and returned to his post outside.

Jenny nervously walked toward them, stopping a few feet from the table. With Stefano's hand on his gun, the men waited for her to say something.

"Mr. Ponti?"

They eyed her intently, then Schielzo asked, "Who wants to know?"

She placed the bag before them and softly said, "My name is Jennifer Nicols. I was asked by Chickie Santorella to find you, and to give you this."

The men reacted with interest as Ponti asked, "What do you know about Chickie? Where is he?"

Jenny looked down and almost in tears, replied, "He's dead. They're all dead."

She began to unzip the bag. Even though Jenny had been cleared by the outside bodyguard, that didn't stop Stefano from pulling out his gun and putting it to her temple. She stopped, raised her hands and stepped away. The gun was lowered, but just a little.

"What happened? Who killed them? We've heard some crazy things," Joey pressed.

Unsure how to explain what everyone at the cabin experienced, she answered, "Not a clue, Mr. Ponti. All I know is, Chickie told me some guy named Donny stole your money, and some other guy named Richie was planning to keep it for himself."

Joey Ponti turned to his captain and said, "See. I knew Chickie'd find out what happened. But fuckin' Paldino wantin' to rob me? That prick was just like his old man. I hope he fuckin' suffered."

Before Schielzo could respond, Jenny assured the boss, "Yes, sir. He did." Then she started weeping as she recalled the ice pick repeatedly going into him, and finished with, "Horribly."

Ponti looked deeply into Jenny's eyes and told her to, "Keep goin'."

With Stefano's gun still pointed in her direction, she said, "What I *do* know is that Chickie saved my life and got me out of a place I'd never want to go back to again, not even in my dreams. If it weren't for Chickie…"

She cried even harder.

"Easy honey. *I'm* Joey Ponti. Relax and tell me who did this," the boss said, hoping to console her *and* to get the information he needed.

She tried to continue, "Mr. Ponti, if I were a religious person, I'd swear on the lives of my parents and *everyone I know* that if I told you who…or *what*…killed those people, you'd never believe me. Since I drove away from there, I've done everything possible to forget what I saw and heard." Then with conviction, she gazed at the Mafia boss of New Jersey and said, "The last thing Chickie Santorella told me was that his only concern was to find *this*." She pointed to the bag. "When he found out about the guys wanting to rip you off, and when he knew he wasn't going to make it back here, he told me it meant everything to him to not let you down. I promised him that if I got out of there alive…I'd find you and bring it to you."

Joey motioned to Schielzo, who slowly unzipped the bag. Bundles of cash were inside, making Joey's disposition a little happier, but just a little. Jenny composed herself as the captain rummaged through the money. He looked at the don and said, "A million. Maybe a little more."

Joey's attitude changed again as he angrily barked, "That's *it*?"

Schielzo nodded. There was nothing else to say.

After a few seconds to calm down, the boss said to Jenny, "You did good to return my money. Grazie, bella." Then he slyly continued, "You take anything outta this?"

Looking Don Giuseppe Ponti squarely in the face and without hesitation, the young woman shook her head and answered, "No, sir. I never even looked in it. It wasn't for *me*. It was for *you*. That's how Chickie wanted it."

Appreciating her loyalty and show of respect, but still skeptical, he continued to question her.

"So, Jennifer Nicols…why you being so good to me? What's in it for you? Why you doin' this for people you don't know?"

"I'm not doing this for you *or* me, Mr. Ponti. Like I said, I'm doing it for Chickie Santorella."

The don solemnly looked at his captain and whispered, "Fuckin' Chickie. One of the best." Then he rose from the booth, reached into the bag, pulled out two bundles of cash and handed them to Jenny. She gathered her composure and bowed her head as she thanked him.

The mob boss pointed his finger and said, "Now get outta here, and forget you ever saw this place, me or this bag. Capisce?"

Jenny said nothing. She gave a *very* respectful nod to those in front of her, put the cash in her pockets, turned and left the dining area. Smiling to the men who opened the door for her, she departed the restaurant, walked in the direction she came from and turned the corner.

A couple of blocks away, and when she was sure no one was following her, Jenny stepped to the rear of a new, black Jaguar convertible with an Ohio license plate. She tapped the remote, causing the trunk to pop open, revealing two dirty duffel bags inside

She unzipped one that, just as the other, was filled to the top with cash. She jammed the two bundles from Don Joey into it, zipped it closed and shut the trunk.

Jenny Nicols got behind the wheel, started the Jaguar, lowered the convertible top, hit the CD player that blasted Rod Stewart's "Young Turks," revved the engine, put it in Drive...and cruised away.

THE END

CAST OF CHARACTERS

Antonio Agostini Known as *The Big Hand*. Don of the New York family the Ponti family reported to. Pronounced: Ag-o-steen-ee.

Antonio Agostini Jr. Known as *The Little Hand*. Took over the family when his father passed away. Pronounced: Ag-o-steen-ee

Bobby Battaglino Son of Tony Battaglino. Worked for the Ponti family. Best friend and right-hand-man of Carmine *'Chickie'* Santorella. Pronounced: Bat-a-leeno.

Tony Battaglino Bobby's father. Occasionally drove trucks for the Ponti family. Mike Santorella's longtime friend and associate. Pronounced: Bat-a-leeno.

Andy Cappomaggi Chosen by Mike Santorella to do the hits at the cabin. Pronounced: Capo-ma-gee.

China Asian hooker who was also a good fighter.

Luigi Colucci Known as *Little Calooch*. Alphonse Salvucci's nephew who took over the Salvucci family. Pronounced: Ka-loo-chi.

Dallas The not very honest hooker-in-charge.

Kent Dooley	Stan Worley Jr's friend.
Dennis Dragona	Don Vincenzo Ponti's driver.
Sheila Dunay	Mayor William Dunay's daughter.
Vivian Dunay	Mayor William Dunay's wife.
William Dunay	Known as *Willie*. Mayor of Gabbs, NV, and owns The Gabbs Hotel.
William Dunay Jr.	Known as *Willie Jr*. Mayor William Dunay's son.
Lenny Flora	Trusted lieutenant Paul Schielzo sent to the cabin in 1999.
Gary Gentile	The first to be killed at the cabin, Feb 5, 1964.
Antoinette Goode	Full Shoshone real estate agent and historian. Mayor Dunay's cousin.
Ray Goode	Antoinette's husband. Owns the local construction company and lumber yard.
Randy Jones	Muscle-bound weed dealer from Florida who gets thrown overboard wearing cement buckets, mid-June, 1982.
Pete Johnson	Shoshone name is *Swift Wind*. Native American killed in 1925 by Stan Worley Jr. and Kent Dooley.
Julie	Kent Dooley's girlfriend.
Laura	Mayor Dunay's hotel receptionist, and his cousin.

Martin McCarthy   Known as *Little Marty*. Works for the Salvucci family. Went to Gabbs in mid-December, 1968 and never came back.

Jenny Nicols   A young hooker with a kind heart who just wants to get back to Ohio.

Annette Oliveri   Shoshone wife of *Nick The Dick*, and mother of Donatello '*Donny*' Oliveri.

Donatello Oliveri   Known as *Donny*. Son of Nick and Annette. Named after Vincenzo Ponti's middle name. Became casino manager of The Ramblin' Rose.

Nick Oliveri   Known as *Nick The Dick*. Owns *Nick's Seafood Restaurant* in South Lake Tahoe. Husband of Annette, and father of Donatello.

Christine Paldino   Enzo's wife. Richie's mother. Pronounced: Pal-dee-no.

Enzo Paldino   Husband of Christine, and father of Richie. Second-rate mobster. The last person killed at the cabin. Pronounced: Pal-dee-no.

Richie Paldino   Son of Enzo and Christine Paldino. A vicious dickhead, just like his father. Pronounced: Pal-dee-no.

George Pipher   Casino manager of The Cactus Flower/The Ramblin' Rose. Worked for Ponti family for decades running backroom casinos and card games. Pronounced: Pie-fer.

Carmine Ponti   Son of Vincenzo Ponti. Killed in 1956 by Big Allie.

Giuseppe Ponti   Known as *Joey*. Son of Vincenzo Ponti. Brother of Carmine Ponti. Godfather of Carmine '*Chickie*' Santorella.

Vincenzo Ponti   Known as *Don Vincenzo*. Head of the Ponti family. Father of Carmine and Giuseppe Ponti.

Albert Povich   Known as *Pig Al*. Was the last contract hit at the cabin on November 28, 1990. A lawyer about to rat on the Ponti family.

Francesco Qualiano   Chickie's first hit at the cabin on his 19th birthday, 1976. Pronounced: Kwal-ee-an-o.

Quishindemi   Known as '*Bobtail Horse*.' Old Shoshone brave that told the legend to Lou Rittberg in 1925.

Lou Rittberg   Young resident of Worley, NV, who wrote the story he was told about the legend.

Alphonse Salvucci Jr.   Known as *Big Allie*. Took over the Salvucci family the day his father died in 1956. Killed Carmine Ponti. Pronounced: Sal-voo-chi.

Alphonse Salvucci   Known as '*Little Allie*.' *Big* Allie's son. Killed August 10, 1958. Pronounced: Sal-voo-chi.

Carmine Santorella   Known as *Big Carmine*. Mike Santorella's father.

Carmine Santorella   Known as '*Chickie*." Mike and Diana Santorella's son.

Diana Santorella   Mike's wife. Carmine's mother.

Mike Santorella Longtime member of the Ponti family. A made man and family captain. Carmine '*Chickie*' Santorella's father and Maria's husband.

Paulie Schielzo A Ponti family captain, and Gary Gentile's boss. Pronounced: Shel-zo.

Stefano One of Don Giuseppe's bodyguards.

Frank Temple Hertz car rental manager in Reno Airport.

Tenupah Dome-up Known as *Man From The Sky*. The wisest and most powerful of all the Not-tsoo-Dainnahpeh…also known as the medicine men.

Sammy Trombino Richie Paldino's right-hand-man. Not the brightest, but loyal. Pronounced: Trom-beeno.

Wayne Welstone Known as *CC*, for being a corrupt cop. Member of the Salvucci family. Went to Gabbs in mid-December, 1968. Never came back.

White Elk Shoshone wise man. Grandfather of Antoinette Goode.

Stan Worley Failed miner and founder of Worley, Nevada. Father of Stan Jr.

Stan Worley Jr Son of Stan Worley.

CHICKIE SANTORELLA'S SUNDAY GRAVY
by
Diane Lombardi-Fleming

The Gravy:
3 – 26 ounce cans of crushed tomatoes
3 cloves of garlic, slivered thin
½ cup of onions, finely diced
2 tablespoons of olive oil
¼ cup fresh chopped parsley
6 fresh chopped basil leaves
1 teaspoon sugar
Add salt and pepper to taste
Add crushed red pepper flakes to taste

Choose the pot with a lid of your liking. Add olive oil and slivered garlic. Heat the oil and garlic and allow it to cook slowly until the garlic just begins to toast. Add the onions and continue to sauté until the onions are translucent, and the garlic is light brown. Turn off the heat and allow everything to cool for a moment or two before adding the tomatoes (if the pot is too hot when you add in the tomatoes it will spatter all over the stove and make a mess, which Chickie don't want), then let the pan cool slightly before pouring in the crushed tomatoes.

Add all other ingredients, stir with a wooden spoon, cover the pot and bring to a boil. Then lower the heat to a slow simmer and forget about it while you prepare the sausages and meatballs.

The Sausages:
One link per person that you're feeding. Use Hot or Sweet Italian links (or both), depending on your preference. Heat a small pot or skillet, preferably made of cast iron. When it's hot, add in the links, turn heat to low and

allow the sausage to brown. When one side is well-browned, turn sausages over and brown the other side. Watch and turn the sausages every 5 minutes or so until all they're evenly browned. Turn off the heat and put the links into the gravy pot. Allow to simmer for an hour or more. Gravy can *not* be overcooked. The longer it simmers the deeper the flavors become. But if you have a deadline, an hour will do.

The Meatballs:
1 pound of ground beef
2 cloves of finely minced garlic
½ cup of Italian-style bread crumbs
2 tablespoons of fresh chopped parsley
2 or 3 fresh finely chopped basil leaves
1 egg
¼ cup milk
Grated Parmesan or Romano cheese to taste
Add salt and black pepper to taste

Put all ingredients into a large bowl and mix well. Grab a hunk of the mixture and roll between the palms of your hands into a ball shape. There is no set rule about the size of the meatballs. Once the mixture is rolled into balls, heat the skillet that was used to brown the sausage. Put the meatballs in the sausage drippings until they're well-browned on all sides. Add the meatballs to the gravy for 20 minutes so they can finish cooking and help flavor the gravy. Before washing the skillet the sausage and meatballs were browned in, add a tablespoon (or more) of the drippings to the gravy for additional flavor.

Serve over the macaroni or pasta of your choice. Sprinkle with extra Parmesan or Romano cheese, and a dollop whole milk ricotta cheese.

For a well-rounded meal, add a salad dressed with basic olive oil and vinegar, salt and pepper, and a loaf of crusty Italian bread. For the perfect meal, add a bottle of chianti. Believe me, Chickie Santorella, you'll thank me every time you eat this meal. Salud!

Now *mangia!*